c.1

OCT 18 1989	JUN 1 2 1992
NOV 1 5 1989	AUG 1 0 1992
DEC 5 1990	SEP 3 1992
APR 1 1991	OCT 7 1992
APR 1 9 1991	NOV 1 1 1992
JUL 1 1 1991	MAR 1 8 1993
FEB 1 3 1992	JUL 0 8 1996
MAR 2 0 1992	
MAR 2 4 1992	

HAS CATALOG CARDS

4015

DEMCO

12 pts

LONG LIVE the QUEEN

LONG LIVE the QUEEN

Ellen Emerson White

SCHOLASTIC
HARDCOVER

Scholastic Inc.
New York

Library of Congress Cataloging-in-Publication Data
White, Ellen Emerson.
Long live the queen.
Summary: The President's daughter is a victim of
kidnapping by terrorists.
[1. Kidnapping—Fiction. 2. Terrorism—Fiction]
I. Title.
PZ7.W58274Lo   1989   [Fic]   88-18558
ISBN 0-590-40850-X

12 11 10 9 8 7 6 5 4 3 2 1   9/8 0 1 2 3 4/9

Printed in the U.S.A.   37

First Scholastic printing, May 1989

For my editor, Jean Feiwel, who has always been swell.

Chapter
One

It was almost dark, but Meg kept her sunglasses on because they reminded her of skiing. Despite the fact that it was May, and she was holding a tennis racket. Her theory had always been — when in doubt, delude yourself.

She lowered her racket, having served the last in another series of ten balls. A gardener near the fence lifted seven fingers, and she nodded her thanks. One nice thing about living in the White House was that there was always someone around to call lines. She picked up the jug of water she kept on the baseline, drinking some, and studying the other side of the court. Seven out of ten. Not bad. Then again, *eight* would be even better. She put the jug down and reached into her ball basket.

Leaning back to serve, she noticed that everyone around the court — her Secret Service agents,

1

groundspeople, a couple of reporters — was standing much straighter. Indicating that the President was somewhere nearby.

Meg grinned. "Is it my imagination, or is there like, a head of state behind me?" she asked without turning around.

Her mother laughed. "The serve looks good."

"I don't know, I'm trying to get more on it." Meg walked back to where her mother was standing, the number of agents and other people around having swelled considerably. "Do you feel like hitting a few?" she asked, already pretty sure of the answer.

Her mother looked down at her dress and high heels. "It would lack elegance, Meg."

Meg nodded. It had been quite a while since her mother had had enough energy to play.

"Besides," her mother said, "I expect your father and brothers are waiting for us."

Meg looked up at the sky to try and guess what time it was — not that she was exactly Nature Girl — then remembered that she had on a watch. She hated watches, but apparently hers was some kind of security thing because the Secret Service had requested that she wear it. She had never wanted to pursue the issue further, and even though she'd been wearing it for well over a year now, she still wasn't used to it.

"High time for dinner," her mother said.

Past seven. "Yeah," Meg said, and bent down to pick up some of her tennis balls.

Her mother bent gracefully for one as Meg scooped up six or seven, using her sweatshirt as a sort of pouch. "Is this like, quality time we have going here?" she asked, dumping her balls into the yellow metal basket.

Her mother picked up another one, holding it with

2

her index finger and thumb. "That appears to be the case, yes," she said.

"Madame President?" one of her aides said from the net.

Her mother sighed, handing Meg the ball. "Excuse me."

Meg watched her walk over and confer with the aide, recognizing the Presidential frown of concern even from behind. Her mother sure knew how to walk. It was too dignified to be a sweep, but too fast to be stately. The influence of too damned many Katharine Hepburn movies, Meg's father had always said. "Statuesque" was the word the media used. Meg just liked to sing "Twentieth Century Fox" at her.

Her brother Steven — who was almost fourteen — either swaggered or slouched; her brother Neal — who was nine — bounced, mostly. Her father — well, he just walked. Occasionally, he hurried. Meg, personally, would either slink or slog. Sometimes, to drive her parents crazy, she and Steven would shuffle. They were big on scuffing too.

"Pretty cool," her mother said, suddenly next to her again.

Meg stopped in the middle of her tennis racket guitar solo. Morrison and the guys would have to wait. "Um, just singing," she said.

"So I heard," her mother said.

Meg flushed and took off her sunglasses, going over to pick up the rest of her tennis balls.

They walked to the White House — with the Secret Service, of course — along the cement oval leading to the South Portico, passing shrubbery like the Dwight D. Eisenhower Pin Oak and the Jimmy Carter Cedar of Lebanon. Their dog, Kirby, invariably used

3

the Richard Nixon Fern-leaf Beech. Steven had encouraged this.

Meg glanced over at her mother. "You look tired."

Her mother shrugged. "Long day, that's all."

Meg kept looking at her, noticing the slight hunch to her left side. Since — well, Meg tried to think of it as "the accident" because the words "assassination attempt" made her sick — anyway, even though it had been over six months, her mother was often in obvious pain and *always* exhausted after anything approaching a full day's work. "Um, how do you feel?" Meg asked.

Her mother's posture changed, the hunch leaving. "Fine."

Meg nodded, not believing her.

"So," her mother said abruptly. "You're certainly practicing nonstop these days."

Meg looked back towards the court. "I don't know." She grinned. "Did you read *Save Me the Waltz?*"

Her mother smiled too. "It's my assumption that you're hoping to play at school this fall?"

She was hoping, actually, to start playing some junior tournaments. "Yeah," Meg said. "Sort of." Although her parents had wanted her to go to Harvard — getting *into* college wasn't exactly an issue for the President's daughter — she had chosen Williams. Small, very academic, surrounded by ski resorts. Her kind of place. The skiing, anyway.

"Did you know," her mother said conversationally, "that professional tennis players change their clothes *right* in the *middle* of the locker room?" She paused. "In front of *everyone?*"

Meg grinned. "Oh, you're just trying to scare me."

"I have it on excellent authority," her mother said.

4

"I wouldn't worry," Meg said. "It's not like I'm good enough." She carefully didn't add a "yet," but her mother's look at her was so penetrating that she must have heard it anyway.

"Well," her mother said, and nodded hello to the Marine guards as they went inside through the South Entrance. Actually, Meg nodded too, but they were so busy being alert that they probably didn't notice.

She followed her mother through the oval Diplomatic Reception Room to the Ground Floor Corridor, red-carpeted with marble walls, where portraits of first ladies hung. Her father — who always looked uncomfortable in pictures under the *best* of circumstances — was going to look funny hanging there someday.

Her father's press secretary, Preston, coming down the hall with a couple of press aides, stopped short, giving her mother a crisp salute.

Her mother smiled, returning it. "At ease, Mr. Fielding."

"Thank you, Madame Prez." He winked at Meg. "Get that serve percentage over eighty, kid?"

"Almost," Meg said.

"Good going." He touched his own throat, where a blue silk tie was loosely knotted, indicating the white towel around her neck. "Sort of a fashion risk."

"Meghan à la Balboa," Meg said, and Preston laughed, continuing down the hall with the aides. Meg really liked Preston. Official job aside, what he really was was her whole family's best friend — and about as cool as it was possible to be. He and her father made an incongruous pair — Preston, the tall, suave black guy; her father very straight and WASPy. "Is he like, your favorite person in the world who isn't related to you?" she asked, watching him go.

5

"Yes," her mother said, getting onto the First Family elevator. "Going up?"

"Oh." If she were alone, Meg would definitely have taken the stairs — in lieu of more interesting enemies, she had always made a practice of fighting calories — but with her mother being tired and all — "I mean, yeah."

They rode up to the third floor — everyone in her family almost always hung out in the solarium, which had the biggest television, a library of records and video cassettes out in the hall, and some extremely spectacular views.

Steven and Neal were on the couch, watching *Top Secret* for probably the seven hundredth time, and Meg's father was sitting at the round wooden table where they sometimes had super-casual meals, although her parents didn't approve of eating in a room that had a television in it. Her mother always talked her father into making exceptions for things like the *Academy Awards*. *Hill Street Blues* was Meg's all-time favorite show in life, but the *Academy Awards* were pretty high up on her list. Right up there with *David Letterman* and *Entertainment Tonight*. It was hard to trust someone who didn't admit to watching *Entertainment Tonight* every now and then.

"Good day at school?" her father asked.

Meg looked up. "I'm sorry, what?"

Her father smiled, putting down his Beck's. When he wasn't being the First Gentleman, he always drank from the bottle. "Did you have a nice day at school?"

"Oh. Yeah. Did you?" Meg shook her head. She really had to make more of an effort to pay attention. "Have a nice day, I mean."

"Very nice," he said, smiling more.

Having said hello to Steven and Neal, her mother was behind her father now, her hands on his shoulders.

"You look tired," he said.

"I *am* tired," her mother said, and sensing that there was a hug or a kiss or something coming from that, Meg went over to sit on the couch.

"Don't you guys ever get sick of this?" she asked, indicating the movie.

"Nope." Steven yawned. "Josh called and said for us to give you a big — " he made a smacking sound with his lips — "from him."

Neal giggled, making his own smacking sound.

Since she and Josh had officially been "just friends" for over a month now — and were still pretty self-conscious about the whole thing — that exact message was unlikely. "What did he *really* say?" Meg asked.

Steven shrugged. "Hi."

Neal, watching the movie, made another smacking sound.

Meg looked at them, then at herself. What a motley little set of children. Three pairs of sweatpants, three pairs of irregularly tied sneakers — theirs high-top Nikes, hers Tretorns; and three sweatshirts — one that said Williams, a New England Patriots one, and Neal wearing an outgrown grey one of Steven's. And it wouldn't kill any of them to go do a little hair-brushing.

She looked at her parents — her mother in her elegant tan dress, her hair and makeup perfect; her father in a grey pin-striped suit. She and Steven looked like her mother: dark hair, blue eyes, very high cheekbones. Neal, like her father, had lighter brown hair and always looked as if he were about to smile. She and her mother and Steven were grinners. She and Steven somewhat more raffishly.

"Thank you," her mother was saying into the phone. "We'll be down directly." She hung up. "Do the three of you want to get washed up for dinner?"

"No," Neal said, and giggled.

"Hell, no," Steven said.

"Go get washed up," their father said.

"So, wait." Meg looked from her parents to her brothers. "Am I like, the swing vote here?"

Her parents shook their heads.

When it was just the family, they would eat in the Presidential Dining Room on the second floor. The furnishings were, so Meg was told, American Federal — which seemed to mean mahogany — and the room had the usual dramatic White House chandelier. The wallpaper was blue, with scenes from the American Revolution painted on it, and none of them liked it much. Mrs. Ford had had it taken down during President Ford's administration, but the wallpaper was antique and Meg's parents didn't want to take chances by pulling it down again.

"How was practice, Steven?" their mother asked, giving herself the smallest baked potato.

"Okay," he said through a mouthful of roast beef. "I was mostly shagging because Coach wants me to pitch on Friday."

Their father frowned. "You went six innings yesterday."

Steven shrugged. "So, he had me taking it easy today. Can you pass me the salad, Meg?"

Meg helped herself, then passed the bowl across the table to him. Although no one really talked about it, her parents weren't very happy about him playing — the Secret Service had advised against it. After her mother had been shot, all of their security had gotten much tighter, and because tennis courts were so exposed, Meg had had to drop off the team at school. For the same reason, the Secret Service hadn't wanted Steven to play baseball, but he had gotten so upset that her parents had finally had to allow it. Much to Meg's relief, their security in general had relaxed a little in the last few months, going back to its pre-shooting level. Which, God knows, was intense enough. She had no intention of permanently giving up competitive tennis, but she wasn't looking forward to the discussion about that with her parents. They were beginning to drop not-so-subtle hints, but so far, she had managed to avoid it.

"Your mother asked you a question," her father said, sounding amused.

"She did?" Meg looked at her mother. "You did?"

Her mother grinned. "I did."

"Oh." Meg shook her head. "I'm sorry, I'm just — I mean, lately — I don't know."

"It's called senioritis," her father said.

"No way," Steven said. "She's always been like that."

"*Always*," Neal said, laughing.

"Yeah, well," Meg gave herself quite a large baked potato, "wait until I go away to school. You guys'll be like, crying all the time because you miss me so much."

"No way," Steven said. "We'll have parties every day."

"Wakes, more likely." Her cat, Vanessa, had come in to sit behind her chair, and Meg slipped her a little piece of roast beef, her father lifting his eyebrows at

9

her. "I mean," she straightened up, "you won't have anyone around to tell you swell jokes, or explain words you don't understand — "

Her parents laughed.

" — help keep the country running smoothly — "

"Yeah," Steven said. "And all the flies and bugs that follow you around'll leave."

"Well, of *course* they're coming with me," Meg said. "I wouldn't go anywhere without — "

"One bad thing," Steven interrupted, taking the salt shaker from underneath Neal's reaching hand, "we won't be able to get any good drugs anymore."

"*Told* you you'd miss me," Meg said.

"Well, goodness knows I'll miss the dinner repartée." Their mother nodded as one of the butlers, Felix, paused with the wine carafe. "Meg, have you gotten any further in your thoughts about what to wear to the Prom?"

To which, yeah, she and Josh were still going. "I thought I'd make something out of my curtains," Meg said, managing — just barely — not to laugh at her own humor. The clothes-making scenes in *Gone With the Wind* and *The Sound of Music* were probably her two favorite movie jokes ever. And the time Carol Burnett wore the curtain dress with the rod still in it.

"Is that a no?" her mother asked.

"Yeah," Meg said. "It's a no."

10

Chapter
Two

She sat in the Secret Service car the next morning, trying to finish her English homework, scribbling about Marlow's journey into the Heart of Darkness and all. Yeah, thrilling.

"Try and hit red lights," she said to her agents. Chet, who was driving, laughed; Dennis didn't. Par for the course. She had her regular detail of agents — two for every eight-hour period, with a couple of extras for manning command centers and advance work — for six months, and then the Secret Service would bring in a new detail. Also, within each detail of agents, they rotated shifts every two weeks. The agents she spent the most time with were the ones on the eight-to-four shift, since they were the ones who took her to school. While Chet was fun, Dennis was too damn intense — so attentive that he made her nervous — and she was looking forward to the next rotation.

"Sorry, Meg," Chet said, slowing to pull into the circular driveway in front of the school. They always varied the entrances and exits, and today was a front-door day. "Did my best."

Meg folded her paper in half, putting it inside her book. "I can probably finish up during homeroom." She closed the book, dumping it inside her knapsack. "In the end, we are all alone. Each our own judge." She looked at Chet. "What do you think?"

He laughed.

"The most frightening demons may, in fact, be within ourselves."

He shook his head, parking the car. "Your poor teacher."

"Exploring the hidden darkness can be — " Meg got out of the car, not sure what it could be. She swung her knapsack over her shoulder. "Revealing." She frowned. Illuminating? No, too obvious.

Her agents didn't like her to stand around when she didn't have to, so she headed right into the school — Dennis, as always, a little too close behind her. She walked more slowly, hoping that he would back off, but he almost never did.

"Hey, Meg, wait up!"

Seeing Josh on his way down one of the side halls, she stopped to wait for him, smiling as he came closer. Sometimes, to give him grief, she called him Mr. Shetland, and today was no exception.

"Nice sweater," she said.

He smiled back. "Thought you'd like it." Before, he would have put his arm around her, or taken her knapsack for her or something, but now, he just stood there, looking uncomfortable.

Feeling pretty uncomfortable herself — although it had been her idea to "de-escalate" things in the first place — Meg coughed. "Well," she said.

"Yeah." He straightened his glasses. "Anything new?"

"Not really. I talked to Beth last night." Beth was her best friend back in Massachusetts, where Meg and her family *really* lived. Or had, anyway.

"What's new with *her*?"

Meg shrugged. "Not much. She's going to the Prom with that Harvard guy." Beth was nothing, if not a social success.

"Are they getting pretty serious?"

Meg shook her head. "I don't get that feeling." Behind her, Dennis was a little too close again and she folded her arms, not wanting to turn around and yell at him.

Josh noticed and put his hand on her waist, steering her ahead more quickly.

"Thanks," she said.

He hesitated, then dropped his hand, putting it in his pocket. "Why don't you talk to him about it?"

She sighed. "He's just doing his job."

"Yeah, but he's not supposed to bother you."

"I'm probably just overreacting," Meg said, her arms still folded.

Josh glanced over his shoulder. "Tell your father, or Preston. I'm sure it wouldn't be a big deal for you to get someone else."

"I guess." Meg sighed again. "I don't know. This rotation's almost over."

"In other words."

"Yeah." She stopped at her locker. "Did you do your English?"

"The demons of darkness are potent, but elusive," he said.

She laughed. "Yeah. I did it too."

Josh came over after dinner — romance or not, he was still her closest friend in Washington — and they sat in the West Sitting Hall, which was considered the First Family Living Room. It was one of the few rooms in the house where they were able to have furniture from their house in Massachusetts, which made it seem all the more comfortable.

He was wearing another Shetland crewneck, this one sort of deep-sea blue, and she touched his sleeve. "Gosh, this is *so* nice," she said.

He smiled. "It's kind of cold out."

"Right." She leaned forward to get her Coke from the coffee table. "How was practice?"

Josh shrugged. "Okay. Nathan hit so damn many home runs that we had to spend about an hour in the woods looking for the balls."

Meg grinned. Their friend Nathan, who was at least as big as the average NFL linebacker, left nothing to understatement when it came to sports. On the high school's baseball team, he played first base, Josh played second, and another good friend of theirs, Zachary, played center field. Because of this, Steven approved of all of them.

"Did you find anyone to hit with?" Josh asked.

Meg nodded. "Mr. Gaines, from CBS." Another nice thing about the White House was that she could always find singles partners.

"He's supposed to be really good, isn't he?"

She nodded. "Yeah."

"Did you beat him?"

She allowed herself a small grin. It was important to be a good sport. "Yeah."

"Badly?"

"No. Two out of three." She frowned at her Coke can. She couldn't stand the taste of Tab since they'd taken the saccharine out, but Coke didn't do much for her either. "Have I told you how unhappy I am about Nutrasweet?"

"Many times," Josh said.

"You want to hear about it again?"

He shook his head.

"Oh." She put the can down. "Hey, I know what. Let's go look at dresses."

"Mmmm, boy," he said.

"I meant, my *mother's* dresses."

"Sounds fun," he said.

"You know, for the Prom. You can help me figure out what to wear — I'm sure she'll let me borrow one." Well, sort of sure. Meg stood up. "Come on."

He hesitated. "I don't know, I — "

"Come on," she said. "It's stupid to keep putting it off because — "

"What about your parents?" he asked. "I kind of don't think I should go in their room."

"They won't mind," she said. "Besides, they're out at some reception."

He looked worried, but followed her down the hall.

Actually, her parents *had* had very strict rules about them hanging out in bedrooms together. Not that she and Josh had ever done anything particularly controversial. Even by *nervous* parents' standards. Since her

15

social life outside the White House was completely in the public domain, and the odds of *really* being alone inside the White House were pretty slim, neither of them had ever felt comfortable enough to get too carried away. As time went on, Josh had gotten more and more frustrated about this, while she — in many ways — had been kind of relieved. It had made life significantly less complicated.

"What," Josh said, smiling at her.

"I'm sorry." She shook her head. "I was just — "

"Thinking," he said.

"Yeah."

They went into her parents' room and through to her mother's very neat — and very large — closet space, lined with suits and dresses, skirts and blouses and gowns.

"Jesus," Josh said, staring at the rows of clothes.

"Want me to do my Daisy Buchanan impression?" Meg asked.

He laughed.

"Is that a no?"

"When does she find time to buy all this stuff?"

Meg shrugged. "They come to her, mostly."

He pointed to the tags on all of the hangers. "What are those?"

"They always write down when and where she's worn the outfit so, I don't know, she doesn't repeat."

"Hunh." He leaned over to study one of the tags. "Who are 'they'?"

She shrugged again. "I don't know — the Cast of Thousands." She and Steven always called the White House staff the Cast of Thousands. For obvious reasons. She held out one of her favorite gowns, a dark sapphire-blue, very simply cut. "What do you think?"

"Well, I don't know," Josh said. "When was it worn last?"

She grinned. Josh was pretty cute when he wanted to be. Sometimes even when he *didn't* want to be. "Well, I don't know *either*," she said, and checked the tag. "Right after Labor Day."

"*Where* was it worn?"

"A thing for NASA."

"It's nice," he said.

"It's *really* nice."

He held out a strapless black dress. "This one's pretty."

"No *way* would she let me wear that," Meg said.

"Why?" He looked at it again. What there *was* of it. "Oh."

"Yeah." Meg put the black dress back and took out a white one, with a scoop neck and three-quarter sleeves. "This, she'd let me wear."

"Kind of bridal," he said.

"Yeah." She hung it up, taking out a shimmery golden dress. "How about this?"

He shook his head.

"She looks — monarchial — in it."

"Is that a word?" he asked doubtfully.

She frowned. "I think so."

"I *don't* think so."

She frowned, making a mental note to look the word up later, although she almost never remembered to do things like that. "She looks — queenly."

He laughed. "Got it."

"In *fact*, she — " Meg stopped, suddenly hearing her parents out in the bedroom.

"I thought they were out," Josh whispered.

"I guess they're back," Meg said, and raised her

voice, hearing her mother coming towards the closet. "Hi, Mom."

"Oh, hi." Her mother came in, pausing in the act of taking her hair down when she saw Josh. "Hello, Josh."

"Um, hello, Mrs. Powers," he said, looking embarrassed. "We were just — "

"He wanted to try on some of your clothes," Meg said helpfully.

"Oh." Her mother smiled. "Are there any you'd like to take along with you?"

"Um — they're all very nice," he said.

"Well, just help yourself," she said.

They followed her out to the bedroom where Meg's father was tuning the television to pick up the Red Sox on satellite.

"So *that's* why you're home early," Meg said.

"It was, perhaps, a factor," her mother agreed, taking off her earrings.

"I don't suppose I'll ask what you all were doing in the closet," her father said, concentrating on the television.

"The key question is, what were we all doing coming *out*," Meg said, quite amused — as was generally the case — by her own humor. A serious character flaw, no doubt.

"Actually," Josh said, "we were just going to go upstairs and watch a movie."

"That's right," Meg said, "we were. Do you guys want to too?"

"No, thanks," her father said, hanging his dinner jacket over the back of a chair and sitting down to watch the game.

"No, thank you," her mother said, indicating her

18

desk, and piles of papers and folders. "If your brothers are up there, tell them we're home."

Predictably, her brothers *were* up there, watching some space epic or other, and she and Josh ended up in the Washington Sitting Room, which was part of a third-floor bedroom suite.

Meg broke the silence. "Want me to sing 'I'm Coming Out'?"

Josh laughed. "Not really."

"I do it really nicely."

He laughed.

"Dulcet tones, people say."

"Unh-hunh," he said.

"No one takes me seriously."

"Gosh, wonder why," he said, and sat down on the red-and-white upholstered couch.

She sat next to — but not *right* next to — him. "Do you think finals'll be bad?"

"Physics'll be the worst."

She nodded, and they sat there without speaking for a few minutes.

"This is pretty hard, Meg," he said.

She nodded. "Would you, um," she didn't look at him, "feel better not seeing me at *all*?"

"No," he said. Instantly.

"I don't want that either," she said.

He sighed. "I don't see why we can't just wait until September. And then, you know, go away to school."

They had already had this conversation about thirty times, without much progress. Maybe she *should* have let it happen that way — just let them drift apart, never initiating any sort of confrontation about it, taking advantage of the fact that he was going all the way out to Stanford and that they wouldn't have to worry about running into each other. But, as she'd felt him getting more and more involved, while she — it hadn't seemed fair. She still wondered — like now — if breaking up had been such a great idea, but it wouldn't have been right to — she sighed.

"I need you as a friend," she said. "I need you *more* as a friend."

He nodded. Unhappily.

"Are you mad?"

He shook his head.

"I'm sorry."

"I need *you* as a friend too," he said. "I'm just — it's hard."

She nodded, wanting to touch his hair, or hold his hand, or *something*, but not sure if she should.

"Is it okay if I put my arm around you?" he asked.

"I'd like that," she said. "I'd like that a lot."

Chapter
Three

The next day, she played tennis with the Assistant
to the Deputy Secretary of the Interior, Mr. Kirkland.
His reputation had preceded him — he had won more
than one government employee tournament, *and* he
was only thirty-four — and apparently, her reputation
had too because when he won service, he smashed the
first ball in for a very intimidating ace. And the second
one. By the third serve, she had figured out the spin
and chipped it back, but he won the game on six
points.

"Do you want to switch sides on odd games?" he
asked, at the net.

She looked at him, seeing a not-very-well-masked
confident smile. It might even have been a patronizing
smile. If there was anything in life that Meg hated, it
was being patronized.

"Sure," she said, and switched sides.

The work on her serve these last few weeks had made a difference, and she won her game, although he passed her once at the net. They stayed on serve right up until the ninth game, which she lost, and he took the set 6-4.

"You're quite a fine player," he said. Smiling.

What she wasn't, although she was careful never to advertise it in public, was a good loser. "Thank you," she said, and got ready to serve the first game of the second set, noticing that there were quite a few people — including Preston — sitting in the seats at the side of the court, watching. An audience. Swell.

She bounced the ball three times, pulled in a deep breath, and smashed the ball into the service court. Ace. Only her second one of the match. She spun the next one to his backhand, and he was caught off-guard, Meg easily putting away the return.

She won the game on four points, and they switched sides.

"That's a tricky little serve you have there," he said.

Little. "Thank you," she said.

She won the set — mainly by slashing cross-courts and making him run — then waited on the baseline for him to serve the first game of the third and final set. He was taking his time — toweling off, drinking some water, straightening the strings on his racket — so she decided that her strategy for the third set would be to lob over his head if he came to the net, and to drop-shot short if he stayed back. *Remind* him that he was thirty-four, and maybe not as fast as he used to be.

His strategy, it seemed, was to hit the ball as hard as he could — which meant that if it went in, she lost the point more often than not; if it went out, she won.

22

They were tied, four-all, her serve, when she started double-faulting. Three times, to be exact, and suddenly, he was serving for the match.

Damn it, damn it, damn it. What a time to choke. She bent down to tie her shoe, finding it a real battle to keep from swearing aloud, so pumped up that she wanted to kick this guy from here to Bethesda. She took a deep breath. Okay, okay, she had to work harder, that's all. Work *a lot* harder.

His first serve came slamming in and she hit the return right past him as he ran in to the net. Almost right *through* him. Love-fifteen. She went down the line with the next two, and won the game with a little drop shot he couldn't quite get.

Okay, okay, five-all. Time to make her move. She put everything she had left into her serve, and two aces — tricky little serve indeed — and several hard rallies later, won her service game. Six-five, her favor.

They switched sides, Mr. Kirkland not saying anything this time, and she was aware that it had gotten very quiet around the court. She kept her eyes down, concentrating on not paying attention to anything except the next game.

The first serve came in hard, but she blocked it back. They hit forehand to forehand once, twice, three times, and his shot hit the netcord, falling over onto — her side. Fifteen-love. Hell.

She smashed his next serve right back to him and he adjusted late, hitting it out. Fifteen-all. He double-faulted, and it was fifteen-thirty. She missed with a cross-court backhand, and it was thirty-all. The next point was another long rally — forehand to forehand, backhand to backhand — and he finally hit one into the net. Thirty-forty. Match point.

She bent to wait for the serve, ignoring all of the people around them, blocking out everything except the ball. The point. The victory so close that she could — again, they had a long rally, so long that she felt her arms starting to shake from nervousness. He followed with a hard backhand to the net; she waited, timed her swing, and lobbed it just over his head, just inside the baseline.

Game, set, and match.

Mr. Kirkland looked disappointed, but smiled as they shook hands. "You're a very good player," he said.

She flushed. The fever to win always left almost as abruptly as it would arrive. "Um, thank you," she said. "So are you."

"Rematch sometime?"

"Sure." Feeling shy, she spent extra time gathering up her gear, hoping that the people who had been watching them would leave. Most of them did — more than one coming over to tell her what a good match she had played — and she went over to sit next to Preston.

"Well, no one'll ever accuse *you* of not having the killer instinct, kid," he said.

"It *shows?*"

He laughed. "I'd say so."

"Is it unattractive?" she asked uneasily.

He ruffled up her hair. "Your mother seems to be doing okay with it."

Meg automatically looked towards the West Wing of the White House. "Yeah, but — she's different."

He also looked at the West Wing. "Old Cal Wilson thinks you're a determined little lady."

24

Meg grinned. Cal Wilson was an economic advisor, and *very* Southern. "End quote."

Preston grinned too. "Afraid so."

She glanced over at him, his outfit so jazzily put-together that *Miami Vice* would be jealous. A linen suit, so grey that it was almost blue, with a subtly blue shirt, and a teal silk tie. To her amusement — and her brothers' great glee — Preston had shown up on more than one Ten Most Eligible Bachelors' list. Most notably, *Cosmopolitan.*

"What," he said, smiling.

"I was thinking about you and *Cosmo.*"

He rolled his eyes.

"You know what Beth says?"

"I can guess what Beth says," he said.

Meg just grinned. She and Beth held the theory that despite the fact that Preston lived with someone, what he was *really* waiting for was for one of them — they could never agree upon *which* one — to be old enough before venturing into marriage. They had agreed, however, that this theory might best be kept to themselves.

"So," Preston said, indicating the court. "What's the story?"

The man was nothing if not up-front. She zipped and unzipped her racket cover. "How good do you think I am?"

"Out of *my* league, kid."

She shook her head. "I'm serious. Do you think I'm getting good?"

"Ned Kirkland doesn't exactly lose all the time."

She thought about that, then folded her arms.

"What," he said.

"Do you think Mom and Dad would let me play a

few tournaments this summer? I mean, you know, junior stuff?"

"Pretty high profile," he said.

She nodded.

"I don't know. Can't see them being *thrilled* about the idea."

"Well — " She decided to try the only halfway decent argument she had. "Steven gets to play baseball."

"Steven *lives* to play baseball."

"Yeah, but — " She stopped. She would rather die than whine in front of Preston. "I guess everyone's used to him being really intense and me just screwing around."

He nodded.

"Is there any way I could do it and *not* attract attention?"

"Lose," he said.

She nodded. That'd do it all right. "I, um, I might do a lot of losing anyway."

"If you thought *that*, kid, you probably wouldn't be so interested in doing it."

She had to grin. "Well — maybe."

"How about I talk to Gabler" — who was in charge of the White House security detail — "and find out some logistics? Then you can present the idea a little better."

She nodded gratefully. He knew her parents about as well as she did.

"How about we go inside and find a couple of Cokes?" he suggested.

Cokes. She sighed. "Can I give you my speech about Nutrasweet again?"

He laughed. "Sure."

• • •

"So," Beth said on the phone a couple of nights later. "How's it going with Josh?"

"I don't know," Meg said. "I guess it's better. I still feel like a snake though."

"You're still going on Friday?"

The Prom. "Yeah," Meg said. "It seems like mostly everyone's going with friends, so maybe it won't be so bad." The worst thing about the Prom, at the moment, was that they were having it a week *before* finals — instead of after finals, like normal schools — because the stupid Prom Committee had forgotten to make arrangments until the last minute.

"What are you going to wear," Beth asked, "the blue one?"

Her mother had, after a few "you really don't think we could come up with something a little more appropriate?" remarks, finally agreed. "Yeah," Meg said. "What are *you* wearing?"

"Black."

"Figures. Is it like, completely sultry?"

Beth laughed. "Yeah. Is yours?"

"Slightly."

"Not everyone can carry it off," Beth said, in a kindly "one-day-when-you're-as-cool-as-I-am" voice.

"Unh-hunh," Meg said.

"Where are you guys having yours again?"

"At this hotel out near Dupont Circle. It's not, you know, the Mayflower, but it's okay."

"If you can believe it," Beth said, "they want us to agree to come back to the gym and have the post-Prom party *there*."

"What, to stop drunk driving?"

"Yeah. Stuart wants to go to 33 Landsdowne."

A Boston disco. "Gross," Meg said.

27

Beth laughed. "Yeah, he isn't really your type."

"Is he *yours*?"

"Well — not really. But, he's kind of fun."

"Does he like your hats?" Meg asked. Beth always wore hats.

Beth laughed again. "Yeah, actually."

"That's in his favor."

"Yeah. He says we make a striking couple."

"Oh, Jesus," Meg said.

"I told you you wouldn't like him."

"Does your stepfather like him?"

Beth sighed deeply. "Stuart has a mustache."

Meg laughed. Beth's stepfather wasn't exactly open-minded.

"*And* he drives a Triumph."

"What's he majoring in?"

"Economics."

"Your stepfather must approve of *that*," Meg guessed.

"Yeah, but he thinks he's too slick."

"From the sound of it, he *is*."

"Yeah, kind of," Beth agreed.

"I really wouldn't like him, would I?"

Beth laughed. "No, not really."

After they hung up, Meg was lying on her bed reading *As I Lay Dying* and waiting for *David Letterman* to start, when her mother came in.

"What are you reading?" she asked.

Meg held up the book.

"Are you enjoying it?"

"No."

Her mother smiled, sitting down on the end of the bed.

"Beth says hi."

"What's she up to lately?"

28

Meg shrugged. "Waiting for graduation, mostly."

"Well, I hope you'll get to spend some time with her this summer," her mother said.

"Are we going to go up there at all, or just to Camp David?"

"I don't know," her mother said. "I thought we might try for a week in August. And we'll have that trip to Geneva in July."

Meg grinned. "You make it sound like a vacation."

"The glass is half full," her mother said.

"Wait," Meg pretended to reach for a pen, "let me write that down."

Her mother smiled.

Speaking of which. "What are you going to say in your speech?" Her mother had been invited to speak at her graduation — about which, Meg was both embarrassed and pleased.

"You mean, at the school?" her mother asked.

Meg nodded.

"Oh, I don't know," her mother said. "About how you all have only just begun, and can choose many paths on the highway of life, I suppose."

Meg looked at her uncertainly. "That's a joke, right?"

"Shouldering adult responsibilities, seeing graduation as both an ending and a new beginning — " Her mother shrugged.

"Now I *know* you're kidding," Meg said, almost positive.

"Well — what would you expect me to say?"

"I don't know." Meg frowned. "I was kind of hoping you'd tell some jokes."

"Jokes." Her mother frowned too. "I see."

"Senator Talbot's son is in my class — we could get

him to come." Senator Talbot was extremely conservative and not one of her mother's favorites. His son Jon was nice though.

"I'll think of some jokes," her mother said.

"Good," Meg said. Not that her mother didn't always tell jokes — too many jokes, her advisors worried — in her speeches. "You won't say stuff about *me*, right?"

"I expect I'll have to *mention* you."

"You won't say you're proud or anything, will you?"

Her mother laughed. "If you think about it, there would be a lot more commotion if I went and *weren't* speaking."

Meg nodded. Either way though, it was going to be something of a circus.

"I think it will be more low-key than you expect," her mother said, apparently reading her mind.

"Do you really think so?"

Her mother hesitated. "Well — "

Meg grinned. "Neither do I."

Chapter
Four

It was Thursday, and Meg woke up in a very good mood. A *hell* of a mood. The switchboard, which she used as an alarm clock, only had to call once, even. And, it was sunny.

"Yes," she said to Vanessa, who stretched and purred. "We *do* need to put on 'I Love Rock and Roll.' " She got up, dropping a tape she had made with Beth once into the tape cassette deck of her stereo and "I Love Rock and Roll" came on. Loud.

She decided to wear her Williams sweatshirt — half because she liked it; half because it would annoy her parents a little. And this wasn't a day to wear an *un*ripped pair of jeans.

The tape was a rowdy one, full of songs like "Respect" and "Brick House," and as she got ready for school, she sang them to Vanessa. Who didn't seem overly impressed.

31

At the Presidential Dining Room, she stopped in the doorway. "Good morning, my little subjects," she said, the rest of the family already eating.

"Oh, Christ," Steven said. "Not that again."

"Not *that*," Neal said.

"Good morning," her parents said, her father frowning at Steven for swearing.

Meg stayed in the doorway. "The proper greeting is, 'Good morning, dear Queen.' "

Her family continued eating breakfast.

"*Well*," she said, and swept to her seat.

"What are the odds of Her Majesty returning to her chambers and putting on something more presentable?" her father asked.

Meg pushed up one sweatshirt sleeve, amused. "The Queen is content, as is." She picked up her orange juice, then stopped, looking around the table. "No kippers? I *say*, you Americans are a savage lot."

Both of her parents laughed.

"What *are* the odds of your going and changing, Meg?" her mother asked.

"I *like* to think I change and grow every day," Meg said, and very solemnly sipped some orange juice.

Steven pretended to throw up, Neal giggling and imitating him.

"Anyway," Meg said, sipping, "this particular queen feels that comfy is as comfy does." She glanced up at the butler waiting by her place. "Just a mimosa, please."

Her father's eyebrows went up.

"Remember the time difference," she said. "I'm *accustomed* to a cocktail right about now."

Her mother sighed, pushing away the morning news

32

summary. "Don't you have homework or something that needs finishing?"

Meg shook her head sadly.

"What your mother means," her father said, "is that maybe she's trying to concentrate."

"No news is good news," Meg said, and reached across the table to grab the Lucky Charms box from Neal, the two of them scuffling slightly.

"Neal, give your sister the box," their father said, sounding tired.

"She should *ask!*" Neal said.

"She *should* ask," their mother said, frowning at Meg.

Meg sat back, folding her hands in her lap. "I guess the colonies have had a bad effect on me." She smiled across the table at Neal. A — monarchial — smile. "Will you please pass me the cereal, sweetpea?"

"Talk about queer." Steven pushed away from the table, putting on his Red Sox cap — their father wouldn't let him wear it when they were eating — and grabbing his knapsack. "Later."

"No royal kiss?" Meg asked.

"No way," he said.

"No *presidential* kiss?"

"Right," he said, and grinned sheepishly at their mother. They weren't big on hugging — at least, she and her brothers weren't — but since her mother had been shot, they were all a little more careful to say pleasant good-byes. "Um, see ya."

"Savage." Meg checked her watch — it *was* kind of on the late side. "I'd better get going too." She grabbed a handful of Lucky Charms from the box. "Mmmm, can't tell you how happy I am about these purple marshmallows they added."

33

"Charming," her father said, watching her.

Meg grinned. "Want to see *charming?*"

"No," her mother said quickly.

"Your loss," Meg said, and grabbed another handful for the road. For the car, anyway. "Um, let's be careful out there," she said, which was her good-luck-charm good-bye. Courtesy of *Hill Street Blues.*

"No presidential kiss?" her mother asked.

"Elected officials kiss *queens,* not the other way around."

Her mother stood up, her expression amused.

"That's okay," Meg said. "You can owe me."

"Are you staying after tonight?" her father asked.

"For a while, maybe. Then I thought I'd come home and — "

"Tennis," her mother guessed.

Meg shrugged. "Kind of tough to find a cricket game around here." She picked up *her* knapsack. "See you later."

All of her teachers had just about given up on getting anyone to pay attention — finals or no finals — so, school went pretty quickly. Josh had to make up a calculus test and she'd promised to wait for him, so she hung out in the auditorium for a while, watching the juniors rehearse their *Farewell, Seniors* show, then went down to her locker to get her books.

The halls had pretty much cleared out, and she sat on the floor, opening her physics book. Glancing at it was *sort* of like studying. Aware of Dennis nearby, she looked up.

"I told Josh I'd wait for him," she said, "then I'll be ready to go."

He nodded.

"Twenty minutes, maybe."

He nodded, withdrawing somewhat.

She decided to go through the chapter summaries, and was on chapter eight when Dennis came back over, frowning.

"Let me have that for a minute," he said, indicating her watch. "There's some kind of signal problem."

She glanced at it automatically. "What do you mean?"

He shrugged, holding his hand out. "I don't know — maybe you banged it during gym."

Volleyball. Most likely. She handed the watch to him, her arm feeling strange without it. *Looking* strange too, with the watch-shaped tan line. She grinned at him, pushing her sleeve down. "You want me to be like, extra careful?"

He didn't really respond, adjusting his earpiece.

So what else was new. She bent over her book.

"Hi," Josh said, jogging down towards her, already in his baseball practice clothes.

She closed the book. "Hi. The test go okay?"

"I don't know, pretty much." He sat down next to her. "Feel like watching practice for a while?"

"No, I'm going to go home and work on my serve." She reached over to snap the elastic strap he used to keep his glasses on when he played sports. "What's next — clip-on sunglasses?"

"Yeah," he said. "Don't tell anyone."

She laughed, putting her physics book into her knapsack and zipping it up.

"Well," he said. "Guess I'm late for practice."

She nodded. "He's going to make you run laps."

"Yeah," Josh said, without enthusiasm, and put his hand out to help her up, Meg taking it. Briefly.

Today was a side-exit day and he walked her to the

door, Dennis behind them, Chet just ahead of them.

"You want to come over tonight?" she asked. "Hang out for a while?"

"Sure," he said. "Eight okay?"

"If you come at seven-thirty, we can watch *Entertainment Tonight*."

"Ooh, boy," he said, and put on his baseball cap. "Hit lots of aces."

"Hit lots of home runs."

"You *know* who's going to be hitting home runs."

She grinned. "Well, have fun chasing them."

As she walked outside, she glanced back to see if he was still there, which he was.

"Tie your shoes," Dennis said.

"What?" She looked down, so used to wearing them *untied* — except when she was actually *playing* tennis — that tying them never occurred to her. "Okay." She bent down.

"Wait until you get to the car," Chet said, without turning.

"It'll only take a — "

He turned. "Wait until you — " He stopped, staring at her left arm. "Meg, where the hell's your — "

Out of nowhere, there was an explosion in the road ahead of them, followed by a second one, and then a third, as a car and a van came speeding through the smoke, veering right up over the sidewalk at them.

"Get her inside!" Chet yelled, his gun already out, blocking her.

Meg stared, too stunned to react as men in masks burst out of the car and van, firing automatic weapons. The smoke was worse, but she saw Chet stumbling back, blood spurting from his chest and neck, and horrified, she turned to try and find Dennis, who was facedown on the sidewalk, blood spreading out underneath him. The school door was opening — Josh! — and she had just enough time to yell "Get down!" before she felt herself being lifted right up off the ground and slammed into the van, the impact of the metal flooring jarring up through her hands and knees. Men piled in after her, still shooting as the van skidded away.

The door slammed, the light dimming, and the van was loud with mask-muffled shouting, the air so thick with the smell of nervous perspiration that she couldn't breathe. Her arms were being wrenched up behind her back, tight metal digging into her wrists. Then, she was on her back, a man straddling her, aiming what looked like a machine gun at her face.

"Where else you bugged?" he shouted.

She just stared, breathing hard, too scared to move. He hit her across the face with the gun. "Tell me!"

She felt bright, sickening pain first; then blood rolling down the side of her face. He hit her again, harder, and she felt tears — it couldn't be blood from her *eye* — joining the trickle of blood.

"Answer me!"

"I — " Her vision was blurred by warm liquid — "I — "

A hand dug in, dizzyingly, somewhere between her neck and shoulder and she groaned, her heart beating so hard that she couldn't really hear anything else. "Tell me!" he yelled.

"Okay," another, much calmer, voice said. "She doesn't know. Just get to it."

A light flashed into her eyes and hands pried her

mouth open, something metal touching her teeth, Meg struggling away in complete terror.

"Put her out first," the calm voice said.

"Fuck that! She — "

"Put her out," the man said.

Chapter
Five

Dark. Hot. Pain. Most of the pain was in her mouth, along with thick liquid, and she choked a little, her lips too numb to spit it out right. Everything felt heavy, like she'd been in an accident, or — Jesus Christ.

There was something metal on her left wrist, then chain links, then another cuff around what felt like a bed frame — oh, Christ. Shooting, Chet and Dennis lying on the — oh, Christ, oh, Christ, oh, Christ. Panicking, she yanked at the handcuffs through the dizziness, trying to sit up, to run away — except she couldn't, she — oh, God. She yanked harder, fighting to sit, to stand, to — but the cuffs were tighter, and it was darker, and — the door slammed open.

Oh, Jesus. She sat very still, very stiff. The man came in, his face misshapen by a stocking mask, and she gulped down a moan of fear, moving back away from him, finding herself in the corner of a wall.

He came closer, not speaking, and she held her breath, shaking so hard that the bed seemed to vibrate.

The man just stood there, looking at her, then laughed, very quietly.

Her voice wouldn't work and she swallowed, feeling nausea up in her throat. Her tongue hit a deep hole and she realized, the nausea much worse, that she was missing *teeth*. That half the side of her mouth was — oh, Christ. Oh, Christ, oh, Christ, oh — control. She had to find some control, couldn't let him —

"W-what's going on?" she asked, her voice higher and shakier than she'd ever remembered hearing it.

He didn't say anything.

She swallowed. "Are you like — Shi'ites?"

This time, his laugh was more genuine.

"Are you someone *like* that?" she asked.

He didn't answer, reaching up to turn on an overhead bare lightbulb. The sudden light hurt her eyes, but she kept them open, getting her first good look at him. He was tall — at least as big as her father — with dark hair bunched up under the mask. He was wearing a dark blue T-shirt, jeans, and leather high-tops. The familiarity of seeing New Balance basketball sneakers was surprisingly comforting.

"Are we in *America*, at least?" she asked.

His hand came towards her face and she flinched away, not sure what he was going to do. It closed around her jaw, his thumb pressing in right where the teeth were gone and she winced, trying to pull away.

His fingers tightened. "If I hit you there, it's *really* going to hurt," he said, in the very calm voice she'd heard in the van.

She stopped pulling, her muscles tensed against the pain, back to being terrified.

40

"Right," he said, and turned her face towards him, studying the right side of her forehead. "Your head hurt?"

Her *mouth* hurt. She sat as still as she could, her heart beating so hard that she couldn't get her breath.

He released her and she sank back against the wall, bringing her free hand up to hold her jaw, shutting her eyes so she wouldn't cry.

"Didn't expect us to leave that transmitter in, did you?" he asked.

She opened her eyes, confused enough to forget the pain.

"They probably told you it was a filling," he said.

A filling. She flashed on going to the dentist right after her mother had been elected and yeah, she had had a cavity — only the second one ever, and — Steven and Neal had had cavities too. Steven and Neal — oh, Christ. What if these people had —

"Lucky you have good teeth," he said. "I would have taken them *all* out."

Meg didn't even really hear that, terrified for her brothers. "Am I the only — " She didn't want to give them ideas. Didn't want to say anything that might — how the hell had they known about her teeth when *she* hadn't even — "Give me your watch," Dennis had said, "there's a problem with the signal." "Tie your shoes," he'd said, even though she was never, ever supposed to stop unnecessarily when she was in transit — oh, Christ. She looked up, aware that the man was watching her. "That bastard sold me out," she said.

His smile was especially scary through the mask. "Looks that way."

"Well, is he — " She stiffened, realizing for the first

time that she wasn't wearing her jeans, or her Williams sweatshirt, or — Jesus *Christ*. She looked down — which hurt her head — seeing an unfamiliar grey sweatshirt, grey sweatpants, and white socks. Feeling very exposed, after the fact, she brought her knees up close to the rest of her body, covering her chest with her free arm.

The man's smile widened. "Was beginning to wonder if you'd notice." He paused. "You have some interesting tan lines."

"I don't — " She swallowed, very nauseated. "I mean, why — "

"Wild guess," he said.

Because they couldn't take chances. Because she might have been bugged. She probably *had* been. She swallowed again, remembering how many men had been in the van, not wanting to imagine them all — she would be able to tell if they had done anything *really* awful — right? — but the thought of them all looking — "Did you — do anything?" she asked, trying to block out any thoughts.

He didn't answer.

"You can't tell me *that?*"

He moved his jaw. "Time was a factor," he said finally.

She decided to take that as a no, letting some of the tension out of her muscles, but keeping her arm across her chest. "It's not like they go pawing through my drawers, putting bugs on everything," she said stiffly, although now that she thought about it, they probably *did*. Why the *hell* hadn't her parents warned — because, of course, they wouldn't want her to worry. Because — she couldn't think about her parents. If she thought about her parents, or her

42

brothers, or — Josh. Jesus Christ. The school door opening, all of the shooting and smoke — what if he — she closed her eyes, moving her hand up to cover them.

"Need to use the bathroom?" he asked.

Yes. But it could wait. "Can you just — " She swallowed. "Were people hurt?"

"No kidding," he said.

Oh, Jesus. "People — my age?"

He smiled. "What, worried about your *boy*friend or something?"

She looked up uneasily, afraid to say yes, but really wanting — needing — to know.

The man smiled more. "He's in the hospital — I don't know if he died or not."

That was terrifying, but there was something so glib about the way he said it, that she tried to see his expression through the mask. The smile was all that showed. "Are you lying?" she asked, feeling her voice shake.

"Maybe," he said.

"*Are* you?"

"Got shot about five times," he said.

"I know you're lying," she said, shakily.

"If he isn't dead yet, I can send someone to finish the job."

That made her cry, and she lowered her head, not wanting to give him the satisfaction of seeing.

He nodded. "Figured you for a crier."

She couldn't stop, and had to lower her head more, blocking her face with her hand.

"Doing the President proud," he said.

"Doing *your* parents proud too," she said, trying to stop.

He laughed. "You need to use the bathroom, or not?"

She nodded, not lifting her head.

"Okay." He took an extra pair of handcuffs out of his back pocket, snapping one end around her already cuffed hand, then bringing her right hand over to cuff it. When he unlocked the cuff around the bed frame, her left arm fell, and it was so numb that she had to use her right hand to lift it off the mattress. She tried to move her fingers, wincing as some of the blood came stinging back in.

"Must hurt," he said. There was no sympathy in his voice, and she didn't bother looking up, gently massaging her left hand with her right, hampered by the handcuffs.

"Let's go."

She slowly flexed her hand. "Did you throw away my shoes too?"

He bent down, picking up a pair of cheap blue sneakers and dropping them on the mattress.

Her legs felt very tired and heavy, and she manuevered them over to the sneakers, slipping them on. They were only a little too big, and she tried to tie them, but couldn't with the handcuffs.

"Come on," he said impatiently. "Let's go."

She swung her legs over the edge of the mattress, uneasily, holding her wrists just above them. "Do I have to wear these?"

"You should thank me for letting you wear *anything*," he said.

Instead of feeling embarrassed this time, she was only angry. "Yeah," she said, stiffly. "Thanks for the dental work too."

He just looked at her, and she stood up, her legs

unsteady. Standing made her so dizzy that she sagged back down towards the bed, noticing for the first time how much her head hurt, how much she — aware of how irritated he was getting, she slid her right foot forward for one step, then lifted her left one for another. What if he was lying? What if he was *pretending* to take her to the bathroom, but was really going to kill her, or — she felt a wave of fear worse than the dizziness and stood very still, too afraid to move.

He made an impatient sound and grabbed her arm, yanking her forward. Then, they were out in a dark, empty corridor, with a wall to her left, a door straight across from her, and a hall that went about ten or fifteen feet to her right before turning a corner. A house? Some kind of storage building?

"In there," he said, indicating the door.

She turned the knob and saw that it was, indeed, a bathroom. There was a light switch just inside the door and she pushed it up, going in and closing the door behind her. She leaned against it briefly, feeling for — and not finding — a lock. Not that she had expected one.

Okay, okay, don't panic. Don't lose it. She forced herself to look around the room. Small, windowless, the sink rust-stained. Like a gas station, sort of.

"Don't take all night," he said through the door.

Night. Did that mean that it was night? Yeah, he would have said day otherwise. Was it still today? Or had she been unconscious for a long time? Or — he probably wasn't kidding about her hurrying up.

She saw that they had — at least — put underwear on her. Men's underwear, apparently new. She was very careful not to touch anything — especially in a place like this — but stayed at the sink as long as she could, washing her hands, her face, her neck, her face again. Her mouth really hurt, but what if they were in a place where you couldn't drink the water? It wouldn't be safe to —

The man opened the door. "Let's go already."

"Is this water safe to drink?" she asked.

"No kidding." He grabbed her elbow, pulling her roughly into the hall.

"I can't rinse my damn mouth, at least?" she asked, knocked off-balance.

"Try *shutting* your damn mouth," he said.

What she tried to do, was get back into the bathroom, and he slammed her up against the wall, keeping her there with one forearm pressed into her throat, yanking a gun out of the back of his jeans and pointing it at her face.

"You want me to kill you?" he asked. "You want me to kill you right now?"

She stared at the gun — a *real* gun — a gun that he might — that he was about to — that —

"Answer me!"

She shook her head, too scared to open her mouth.

"*Answer* me," he said.

"No," she said, her voice so small that *she* could barely hear it.

He looked at her for a long minute, then nodded, stepping away so suddenly that she fell, landing hard on her right elbow.

"Come on, get up," he said, kicking her in the ribs, and she groaned. "Hurry up."

With an effort, she pushed herself to a sitting position, then all the way up, hunching over on her side.

"Get in there," he said, gesturing with the gun.

She nodded, walking quickly into the room, not

protesting as he used the extra pair of handcuffs to cuff her to the bed frame before uncuffing her right hand from the other pair, testing the lock with one hard yank.

"Are you coming back?" she asked.

He didn't answer, turning to leave.

She watched him, relieved, at least, that he was wearing a mask. That meant that they weren't going to kill her. As long as she couldn't identify them, she would be safe.

"I won't try and look at you," she said as he reached up to turn the light off.

He turned it back on. "What?"

"I just meant — " She blinked from looking at the bulb. "I mean, I'm not *stupid*."

"Only wore it to scare you," he said.

She frowned. "I don't — "

Very slowly, he pulled the stocking mask off. "Maybe this'll scare you more," he said, and smiled.

She stared at him, at his *face*, a surprisingly normal face, and her stomach both twisted and fell. His face. Jesus Christ, that meant — Jesus Christ — "I thought — " She gulped, her voice barely coming out. "Y-you aren't going to let me go?"

"No." He smiled. "I'm not."

Chapter
Six

After he left, slamming the door, it was very, very
quiet. Very, very *dark*.

Okay, okay, don't cry. *Really* don't cry. She pressed
her sweatshirt sleeve across her eyes, fist clenched,
concentrating on swallowing to keep control. Okay,
okay, be calm. She had to try and be calm. To figure
out what she was going to do. If there *was* anything
she could do.

They would find her. Every damn security agency
in the country would be working on this, and they
would have to — except they already would have. She
could be anywhere in the world, and there was no way
that they would — be calm. She had to be calm. Her
mother was the *President* — she would be able to do
something. All Meg had to do was wait. And try to
be calm. To be *brave*.

Her mother would be brave. Her mother would be

completely, totally, *amazingly* — oh, Christ, what if something had happened to her brothers too? And what if Josh really was — she couldn't think about it. If she thought about it, she would start — she was *already* crying. Oh, hell.

She forced herself to lean back against the bed frame. To take a few deep breaths. She closed her eyes, tears still pushing out and down her face. Oh, God, her mouth hurt. Her mouth, and her head, and her side — her mother would be brave. Her father would be brave. *Preston* would be brave. She, at least, had to try. Jesus.

Tentative in the darkness, she pressed down on the mattress with her hand, moving herself into a more comfortable position. Her handcuffed hand was already falling asleep and she flexed her fingers a few times. Handcuffed. Jesus Christ, she was actually — she had to be calm. The only way to — very, very calm.

Her mouth was really hurting and, very cautious, she touched the hole with her tongue. It was still bleeding — although not as much — and seemed very deep. Two molars, probably. Maybe even three. She shivered, remembering the light in her eyes, the cold metal on her teeth — Thank God he had had them knock her out. It would have been — Thank God.

Maybe he was lying about killing her. They'd have to be *crazy* to kill the President's daughter. Kidnapping was bad enough. Kidnapping. Even with Dennis's help — was he out there with them? Or, with all the blood she'd seen, was he — it was still hard to believe they had pulled it off. And they must have. If it was night, hours had passed, and she should have been located by now. But how had they managed — he was smart. Extremely smart, with the same aura of professionalism she associated with Secret Service and FBI agents. Calm, clear, unemotional — what if he was an insider too? What if — he didn't seem like a terrorist. At least, not the crazed revolutionary types she pictured. This guy was American; this guy was obviously well-educated. And there didn't seem to be anything fanatical about him. Neat, dark hair; lighter, expressionless eyes; straight nose. Christ, he could be any one of the youngish ambitious men that overpopulated Washington, wearing well-cut suits and carrying briefcases. Actually, with a suit and a pair of Ray-Bans — had she seen him before? Had he maybe been in the streets around the school, or at one of her tennis matches, or — she had probably seen him before. He hadn't planned the thing overnight.

Her mouth hurt so much that she decided to concentrate on *that* for a while, resting her head against the wall. It was throbbing, like the beginning of a terrible earache, and the whole side of her face felt hot. He could have let her rinse it out, at least. Although that might have made it hurt even more. But this way, it was sure to get infected. Not that she didn't have worse things to worry about.

There hadn't been a mirror in the bathroom, and she reached up to touch her forehead, feeling a huge bump. There seemed to be a split in her right eyebrow and she touched it cautiously, feeling what had to be blood. The water from washing her face had been brownish-red, and the washing must have opened it up again. She let her hand fall, wiping the blood on her sleeve. Not *even* her sleeve. Or her sweatpants, or her underwear, or — think about something else.

There was a tiny crack of dim light at the bottom of the door and she focused on it, afraid of the darkness.

The light chain was somewhere near the middle of the room. If she could reach it, maybe — but he wouldn't like it. And he might come in and hurt her. *Kill* her.

Kill her. Christ, this couldn't really be happening. One minute, she was talking to Josh; the next — she couldn't think about it. If she thought about any of it, or him, or — it just couldn't be happening.

And crying sure as hell wasn't going to get her anywhere.

Of course, it wouldn't *hurt* either. He might come in and laugh at her, but — to hell with him. There'd be something wrong with her if she *weren't* crying in this situation.

Only — would her mother be crying? No. Her mother would be *plotting*. Okay. She would try plotting. Do something constructive. Something to stay in control.

Maybe the handcuffs weren't fastened right. It was highly unlikely, but she pulled at them anyway, the metal edges hurting her skin. First, she tried a slow, gradual pull, then a few quick yanks, the metal digging deeper. She traced the cuffs with her free hand, searching for the locks, pulling the chain to see if anything were loose. Defective. Nothing was.

What about the bed? She felt the frame, shook the bars. Thick, solid metal. Iron, probably. What about weight? Maybe if she lifted the bed with her handcuffed hand, the weight would make them open. It was worth a try, anyway. She moved her legs over the edge of the mattress, a little afraid of standing up in the dark and leaving the security of the bed. Which proved that everything was pretty goddamn relative.

She stood up carefully, letting the dizziness ebb away before turning her attention to the bed frame. She

51

pulled on the cuffs — no result. Maybe if she pulled *really* hard, she could — she tried it, using both hands on the chain. The bed scraped over a foot and she stopped instantly, afraid that someone might have heard the noise.

She waited, holding her breath, but the hall was quiet. Would it be safe to risk lifting the bed? And if she could get to the light, if she could turn it on for even a second, she would feel a lot safer. Less afraid. She reached out as far as she could, letting her arm swing in the darkness.

Oh, Christ, what if there were spiders, and rats, and — she would have seen them when the light was on. This was just a room. A small empty room. A room in God-knows-what, God-knows-where, that she would be in until these people decided it was time to — she tugged on the bed to distract herself, pulling it over another foot or two, towards the middle of the room. She swung her arm again, and the light pull brushed over her wrist. She felt around, the darkness seeming thicker than normal air, until she was holding it tightly in her hand. Even just holding it made her feel safer and she gripped the little chain, deciding whether or not to risk turning the light on.

The hall was still very, very quiet.

Okay. She turned the light on. It *was* just a room. Maybe ten-by-ten, no windows, the walls closer to grey than white. There was no furniture except for an old wooden chair next to the door, and the bed frame — black iron — was even more solid than she'd been afraid it was. The mattress was covered by a white sheet, and she elected not to look underneath it. The sheet looked brand-new and was perfectly clean except for the bloodstains where her face had been.

Her clothes smelled new too, and it was strange to think of him, or someone, going out to shop for all this unisex stuff. Strangely civilized. Smart too, since a cashier would be likely to remember a man buying women's clothes. Not that this guy struck her as someone who would slip up on a detail like that. Not, apparently, a guy who had slipped up anywhere. So far. When he got in touch with her parents though, *that's* when they'd trace him. He had to have demands, or a motive, or *some*thing. And that's when they'd get him.

Should she turn the light off? Not take chances? Or bend down and check out these handcuffs a little more closely? That was an easy choice, and she crouched down next to the bed, studying the shiny metal. Nothing she could break, nothing she could bend, nothing she could do. Where, for Christ's sakes, had he gotten *handcuffs?*

Jesus, was she tired.

Slowly, she straightened up, not sure what to do next. The smart thing would be to turn the light off, move the bed back, and wait. If he didn't know that she could turn the light on, that was an advantage. Of some kind, anyway.

Okay. Whether the darkness was scary or not, she'd do it. As she reached out for the light chain, the door smashed open and he stood there, looking at her.

Part of her wanted to burst into tears, wet her pants, cringe; the other part just stood there, looking right back. The same part was also, out of nowhere, mad as hell. "Got a *problem?*" she asked, and consciously turned her back on him, giving the bed an awkward kick back towards the wall.

He came over behind her, so close that they were

almost touching. "Maybe you ought to think about being a little more scared," he said quietly.

She pushed the bed to get further away from him. "Maybe *you* ought to go to hell."

She saw his fist go back, then found herself crumpled on the floor, handcuffed arm twisted awkwardly, blood gushing from her nose and over her upper lip. She stayed there for a minute or two, disoriented, then lifted her free hand towards her nose, touching the blood. Then, she tried to get up, but was so dizzy she had to sink back down.

He smiled. "Need a hand?"

"Fuck you," she said, and blinked, surprised both by the reaction, and that she was crying.

He shook his head. "Mom and Dad wouldn't like that much."

She kicked at him with her left leg and he stepped out of the way.

"Getting angry?" he asked.

"No!"

"Not even a little?"

Bastard. "What, is that the part you get off on? Or just the beating me up?"

"I'm getting off on just about all of this," he said, his voice both vicious and pleasant.

She slouched down, covering her face with her arm, still stunned by the fact that someone had just *hit* her. With his *fist*. Dizzily, she wiped at the blood with her sleeve.

"Crying?" he asked.

She lifted her head just enough to look at him. "They have agencies you don't even *know* about working on this. Agencies *I* don't even know about."

He nodded seriously, folding his arms and leaning

against the wall. "Consider yourself pretty important, do you?"

"No, I" — frowning hurt, so she stopped — "I mean, *I* don't have anything to do with it."

"Yeah," he agreed. "Good thing 'family' is such a big priority with your mother."

"No, she — " Meg stopped again. "It doesn't work that way."

"If she were a good mother, you wouldn't be here right now."

"It could have happened anyway," she said, hearing the uncertainty in her voice. "I mean, they're pretty rich."

"But *that* would just be ransom," he said. "You'd get out of it all right. But," he shook his head, "because she doesn't love you — "

"It's not her fault," Meg said defensively, almost forgetting the blood and pain. "I mean, just because she's — "

He nodded. "Worries about you kids first and foremost. Always there for you."

These were old arguments, old accusations. Things her family had worked to put to rest. To understand. Things that were none of his goddamn business. "I think you're just trying to upset me," she said, uneasily.

He shrugged. "Seems to be working."

Since she *was* upset, she changed the subject. "You know, you'll never get anything. There's no *way* they negotiate with terrorists."

He shrugged again. "Tough price to pay."

"*Especially* because it's her family, they can't," she said. "You should be smart and let me go."

He nodded. "That'd be smart, all right."

Her nose was hurting more and she lowered her

head, despite the blood, to try and ease the pain.

"Tip your head back," he said.

Feeling dizzy, she lowered it more.

"Come on, tip your head back," he said, sounding impatient. "You want to bleed for the next week?"

She looked up slightly. "What's it to you?"

He frowned, stepping away. "Hey, if you *enjoy* it."

"Not as much as you enjoyed *doing* it." But she tipped her head back, feeling the blood run down somewhere inside her head. Afraid that she was going to cry some more, she closed her eyes, taking a deep breath to distract herself. Talking was a hell of a lot *better* distraction, though. And he looked like he might be about to leave. "Don't I have to talk into a tape recorder, or have my picture taken, or something?" she asked.

"Watch a lot of television?"

"Well — yeah."

He nodded. "Thought so."

"Well — " She frowned, which hurt. "I wouldn't do it anyway."

"Oh, yeah?"

"Yeah," she said, trying to sound defiant. Brave.

He took a quick step towards her, his fist up, grinning when she flinched. He lowered his fist. "If you say so," he said.

"Yeah, well — I wouldn't." Actually, she probably would. Which was a humiliating thought. "You, um, you must want *something*. I mean, otherwise, what's the point?"

"I thought you said I wouldn't get anything *anyway*."

"Well, yeah, but — " She frowned again. "I mean — it seems like sort of a waste."

He shrugged. "Doesn't affect me."

"I don't — " How the hell could it *not*? Unless —
"You mean, you're working for someone?"

He grinned, firing his hand at her as though it were
a gun, the gesture both frightening and mildly
amusing.

"You were supposed to say 'Bingo,' " she said.

His grin broadened.

"Well — who are you working for?"

He didn't answer, taking out a Swiss Army knife
and cutting the light pull so that it would be out of
her reach.

"Do they know how totally stupid this is?" she asked,
watching him put the knife and the string in his
pocket.

He shook his head, grinning again.

"Well" — he could at least *talk* — "who are they?"

"Right," he said.

"Are we like, in their headquarters or something?"
she asked, mentally crossing her fingers.

He laughed.

"Are we?"

"Hmmm," he said. "Now where's the first place you
think they'd look?"

That gave her some hope, but she was careful not
to show it, wiping some blood away. "You mean,
they're letting people know who they are?"

He shrugged affirmatively. "The only thing they can
get out of this is publicity."

That meant that someone would find her. The FBI,
the CIA, *someone*, would find her. All they had to
do —

"Before you get your hopes up, my" — he gave the
word extra irony — " 'employers' don't know who, or
where, I am."

Hell. Naturally. "Going to be tough to send you that W-2 form," she said.

He started to laugh, but stopped himself.

"How did they hire you, if they don't know who you are?"

He shrugged. "Word gets around."

Looking at him, she could believe it. *She'd* hire him if she wanted a really difficult crime committed. "Did they pay you a lot?"

He nodded.

"How much?"

"Right," he said, and shook his head.

She studied him, wondering if money were the only motivation. "It must be a hell of a *lot* of money. Or do you like, hate the government or something?"

He shrugged. "Hard to resist the challenge."

And, apparently, he had risen to the occasion. What a waste of ability. "You know, if you were nice," she said, "you could really accomplish a lot."

He laughed. "Oh, undoubtedly."

"You could really *help* people."

"Unh-hunh," he said.

Undoubtedly. He sure didn't *sound* like a terrorist. At least, not her image of one. "Did you go to a good school?"

He laughed again. "Want to see my class ring?"

Automatically, she looked at his hands. No rings, of course. A plain black Timex, nothing distinctive. She tried to read the time, and he took the watch off, putting it into his pocket.

Damn. "Well — how do you communicate with them?" she asked. "I mean, how are you going to know what to do to me or anything?"

He smiled, very slowly looking her over. "I have a

58

few ideas of what I'd like to do to you."

She couldn't help shivering, moving her arm to try and cover herself.

"*More* than a few."

"I get the point," she said stiffly.

"The *point*," he said, "is that once I have you, it's my show. They can do or say whatever they want, but the deal was autonomy."

Meg frowned. "So, they take all the credit, yank everyone around thinking they have me, but *really* don't have anything to do with it?"

"Bingo," he said.

Chapter Seven

When he was gone, with a mocking "Sleep well," she couldn't stop shivering. It seemed even colder and darker sitting on the floor and, with a lot of effort, she managed to pull herself up onto the bed. Spots of color seemed to be bouncing against her eyes, and she closed them, the throbbing in her nose joining her jaw and her head. Moving around had started a fresh rivulet of blood, and she tilted her head back against the wall. Her whole face felt sticky and she touched the blood, wondering — for the first time — if her nose were actually *broken*. Jesus Christ.

She closed her eyes more tightly, praying that the pain would fade. People got beaten up all the time and still managed to — Christ, Steven had come home with so many black eyes and bloody noses over the years that they — Steven. Was her family safe? And Josh? She was almost sure that he had been lying about

Josh being — but what if he *wasn't*? What if — thinking wasn't going to help much. And, if she started crying, it wasn't going to help at *all*. The important thing was to stay cool, and — why the hell hadn't they ever briefed her about something like this? All that security — and here she was, lying in some *place*, and — weakest link, they were probably saying to her mother. Human error. Lack of precedent. We're really sorry. One thing for sure — all hell must be breaking loose.

The blood seemed to be stopping and tentatively, she wiped at it with her sleeve. Talk about gross. Her eyes seemed to be swelling shut, which was going to make it even harder to stay awake. But she couldn't sleep — she had to be ready. He — or someone else — might come in and — and — it was hard to decide which would be worse: them coming in to kill her, or coming in to do something — obscene. Something — her stomach literally seemed to turn over and she forced down a swallow, not wanting to throw up. Not that there was much of anything inside. What a day to decide to skip lunch.

Okay, okay, she had to think. He'd said "Sleep well," so he probably wasn't coming back until the morning to bring her food or whatever. And although he might be planning to kill her, he didn't seem to be planning to do it *yet*. So maybe he was lying about not negotiating. Otherwise, it would have made a lot more sense just to assassinate her — Christ — or — the only thing she could tell for sure was that he seemed to be feeling pretty safe. Seemed, to a degree, to be playing this by ear. So, all she could really do was wait. He was pretty cocky, but that didn't mean that she wasn't about to be rescued. Except she knew enough about security to know that the longer this went on — unless it stretched into *days* and they could get intelligence — *weeks?* — the less likely it was that they would be able to find her. Unless he was stupid enough to have her right in downtown Washington or something. Yeah. Sure.

The smart thing, was not to do anything to make him angry. Turning on that light was the *stupidest* thing she'd done since — well, since not telling anyone that Dennis made her nervous and could she have a new agent put on the detail. Christ, if only she'd — well, it was too late to be worrying about *that*. What she had to do, was stay calm and make him like her. If he liked her, then he wouldn't want to hurt her, or kill her, or — just thinking that word made her stomach twist again. But if she could make him like her — the Stockholm Syndrome, that's what they called it. On *Hill Street Blues* and everything, they were always talking about the Stockholm Syndrome. Which had happened in some bank — in Stockholm, no doubt — where the hostages had started liking the robbers and — oh, yeah, like she was going to start *liking* this guy. It would be a long cold day in hell before — Patty Hearst. Jesus Christ, this was going to be even bigger than the Patty Hearst — maybe that's why he wasn't killing her yet, maybe he was going to terrorize her into — aware that she was sitting up stiffly, muscles tensed, waiting for him to come bursting in or something, she forced herself to relax. She maybe didn't *want* to sit here and wait, but she didn't have much choice. All she could do was try to stay calm, stay cool. *That*, she had some control over.

She closed her eyes, trying to think some soothing thoughts. It could be worse. She could be *dead* already.

She could have been shot and lying here in even *worse* pain. She could be lying here *without* the unfamiliar sweatshirt and sweatpants. The thought of which was too terrifying to pursue. Both arms and legs could be handcuffed, she could be gagged, or blindfolded, or — she could have her period. *That* would be a nightmare. And she had just gotten over it, so as long as they didn't keep her for weeks — these were not soothing thoughts.

She pulled in a deep breath, slowly letting it out. The air hurt the hole where her teeth had been, but using her nose to breathe hurt even more. Relax. Stay calm. Think productively. Take another breath. Sleep was a very tempting idea. But they might come in or, to be realistic — she must be getting calm, she was thinking about this calmly — if they were going to kill her, it would be stupid to sleep the rest of her life away. She shouldn't waste it like that.

Which, in a strange way, struck her funny. What was she going to do — sit here and compose poetry? Make peace with Her God? Although, if she was *in* this situation, Her God was obviously on vacation. Probably still not back from the one he took the day her mother got shot. Which was pretty blasphemous, and she found herself glancing up at the ceiling. That'd *really* make her day, seeing a lightning bolt right around now.

She should probably be praying. Seemed like an appropriate time for it. But — well, that kind of fox-hole stuff always seemed stupid to her. Like, when her mother had been shot, she didn't pray because she *never* did. If she were God, people who prayed only when they wanted something would really bug her. To be able to justify praying at a time like this, she should pray *every* day. Thank God for sunshine, and whiskers on kittens, and all. And as for the old "if you get me out of this, I'll never yell at Steven and Neal again, or be cranky, or selfish, or — " Yeah, right. She'd probably make it about twenty-four hours.

So, she wouldn't pray.

On the other hand, it couldn't *hurt*.

She had to grin, amused by the convenient little mind reversal there. When in doubt, rationalize. No, she wasn't about to turn around and start praying, but it was funny that part of her *wanted* to.

Damned if she wasn't calm. Calm*er*, anyway. God's work, perhaps? she thought and almost laughed. Be pretty amusing if she came out of this a born-again Christian or something.

"When God closes a door, somewhere he opens a window," she said solemnly, being the Mother Superior in *The Sound of Music*, and this time, she *did* laugh.

There was a movement out in the hall and she stiffened. Was he out there listening maybe? Or if not him, someone who was guarding her? She could imagine the guy reporting in: "I don't know, boss, she's just sitting in there, laughing her head off."

The movement stopped, but she stayed tensed, waiting for whatever might happen. Not that she should be surprised that someone would be out there. If — when? — the place got raided, the guy would want to be in position to use her immediately as a hostage.

Her left arm was numb, and she clenched and un-clenched her fist, trying to get the blood circulating. Which reminded her how much her jaw and nose hurt, how cold it was, how much calmer she had felt a minute ago. Any *second* now they might come in here and — oh, Christ. Oh, Christ, oh, Christ, oh, Christ. He was going to kill her, in some horrible violent scary way, and there wasn't anything she could — oh, Christ. What was he going to do? Just like, come in here with the gun, point it at her, and — ? Or would he make it even more horrible, make the insult to the United States government all the more — oh, God.

She wanted to cry — to *whimper* — but they might hear her and come in. Of *course* he was going to kill her — he wasn't wearing a mask. And they weren't going to rescue her. That was movie stuff. *This* was — the panic faded into slight amusement. Real life, she'd been going to think. Speaking of movie clichés.

She slouched back against the iron frame — he could have given her a damned pillow, at least — letting her eyes close. Time for some more deep breaths.

She must have fallen asleep at some point because when the key turned in the door lock, she had to wake herself up. Everything hurt more than ever and she groaned, trying to find a less excruciating position. Her eyes didn't seem to open right and she squinted in the direction of the door, seeing the same man.

"It's *Prom* Day," he said with a Jack Nicholson grin.

Josh. Tears immediately in her eyes, she looked away.

"What's the matter?" He came over to the bed, prodding her shoulder. "Got a — *problem?*"

She turned away as far as she could, blocking the exposed side of her head with her arm, in case he decided to hit her.

"Giving me the silent treatment?"

She didn't answer. The idea of making him like her worked a lot better in the abstract.

"I see," he said, and folded his arms. It was quiet for a minute, then he spoke again. "The President gave a *brave* angry speech last night."

Meg looked up.

"*Thought* that might interest you."

Meg swallowed, her throat so dry she wasn't sure she would be able to speak. "W-what did she say?"

"Oh, I don't know." He bent down so that his face was at a level with hers. "That your life is a sacrifice someone in her position has to make. That it's too bad, but" — he shrugged — "those are the breaks."

"S-she didn't say that."

"She said to hell with it, and to hell with *you*."

Meg shook her head, staring at his eyes to try and read the lie.

"Okay." He straighted up. "How about 'cannot, have not, and *will* not negotiate with terrorists'?"

That, she probably said. Meg swallowed again, the muscles in her throat so tight that it felt as if she were choking. "That just means they've figured out where you are and they're going to get you," she said, hearing her voice tremble.

"Unh-hunh." He sat on the edge of the bed, Meg moving as far away as possible. "She's got balls, your mother," he said conversationally. "After she told the country she didn't care what happened to you, she said that what terrorists wanted more than anything was publicity, so she was requesting a complete news blackout."

Jesus. Serious grist for the Beltway mill. "Did they go for it?"

He shrugged. "Seems that way. Except for reporting what happened."

"What happened?" she asked, looking right at him.

He grinned. "You mean, did he die yet?"

She held her breath, waiting for the answer.

"Hell, yes," he said. "Told you he got shot about ten times."

Oh, Jesus. "You said five," she said, voice trembling again.

"Doesn't make him any less dead."

Oh, God. He was lying. He *had* to be lying. Josh was so sweet, so — so *nice*. Not someone who deserved — not that anyone deserved — he had to be lying, that's all. Keeping her off-balance. Trying to —

"So, the Prom," he said, very cheerful. "Tonight the night you were *finally* going to sleep with him?"

She hunched down, not looking at him.

"Now you must *really* regret waiting," he said pleasantly. "Being a good little girl."

Bastard. "For all *you* know, I've slept with half of Washington," she said.

"Really?" He pretended to look shocked. "Men *and* women?"

Whatever else he was, he was smart. Smarter than just about anyone she had ever met. "And *pets*," she said, spitting the words out.

He looked away, but she saw a little grin. "I'll leave you to your memories," he said, and got up.

"Aren't you going to bring me some food?"

He paused, halfway to the door. "Why?"

"Well — I mean — " Why, when you're going to be dead anyway. She swallowed. "Y-you aren't?"

"Would you *trust* it?"

No. "No," she said.

He nodded. "Smart girl."

"Well, wait," she said, as he turned to go. "Couldn't I at least have a book or something? Or a radio? Or — "

"No."

For some reason, the flatness in his voice brought tears to her eyes, and she rubbed her hand across them. "Well — what about a pillow? I mean, I really — "

He shook his head, opening the door.

"Could I have a *blanket*, at least?" she asked, feeling panicky. "It's so cold in here, I — "

The door slammed, and she was alone again.

Chapter
Eight

Hours passed. And it *was* cold. And she was tired, and hungry, and *thirsty*. She slept on and off, but mostly sat in the darkness, her brain feeling both numb, and as if it were on fast-forward. She didn't want to think — especially about the future. Especially about the *present*. Which just left — everything *else* she didn't want to think about.

Her head felt so thick and dull, she couldn't seem to think anyway. Just flashes, really. Their house in Massachusetts. How quiet it was, how safe. The smell of the Vick's Vaporub their housekeeper — and surrogate grandmother — Trudy had always put on her late at night, when she had nightmares. She'd always been one to have a hell of a lot of nightmares when she was little. Mostly, not being able to find her parents, not being able to go somewhere with her mother, and — ironically enough — being grabbed and taken away. Although in the dreams, it was always monsters.

Which was also ironic. Like, just because this guy was civil, he wasn't a *monster*? Yeah, right.

Her handcuffed arm felt completely dead, and she rubbed it with her other hand, trying to get the feeling back in. It didn't matter what position she sat in — it still fell asleep after a few minutes. Not that it really mattered — she'd be lucky if she ever got a chance to *use* it again. If he wasn't going to feed her, he obviously wasn't planning on keeping her around too long.

But she wasn't going to think about that. There was no point in — unless it was going to be something horrible. Something *barbaric*, something — it wasn't fair, this shouldn't be happening to her. He was right — if her goddamned mother loved her, this *never* would have — *no*, damn it. She wasn't going to think like this. It wouldn't solve anything. Christ, thinking about the pain in her head and face — and, increasingly — her stomach, would solve more.

She huddled up against the wall, shivering in the thin sweatshirt. It wasn't that she was *cold*, so much as — she just couldn't stop shivering.

Think. Think about other things. About *anything.* Anything *else.* Except all she kept coming back to now was her mother. The way their lives had always revolved around whether she was home or not. When she was coming back, what they would do when she got there. It was always so strange, sitting — for example — in Beth's kitchen and watching Mrs. Shulman make dinner or whatever. After the divorce, Mrs. Shulman had dated a lot of significantly younger men, then married a significantly older man — but at least

70

she was always *there*. There for meals, there for holidays, sometimes even there after school.

"Yeah, well, your mother may not be around," Beth had always said, "but at least when she is, she has a clue."

"If she had a clue, she'd *be* around," Meg would say, and they would agree to disagree.

She thought about her father teaching her how to ride a bicycle, Trudy taking pictures so that her mother would be able to see them later. About all of the plays and tennis matches and assemblies her mother had never been able to come to — big vote on the Panama Canal or something stupid — and how it was almost worse if she *did* come, because the press would come too, and everyone would ask The Congresswoman, or The Senator, or The Candidate, or whatever the hell she was that particular year — *damn* her.

And damn that bastard out there for making her think these things. Her family had spent a lot of time talking about these very things. Accepting them, in fact. Her mother was a difficult person, she was a complicated person, but she *was* a good person. And she *did* love them; she always had. And Meg wasn't going to let this son of a bitch change that.

She had to think about good things. About Christmases they'd had, or times they'd gone skiing, or even how much closer they'd gotten since moving into the White House. Suddenly, her mother *was* there for meals, and birthdays, and just plain old conversations. She worked harder than she ever had, but then again, she worked right downstairs. She still had to travel, but as a rule, especially if it were overseas, the family went with her. All in all, things had gotten much better in the last couple of years. Now, it was the *outside* world that was making things terrible. Both last fall, and — but she was *not* going to think about it. She wasn't.

Only, that made her think of something else she'd been avoiding. Some*one* else. Josh. The guy had to have been lying — but what if he wasn't. What if — she'd seen poor Chet and goddamn Dennis and all the blood — and Josh could easily have — good things. "Think good thoughts," her father had often said, "life is short." He certainly had *that* one right.

She huddled lower, very close to crying. Josh was so nice. So nice to *her*. If only she'd broken up with him *completely*, so that there was no chance that he would have been *near* her, and no chance that he — or not broken up with him at all. Not done anything to make him unhappy. If, yeah, she'd slept with him. She should have — oh, Christ. She *knew* she had Secret Service agents, she *knew* she had them for a reason — letting Josh be a target was at least as bad as her mother letting *her* be one. If anything had happened to him — now she *was* crying. She pressed her face — nose be damned — into her arm so no one would hear.

She was still crying when she heard the key in the lock, and sat up, rubbing her face with her sleeve so he wouldn't be able to tell.

The man came in, cocky as ever. "Keeping yourself amused?" he asked.

She didn't say anything, blinking as the light came on, and he smiled when he saw her face.

"Now did I have you pegged as a crier, or *what*," he said.

"Fuck you."

He shook his head. "Those manners sure are going downhill."

She hated him. She *hated* this arrogant son of a bitch. Smelling food suddenly, she realized that he was holding what was left of a hamburger. A Big Mac. A delicious beautiful Big Mac. Without meaning to, she licked her lips, which — judging from his grin — he found very funny.

"Give me a minute to finish this," he said, sitting down, "and you can go to the bathroom."

The hamburger smelled so good that she couldn't look at him, her stomach actually hurting with hunger.

"All this excitement makes me hungry," he said.

Bastard. The smell was almost dizzying, and she hunched over, refusing to give him the satisfaction of watching.

Just before finishing the last bite, he stopped. "I'm sorry — did you want some of this?"

She shook her head, to his obvious amusement.

"I mean, if I thought you were *hungry*, I would have brought you something." He came over to the bed, going through the handcuff routine until she was free of the bed frame, her hands cuffed in front of her. "Okay, let's go."

Her legs were stiff and weak, and each step was an effort. She stayed in the bathroom as long as she could, enjoying the change of scene. Rinsing her face and mouth set off jagged shocks of pain, but she didn't stop, drinking from her cupped hands and washing her face over and over again.

He threw the door open. "I say you could stay in here this long?"

She gave him an "*ask* me if I care" look, and kept drinking.

"Get out here." He pulled her into the hall, Meg too tired to fight him, water splashing all over her sweatshirt.

"What's your hurry?" she said, as he shoved her back into the room. "The boys putting together a stir-fry?"

He grinned — almost laughed. "We're making our own sundaes."

To her horror, she almost laughed too.

"The blackout still on?" she asked as he cuffed her back to the bed.

He nodded, checking the locks.

Maybe she could trick him. "Your 'employers' must have called you all upset."

He put the handcuff keys back into his pocket. "They don't know where I am, Meg," he said pleasantly.

Meg? She scowled at him. "You can't call me that."

"I can do whatever I want," he said.

"Yeah, well, you *can't* call me that."

"Right." He paused. "Meg. Anything you say." He turned and walked to the door.

"When are you coming back?" she asked, hating herself for it.

The door closed.

It was a long night. The longest night she could ever remember. Longer than Election Night ever *thought* of being. The only smart thing to do would be sleep, but she was too tired. Too *hungry*.

She curled up on her side, bringing her knees up for warmth, trying to use her shoulder as a pillow. It wasn't like her arm wasn't *already* dead. Lying here and thinking would be a disaster, so she tried to remember the title of every book she'd ever read. Every movie she'd ever seen. Every album she had. The *songs* on the albums. The words to the songs.

It was so boring that she managed to fall asleep for a few minutes here and there, but it wouldn't last, and she'd be staring into the darkness again.

The only thing she was sure of, was that the next time he came in, she was going to make her move. He was going to kill her anyway, so she might as well try. Also, she hadn't actually *seen* anyone else, so if she could elude him, she might be able to get away. That hall had to go *somewhere*.

It was so quiet that when he came down the hall, endless hours later, the sound woke her up. By the time the key was in the lock, she was ready, slumping into an exhausted, defeated position. He opened the door, grinning when he saw her.

"Tough night?" he asked.

She didn't answer, not looking up, wanting to make it obvious that she had given up completely.

"*Knew* you wouldn't be able to hold out much longer." He cuffed her wrists together and uncuffed her from the bed. "Bathroom?"

She shrugged dully.

"You expect me to carry you or something?"

She shook her head.

"Then, get moving."

She took her time pushing herself up, using the wall as a support, giving her legs a chance to get some strength back. She took a couple of steps, then sagged down so he would think she could barely walk.

"For Christ's sakes," he said, sounding impatient.

"I'm trying," she said weakly, all of her weight against the wall. She waited until she was sure he was too annoyed to be paying close attention, then shoved past him and out into the hall. Running with handcuffs was awkward, but he'd reacted late and she was already around the corner, well ahead of him, when two men with stocking masks and machine guns snapped into position in front of her. She skidded to such a fast stop that she fell, landing hard on her hands. At first, she was stunned, then she looked up at them, still too surprised to be scared. The situation seemed unexpectedly ridiculous, and she laughed.

"Yeah," she said to them, out of breath, gesturing with the handcuffs, "I'd be scared of me too."

Neither of them reacted, and she turned over onto her back to find the other man standing there with his gun leveled at her, his eyes colder than usual, his gun hand shaking slightly.

"Oh, come on," she said, moving to a less vulnerable position, sitting against the wall. "Would you respect me if I *hadn't* tried?"

He didn't answer, the gun pointed at — almost touching — her face, his arm visibly shaking.

Jesus Christ, he was going to shoot her. This wasn't like the other time, he was actually going to — "Hey, come on," she said, her voice trembling as much as his hand was. "It's not like I — "

"Shut up," he said, quietly. Viciously.

"But — "

"Shut up!"

She did, too scared to breathe, watching his left hand come over to steady his right. He was deciding whether or not to kill her, he was deciding — she sat absolutely still, terrified that even the tiniest movement might set him off, staring at a gun that was pointed at *her*, a real, loaded — she looked at his eyes, seeing nothing rational, or even human, in them.

They stared at each other for what might have been hours, unwanted perspiration blurring her eyes; then, slowly, he let out his breath and lowered his still-shaking arm, shoving the gun back into his jeans.

She let out her breath too, collapsing against the wall, the last minute or two having been the most exhausting of her life. She sat there, dazed, still not quite believing that she was alive. That he hadn't pulled the trigger, that — the other two men were still standing there with their guns, but she knew they wouldn't fire unless he told them to.

He was moving closer and she lifted her eyes to see what was going to happen.

"Look, I won't do it again," she said, almost not recognizing her own voice. "I just — "

He didn't answer, suddenly kicking the outside edge of her kneecap, Meg both feeling and hearing a scream rip out as the top and bottom halves of her left leg twisted in different directions. He kicked again, even harder, then stepped back as she huddled over what looked — and felt — like a severe dislocation.

He stood there, watching her for a second, then crouched down, resting his hand on it. "Next time," he spoke very quietly, "I use a bullet. Understand?"

She didn't say anything, breathing hard, covering her face with both cuffed hands so he wouldn't see her crying.

He increased the pressure, Meg trying — unsuccessfully — to keep from moaning.

"Understand?" he asked.

She nodded, the crying closer to whimpering.

"Okay." He straightened up, indicating for the others to return to their posts. "Now, get back to that room," he said to her.

She looked down what now seemed like a *very* long hallway.

"If you *don't*," he said, "I'll kick out the other one."

And he would. She knew perfectly goddamn well that he would. And if she *still* didn't move, he would probably do the same thing to her arms, and then — she swallowed, pretty close to losing control.

"*Now,*" he said.

She swallowed again, the pain fading in and out of nausea, worse than anything she could ever remember. "C-can you at least uncuff me?"

He shook his head, very slightly smiling.

"Yeah, well, fuck you," she said, and pushed against the floor with her good leg, struggling not to scream as her bad one stretched and jarred with the effort.

It took a long time, using her right leg to propel herself inch by inch, and she kept her hands over her face, having to cry the whole way. She was too weak to get onto the bed, but he didn't help her, just lifting her wrists to recuff her to the frame.

As he stepped back, she managed to look up, away from what had been her knee. "I *ski*, you bastard," she said, hearing her voice shake with hatred.

"Past tense," he said, gave her leg another kick, and left the room.

Chapter
Nine

It hurt so much that she couldn't stop crying, every muscle stiff, her teeth biting into her lower lip. If he was going to kill her — and the reality of *that* was more and more obvious — then why didn't he — they — just *do* it? Instead, he left her lying here hour after hour, her leg ripped to — she cried harder, making small animal noises she didn't even know had existed inside of her.

The floor was cold and hard, and she tried to drag herself onto the bed, the pain so bad that she almost fainted. She tried again, using her elbows to pull herself up, almost biting through her lip as her leg flopped in an impossible direction, her whole body reacting with a convulsive shudder. Arms trembling, she dragged herself the rest of the way up, tasting blood by the time she was on the mattress. She lay there, crying, praying for this to be *over*. For him to hurry up and kill her.

It was a long time before he came back and when she heard the key, she turned her head towards the wall, pretending to be asleep.

He walked over, stood by the bed briefly, then walked away. Thank God. She heard the door close again and relaxed a little, waiting for the key to turn. When it didn't, she lifted her head slightly, wondering if he could still be —

"*Knew* you were faking," he said from somewhere near the door.

She slumped back down.

"Took all the fight out of you, I guess," he said, turning the light on.

She covered her eyes with her sleeve, the crook of her elbow at her nose so *it* wouldn't hurt more.

"Okay," he said, and she heard the chair scrape across the floor to somewhere near the bed, and he sat down. There was the sound of a bottle cap being unscrewed, then liquid pouring into a glass.

She tensed, not sure if he had something sadistic in mind, but heard him put the bottle on the floor. From the smell, scotch. Christ, was he just going to sit there and drink? And *then* what would he do? Oh, Jesus.

"Want a drink?" he asked, his voice sounding a little thick.

She pulled in a few shaky breaths, not wanting to cry in front of him. Again.

He laughed. "Hurts, hunh?"

"*Please* go away," she said through her teeth.

"I don't want to," he said, and laughed again. "Sure you don't want one?"

She tried to turn further away, but moved her leg in doing so and had to groan. Oh, Christ, it hurt. It really, really hurt. Oh, Jesus. Jesus God, did it hurt.

"You'd feel better if you had a drink."

Her breath was coming out in short gasps, a small high note of hysteria somewhere behind them.

"Fine," he said, and she heard more liquid pouring. "It's your own fucking choice."

He didn't say anything else and slowly, she got herself under more control, concentrating so intently that she almost forgot he was there. Almost.

The steady throbbing in her knee was echoing inside her head — along with all the other throbbing, underscored by a constant, searing pain, worse than any — the tears wouldn't stop either, rolling down her face in what must be *grooves* by now, making her head hurt worse than ever.

"It would help you sleep, you know," he said.

That made a certain amount of sense and she opened her eyes, considering the idea. If she could sleep, it would be a lot better than lying here crying and in pain. At this point, she could sleep away every last *second* of her life and not give a damn. Just so this whole thing would be *over* already.

"It's — medicinal," he said.

It wasn't like a drink was going to make things *worse*. She didn't think. It couldn't be poisoned, not with him sitting there drinking it. She nodded dully, rubbing some of the tears away with her hand.

"*Okay*," he said, pouring some in another glass, then topping off his own.

"What is it?" she asked, and he turned the label so she could read it. J & B. Her father drank that. She swallowed a hard jolt of homesickness, wishing she hadn't asked. "K-kind of expensive," she said, not wanting to cry more.

He shrugged, holding out her glass. She reached over, her hand trembling so much — from pain? Shock? Exhaustion? — that she had trouble taking it.

"Can you undo my other hand?" she asked. "So I can hold it better?"

He shook his head.

Naturally. She sniffed the glass, not sure if she had ever even tasted scotch.

"Cheers," he said, his voice mocking.

Instinctively — too many White House dinners — she lifted her glass towards him, then to her mouth. Medicinal. Christ, as long as she didn't choke on it — he would be sure to make fun of her. She tipped the glass up, letting the liquid moisten her lips. It tasted terrible.

He made an amused sound, but didn't say anything, and she tried again, taking an actual sip this time. The taste made her shudder, but the warmth going down felt very good. Soothing. Gaining confidence, she tried a bigger sip, then looked over, aware of his amusement.

"Come here often?" she asked.

His laugh was the most genuine she'd heard it and, smiling a little herself, she took another sip, only re-coiling slightly from the taste. The warmth was giving her courage and she looked back over. "What did you major in?"

This time, he really did laugh.

She took an even bigger sip. Not bad. In fact, this stuff could grow on her. She drank a full mouthful, shivering from the aftershock of — heat? Fumes? *Something.* When the aftershock faded, it seemed cold, and she took another mouthful.

"I'd take it easy," he said.

"*You'd* take it easy," she said. "Then how come the bottle's half empty?"

He didn't answer, drinking.

Thinking about reasons why he might feel like he had to get drunk was scary and she concentrated on her glass. "Half full, I meant," she said quietly.

"What?"

"Half full," she said. "The bottle is half *full.*" She nodded to punctuate that, then took a sip of her scotch. His feet were propped up on the side of the bed frame and she looked down at the heavy leather high-tops, deciding not to think about the fact that he had used them to kick her knee to shreds. "So. You and the boys going to play some ball later?"

He looked at his sneakers and grinned, but didn't say anything.

"How's the blackout going?"

"Couldn't tell you," he said.

"Bullshit." She drank some scotch. "You just don't *want* to."

"You're a chatty drunk, aren't you," he said.

Oh, yeah, like she'd ever been drunk in her life. "How the hell would *I* know?"

"Dream Teen," he said, his voice more than a little vicious.

Bastard. "What am I supposed to do — stumble around drunk, then show up in *Us* the next week?" She shook her head. "Christ."

"They would've covered it up."

"Are you kidding? *The Enquirer* and people print stuff like that *anyway*. All I need's for it to be true." She finished off her drink.

"And it's always lies?" He leaned over, pouring more into her glass. "On account of you being perfect and all?"

She frowned at the pale liquid. "Are you trying to make me drunk?"

"Does your leg still hurt?"

Yes. She nodded.

"Okay then." He poured some more into his glass too.

"I don't know." She kept frowning. "Are you trying to be nice, or mean?"

"Hey, I'm not pouring it down your throat," he said.

True. She took a careful sip, in case it was going to make her drunk soon. "Do you drink a lot? In your life, I mean?"

"I'm not an alcoholic, if that's what you mean."

"No, I — " What *did* she mean? "My parents drink a lot." That wasn't what she meant. "Well, not a lot, I just — I mean, before they would just have like, wine, or my father would have a beer, or — now they have a scotch."

"They share it?" he said, his mouth in the half-smile.

"No, I — " Was he stupid? "Before dinner, I mean. You know, like a drink."

"So they're alcoholics," he said.

"*No.* I just meant — " Could she really be getting drunk already? Nothing was making sense. "The White House made things different, that's all. They worry more."

84

"Bet they're drinking up a storm right now."

"*Coffee*, maybe." During crises, her mother always drank coffee. Most people probably did. "Are you getting drunk for a *reason?*"

"I'm not drunk," he said, his voice belligerent enough to be a contradiction.

He was up to something. He had to be. "Are you — ?" She stopped, not wanting to put any ideas into his head.

"What?"

She shook her head.

"You were asking me something."

She just shook her head.

"*What?*"

She swallowed a mouthful of scotch. "Are you going to do anything — bad — to me?"

His face relaxed. "What do you mean, 'bad'?"

"Well, I mean — *you* know. Bad."

"Oh." He grinned. "You mean, just for example, yanking teeth out of your head wasn't — 'bad'?"

She shook her head. Bringing this up had been a mistake.

"Mangling your leg wasn't — "

"Look," she said. "I just want to know, okay? I mean, if you're going to" — she couldn't actually say it — "I mean — "

"Oh," he said. "*That.*"

She nodded, suddenly exhausted, her knee hurting worse than ever.

He smiled, leaning closer. "Do you want me to?"

"I just want to be *out* of here, *okay?*"

"I'll bet you do." He got up, sitting on the edge of the bed, which was definitely not a positive sign. "The

85

thought *does* keep crossing my mind."

She didn't say anything, her good leg drawn up, her right arm protecting her chest.

"Feelings might be a problem," he said.

"You're worried about *my* feelings?"

"Hardly."

"Oh." She moved her jaw, which hurt. What *didn't* hurt? "You mean, raping *me* would hurt *your* feelings?"

"*Some* sort of feelings would be inevitable," he said, patting her hip in a distracted sort of way.

She frowned. "I don't get it."

"Let's say, for instance, I start hating you." His hand trailed down her thigh, then back up to her hip. "If I *do*, I lose perspective. And if I do *that*, I stop thinking about my job, and — " He shrugged, lifting his drink. "Well, it's not a good idea."

She didn't respond, edging away so he wouldn't be able to touch her as easily.

"Then again, worst scenario, I start *liking* you," he said. "And liking you makes it a hell of a lot harder to do the things I have to do to you."

"*Have* to do to me," she said, almost under her breath. Then, she frowned. "You don't like me at *all*?"

He shook his head.

"Even with me being such a — you know, under the circumstances — good sport?"

He laughed. "Afraid not."

If she hadn't been handcuffed, she would have put her hands on her hips. "Well, for Christ's sakes."

He laughed again, moving back to his chair.

"Well — fuck you."

"Such conviction," he said.

"*Fuck you.*"

"Keep trying," he said. "You'll get it right."

Damn him. She looked down at her hand wrapped around the glass. "Would it make a difference?" she asked, ashamed by the question.

"What?"

She kept her eyes down, feeling herself blushing. "Me making you like me."

A slow grin spread across his face. "In exchange for not killing you?"

She nodded, ashamed.

"Probably not," he said, then paused. "Would you do it?"

"Probably not," she said.

"Just curious?"

She nodded, her face hot with embarrassment.

"It's not the *worst* idea I ever heard."

"Yeah, it is," she said stiffly.

"Yeah?" He leaned forward, resting his hand on her stomach. "You might *enjoy* it."

She shook her head, moving away from the hand.

"You might be" — he shifted his hips slightly — "surprised."

She looked right back at him. "You know what they say about people who carry *guns* around."

He grinned, taking the gun out, holding it between his first two fingers. "What," he said, "*this* little thing?"

He was so goddamn arrogant that she found herself grinning back. "Right," she said, and drank some scotch.

"*Well,*" he said, and put the gun back.

What a — she couldn't even think of a word — somewhere between jerk and psychopath.

"What," he said.

"I don't know." She shook her head. "You must listen to a lot of Screamin' Jay Hawkins."

"My man, Screamin' Jay," he said, nodding.

"You really do?" she asked, surprised.

"Well — not recently," he said.

The fact that he even knew what she was talking about was — weird. Too weird. "You're not anything like a terrorist."

"Ah," he said. "You know a lot of terrorists?"

"No, I — " Something new occurred to her. "Was it like, an inside job? I mean, do you work for the government?"

"Oh, right," he said.

"Well, I still don't get how you pulled it off."

He shrugged.

"They should have been able to stop it. I mean, I don't care about Dennis, or how smart you are, or — "

"They *could* have," he said. "A little quicker with the stun grenades, and they *would* have."

Which she didn't get. Christ, *was* she drunk? "Stun — I don't — "

He grinned wryly. "You have a lot more back-up than you think you do."

"You mean — you paid off *all* of them?"

He snorted.

"Then" — she must be drunk — "I don't — "

"Took a gamble," he said. "Figured it out as far as I could, then it depended on how far they were willing to go."

She shook her head. "I don't get it."

"It's simple," he said impatiently. "Either they were going to shoot everything in sight, *or* they would decide your life wasn't expendable and try to arrest the situation at a different point."

She frowned, her mind feeling fuzzy. "You thought they would *kill* me?"

He shrugged. "Tough call. Me pulling it off makes the government look pretty stupid."

"Yeah, but — they wouldn't've *killed* me." Would they? Jesus.

"It would've *stopped* it."

"So" — there had been so much shooting — "they didn't fire back?"

He shook his head. "Not where you were. Just tried the stun grenades."

"If they'd killed me, you *definitely* would have been killed."

He nodded.

Jesus. What kind of person *was* he? "That's kind of a chance to take."

He shrugged, pouring a little more scotch into his glass. "What," he said, as she kept looking at him.

"I can't tell if you're crazy or not."

"Oh, really?" He put the bottle down.

"Well — you just seem regular. I mean, like you went to a good school and could be doing all *kinds* of things. I don't get — " She frowned. "Were you in Vietnam, maybe?"

He lowered his glass enough to look at her. "How old do you think I am?"

"Well — " He'd be a *lot* older if he'd been in Vietnam. "Not that old, I guess."

He nodded, raising the glass again.

"Maybe you're just like, a mercenary?" she guessed. "Like going around to Central America and Angola and all?"

He just looked at her.

"I don't know," she said defensively. "I just — I can't figure you out."

He shrugged, drinking.

She watched him, trying to make some sense out of this. He was just — a guy. A guy in Levi's, basketball sneakers, and — today — a blue flannel shirt. A nice one too. Eddie Bauer, maybe.

"What," he said, letting out an irritated breath.

"I just — " She looked at him uncertainly. "You *really* don't like me?"

"No," he said. "I really don't."

Chapter
Ten

It was very, very quiet. So quiet that none of this seemed real. But the world, the world where she would be hanging out in the White House solarium or someplace, reading or holding her cat or watching movies with her brothers — that didn't seem real either. But *this* situation, so oddly civilized and violent, was the strangest.

"You were going to kill me this morning," she said, breaking the silence.

He nodded. "Probably should have."

Feeling cold, she sipped some of her drink, hunching her shoulders for warmth. If *only* her leg would stop hurting. "H-how come you didn't?"

"I don't know." He looked at his own drink. "I'd rather do it as planned, not because I lose my temper."

As planned. "You mean," she had to swallow, "you're still going to?"

He nodded, expressionless.

"You don't have to — I mean — "

"Don't beg," he said, "okay?"

"I wasn't," she said. "I just — " Seeing the disgust come into his eyes, she stopped. "I just wondered," she said quietly.

Neither of them spoke for a while, the guy staring straight ahead, drinking; Meg just sitting there.

"What about — " She stopped. At least he could answer *this*. "Did you kill him?"

"Who, your *boy*friend?"

Even her heart muscle felt tense with fear. "My friend, yes," she said, clenching her hand around the glass.

It was quiet again.

"I don't know," he said finally. "I think I saw him out there though."

"On the *ground*?"

He looked at her, not answering.

"Oh, come on. You're doing all this bad stuff to me, can't you just — *please*?"

He sighed. "He has glasses, right? Wearing a dark green cap?"

She nodded, her muscles even tighter.

"We were already leaving. He — " He moved his jaw. "He wasn't involved."

"You're *sure*?"

He nodded, and she felt her shoulders relax a little for the first time since all of this had happened.

"You really wouldn't lie to me?" she asked. "I mean, *this* time?"

"He was fine," he said. "Don't piss me off, okay?"

She nodded, blinking at tears of relief. "Thank you," she said, almost whispering.

92

He shrugged, lifting his glass.

Again, they didn't talk for a while, Meg fighting against thankful tears. He was telling the truth. She was almost *sure* he was telling the truth.

Then, immediately embarrassed by the thought, she realized that the alcohol was having at least *some* effect.

"What," he said.

"I, um," she didn't look at him, "I need to use the bathroom."

He sighed. "Christ."

"I *really* do."

He sighed again, fumbling in his pocket for the handcuff keys. "Got any bright ideas of how you're going to get out there?"

She shook her head, feeling — whether she should or not — very ashamed. He didn't make any move to cuff her hands together once he'd freed the left one, so, carefully, she eased her bad leg towards the edge of the mattress. It dangled horribly, hurting so much — even through the haze of scotch — that she had to groan, new tears coming into her eyes. She brought her right leg over to the edge too and tried to use it to stand up, fingernails pressed into her palms. It hurt too much and she had to cry in earnest, covering her face with her hands.

"Can't get up?"

She shook her head, even more ashamed.

"Christ." He put his glass down, then moved next to her, bending to lift her.

"I can do it!" she said, trying to pull away.

"Shhh." He cupped her cheek with one hand. "I'll try not to hurt you."

She laughed weakly. "Unh-hunh."

He picked her up, one hand around her back, the other under her legs. She had to gasp in pain and he moved his arm further away from her bad knee. Being carried was humiliating, and she covered her eyes with her hand, leaning away from him as much as she could.

"Be easier if you put your arm around my neck," he said.

That was about the *last* thing she wanted to do, but then she remembered the gun in the waistband of his jeans. If she put her arm around his shoulder, maybe she could reach down, grab the gun, and —

"If you go for that gun," he said, "I'll break every bone in your body."

She took her hand off his back, so frustrated that she wanted to hit him. "The hammer, the anvil, and the *stirrup?*"

He didn't answer, banging her leg into the doorjamb and she gasped, having to grip his shoulder for support. Horrified, even through the pain, that she'd *touched* him — voluntarily — she yanked her hand away, covering her face with it.

They were at the bathroom door now, and he pushed it open, then set her down, Meg grabbing onto the doorknob to keep from falling. With her hands free though, it was easier to get around, and she maneuvered herself into the little room, closing the door.

The whole operation was excrutiatingly painful, and after she'd lurched over to the sink to wash, she collapsed onto the floor, gripping just above the knee with both hands, rocking in an attempt to ease the pain. He opened the door, but she was in too much agony to look up, the leg throbbing and jerking in what had to be muscle spasms.

"Oh, Christ." He crouched down next to her, trying

to ease her hands off. "Come on, take it easy now."

"Don't make like a coach when you're the one who hurt me!" she said, trying to protect herself. The leg *really* seemed to be jerking now, hot scary spasms, hurting so much that she couldn't seem to breathe. And it was going to get worse and worse, and he was going to kill her, and, and —

"Planning on having hysterics?" he asked, his voice breaking through the blur of panic.

"You'll be the first to know," she said weakly, and he laughed.

His hands were soothing the muscles, unexpectedly gentle, and she watched him do it, some of the panic — and a little bit of the pain — fading.

"Trust me not to, all of a sudden, twist it?" he asked.

She tensed, just in case. "I don't have much choice."

"No," he agreed. "You don't."

The muscle spasms had pretty much stopped now and he picked her up, still surprisingly gentle. There was something scarily intimate about being carried, and she was so exhausted and afraid that she wanted to rest her head on his — *anyone's* — shoulder. To have him promise that it was going to be okay, that he wasn't going to hurt her anymore, that she was safe. That everything was going to — she held herself rigidly in his arms, pretending that she was being carried off after falling on the tennis court or something, and being taken to the hospital, and — he was lowering her onto the bed, which hurt, but not as much as it could have.

Slowly, he recuffed her to the frame, then sat on the edge of the mattress. Feeling his hand touch her cheek, she opened her eyes all the way, startled by the strange look on his face.

95

"You would, no doubt, have grown into a spectac-ular woman," he said.

"You'd better watch it," she said, just as quietly. "You're going to lose your edge."

Abruptly, he got up. He stood there looking at her, his expression unreadable, then suddenly smashed his fist into the wall above her head, Meg cringing. He must have been even drunker than she thought because although he'd dented the plaster, his expression never changed. He picked up the scotch bottle with his other hand and turned to go, not speaking to her. The door slammed behind him and she was alone in the dark-ness, trembling, not sure where the scotch left off and the *real* fear and confusion began.

If nothing else, she slept *heavily*. Dead, dreamless sleep, waking up with a pounding headache — to go along with all of the other pain — and an unbelievably dry mouth. She licked her lips, trying to moisten them, wishing he would hurry up and come in so she could get a drink of water from the bathroom.

But, he didn't. Not for a long time, anyway. She lay there on the bed, just being in pain, her eyes so heavy that it hurt to keep them open, feeling too tired to worry, or be afraid — or even to think. She was also too tired to sleep, so she just rested her head against the wall, holding her aching jaw. Sometimes, the warmth from her hand made it feel better. Her leg and nose hurt too much to touch at *all*.

When the door finally opened, she shook herself out of her doze with some difficulty. He didn't look that great either — wearing the same shirt, unshaven, shadows beneath his eyes.

"Need to use the bathroom?" he asked, not looking at her.

She nodded, although if he didn't carry her again, she wouldn't be able to make it. "How's your hand?" she asked, *not* kindly, seeing that it was swollen.

He looked down, a little self-consciously. "I'll live," he said, with extra irony.

They didn't look at each other.

"Yeah, well," he said, and came over to uncuff her.

As he fumbled for the keys, there was an urgent knock on the door and instantly, he had his gun out. He glanced at her, then moved to the door, opening it partway. One of the men said something to him in a low voice and she heard him say *"Shit"* before he answered, his voice just as low. Without any explanation, he was gone, and the other man had posted himself inside the room, machine gun ready, staring straight ahead through his mask.

Something had happened. Something terrible had happened.

"Wh-what's going on?" she asked.

The man didn't even look at her, giving no indication that he had heard.

"Is something wrong?" she asked, although from the sound of quick movement and low orders in the hall, the answer was obvious.

The man never spoke, and when the regular guy — Jesus Christ, she didn't even know his *name* — came back with another stocking-masked man, she knew. The way they came in — very quiet, very professional, emotionless. She stiffened even before she saw the syringe in his hand and, seeing it, felt bile come up into her throat.

They were going to kill her. Jesus Christ. Right now, without any warning, or preparation, or — she drew her good knee up, moving defensively into the corner.

"What's going on?" she asked, voice shaking.

None of them spoke, which was scarier than an answer. She edged further into the corner, making her body as small as it could be, hampered by the handcuffs.

"At least tell me what's going on," she said, looking at the regular one, trying to find some sign of the man who had seemed almost — fond — of her last night.

He avoided her eyes, turning to one of the other men. "Hold her down," he said, which was when she panicked, forgetting about the handcuffs, trying to dive through them. The man in the stocking mask caught her easily, pushing her back down on the mattress, holding her there. She fought as hard as she could, twisting and turning, never taking her eyes off the syringe or the man holding it. He was going to kill her. Without even — she struggled harder, adrenaline bursting into her in uneven jerks.

He just stood there, letting the man in the stocking mask do all of the work. "Come on," he said, sounding very tired — and maybe even a little sad. "Don't fight."

When she didn't stop, looking right at him as she flailed at the other man with her free arm, fighting with more strength than she thought she had left, he moved forward, pressing his hand into her left knee. The combination of that, and the other man's weight and fists worked, and she found herself pinned, breathing hard, trying not to cry, her left arm forced out at an unbearable angle along the bed frame.

She watched him come towards her arm with the

syringe, and as their eyes locked, a weight even heavier than the other man seemed to press into her whole body. She had to do something to stop him, *say* something, something to make him change his mind — *anything* to — it was almost over, the whole thing was almost — she had to *think*, had to —

"Nurse Ratched, I presume?" she said and managed, just as the needle went in, a very weak laugh.

Chapter
Eleven

She was aware of pain first. Darkness second. And — dirt. She was lying somewhere, with her face in the dirt. There was some in her mouth and she tried to spit it out, her throat and mouth so dry that she couldn't. She was too dizzy and sick to lift her head, and everything else hurt so much that she let her eyes close again. She wasn't ready to deal with this yet.

The next time she woke up, it wasn't as dark. She lay there for a long time, not trying to move. After a while, she turned her head, lifting it just enough to see where she was. Light. Not much — coming in through boards or something. The air smelled mildewed, but there was a draft. A cold one. Jesus Christ, was she in a *cave?*

Okay, get a grip. Turn over. See what's going on. Using both hands, she tried to push herself to a sitting position, her arms weak and trembly. There was a heavy cuff of some kind on her right wrist and she pulled experimentally, discovering that it was attached to a chain. She wasn't strong enough to sit up, but managed, groaning, to turn over on her back. She lay there, exhausted by that mild effort, letting her eyes — one of which would barely open — get accustomed to the darkness.

Oh, God, she hurt. *Everything* hurt. Pain she didn't remember from before. The thing to do was figure out how badly hurt she was and then — oh, Christ, was she *alone?* Or was he sitting there, watching her? All of them, watching her. Or — it was so dark.

But she didn't see anyone. In fact, she didn't see *anything.* Just a tunnel or something. A rock tunnel. She could be at the end, or it could go back for miles — it was too dark to tell.

Okay, okay, find out how hurt you are. Start with the legs. She moved each foot, cautiously; moved her ankles; bent her right knee. Small, dull pains; some old, mostly new. Bruises probably, no reason to panic. Her left knee felt as bad as it had before, and she didn't try moving it.

One hip hurt a lot, the other one was just stiff. It was her ribs where the serious new pain started, the slightest breath or movement causing sharp twinges. Vaguely, she could remember being punched before she went unconscious. Had they kept on *after* she was unconscious? Had they done anything *else* while she was — no. She couldn't feel anything to indicate that they had done something — awful — and the drawstring, she checked, to her sweatpants was still double-knotted. Good.

She tried moving her head. Her neck. Her arms.

101

Just bruises. And stiffness from lying in cold dirt for God only knew how many hours. Either she had been battered around during the transfer to this place — she could smell and feel a smear of motor oil across her clothes — or they had intentionally hurt her, tried to beat her to death maybe. Jesus.

She touched the cuff on her wrist, then followed the chain with her fingers to a stake driven deep into the rock wall. She yanked on it, neither finding nor expecting any weak points. Christ. Her eyes were more accustomed to the dark now and she looked around, seeing straight square walls, a ceiling supported by a beam here and there. Was this place a *mine shaft* maybe? It obviously went further back — and down? — she couldn't tell *how* far.

Only a little light — sunlight — came in through the battered boards and she realized that the boards weren't a door. That she was nailed in. Nailed in with dirt, and rocks, and — nothing else. No food. No water. No blanket.

No water. She swallowed, her mouth and throat so dry that it was difficult. No water. He and the others might be out there somewhere — but she doubted it. He'd left her here, nailed in, chained, without water. Left her here.

Panicking, she yanked on the chain with both hands, trying to pull free. It wouldn't come — she knew it wouldn't come — but she had to try, fighting with it until she was out of breath and crying, yanking until she was too weak from pain to continue. She collapsed into the dirt, too tired and out of breath to try anymore.

Help. Call for help. She turned her head towards the light.

"Hey! In here!"

Yelling made her throat feel as if it were rupturing and she tried to swallow, not able to come up with much saliva.

"Hey, help! In here!"

No answer.

She felt for a rock, throwing it at the boards to try and break them. It fell down harmlessly inside and she threw another, with the same result. She threw one towards the back of the cave, hearing it go at least twenty feet. She threw a whole handful of small rocks, hearing them hit dirt, other rocks, some more boards maybe. No water.

No water. The inside of her mouth tasted terrible and she swallowed again, the muscles in her throat noisy in protest. Think, damn it, *think*. Maybe she could *dig* for water. Maybe — she fumbled around the dirt until she found a fairly sharp rock, using it to scratch a hole in the dirt, her fingers cramping with the effort. She would dig as long as she could stay awake — which wasn't going to be long — and then, when she woke up, maybe water would have seeped into the hole. Yeah, Nature Girl strikes again.

The ground was hard and rocky, but she was so relieved to be *doing* something that she kept digging. One inch. Another. The ground felt cold. Damp? Maybe. Definitely cold. Energy ebbing, she dug another half inch, then was too tired to continue, dropping the rock and leaning her head against the rock wall to sleep. Too uncomfortable. She curled up in the dirt, trying to find the least painful position, using her right arm as a pillow. Too tired and afraid to think, she closed her eyes.

* * *

"Meg, are you all right?" she heard someone saying. A nice voice. She was safe. This whole thing had been a — she smiled, opening her eyes — except she couldn't see anything. Oh, God, she was blind. She lifted her hand in front of her face, trying to see it. She *was* blind! She couldn't —

"Where are you?" she asked, voice rasping. "I can't see you!" She didn't hear anything. She didn't *see* anything. "*Talk* to me! Where are you?" As she tried to sit up, she heard the chain clink. Both the relief and the fear faded as she realized where she was. That there was no one there. Unless he *was* in here, unless he was trying to — "Are you in here? Are you trying to scare me?" *Trying?* Yeah, right. Succeeding and *then* some. Except she didn't hear anyone. She didn't hear anything at *all*. Wind, maybe.

She rubbed her hand across her face, feeling dirt, and a crust below her nose and lips that could only be dried blood. Her nose was stopped up — also with blood? — and she was having to breathe through her mouth, which felt even drier than it had before. She licked her lips, feeling more than one crack. Oh, boy. This was more and more serious with every — the hole! She felt for the hole in the darkness — so black that she couldn't see her hand moving — finally finding it. An empty hole. A *dry* hole.

Serious, serious trouble. And her mind just felt numb. Blank. She eased herself back against the wall, focusing in the direction of the boards. The only thing she could think of to do was wait for morning.

Daylight only made things seem worse. More hopeless. The only thing she knew for *sure* was that she couldn't sit around waiting for something to happen.

104

She had to *do* something. Think of a way out of here.

The only possible way out was to break the chain somehow. How, being the operative word. She didn't have much energy, so she had to choose. She could chip away at the stake, and the rock wall, trying to loosen it; or she could choose a weakest link, hammering on it until the chain broke. She pulled on the stake, pulled on the chain. The chain. It wasn't as thick. She felt for a rock, then hammered at the place where the chain and stake met. Double her odds that way.

Hammer, hammer, hammer, rest. Hammer some more. And some more. As many times as not, she would miss, scraping her knuckles against the rock wall. When her left hand hurt too much to continue, she switched to her right, hammering and hammering, not sure if ten minutes, or ten hours, were passing.

Her sweatshirt felt damp, and her arms were so heavy that it felt as if her strength were draining out along with the perspiration. But she kept hitting the chain, trying not to perspire, to lose liquid. Each time she lifted her arm, she wasn't sure if she could do it again, but she kept on, on the theory that it was keeping her sane. Oh, yeah, terribly. Although there was nothing in there to vomit, her stomach was upset and she wished she could swallow more easily. More often.

Hammer. Hammer. What time was it? What *day* was it? It had been dark — twice? More times? She'd slept so much it was hard to tell.

Her hair seemed like a great weight, and she pushed it off her neck and shoulders. It felt disgusting — dirty and sticky, hanging in damp clumps. Talk about gross.

"I'm going to get out of here," she said, needing to hear a voice. Even a voice that pathetic and hoarse.

105

"I swear to God I'm going to get out." A voice so small she almost couldn't hear it. " 'I'll *never* go hungry *again*,' " she said, being Scarlett O'Hara. She laughed weakly. Might as well make jokes. Nothing else to do.

Her hands were numb from hitting the wall by accident so many times and she dropped the rock, giving up. She might as well *sleep*. If she was going to have to die, she'd prefer it to happen as soon as possible. Survival was too goddamn tiring.

Maybe she was cracking up. Then again, the last few days had been pretty rough — she was entitled.

"Miss Powers, I'm sorry," she said. "You're going to have to be put to sleep."

Sleep. Good idea. She fell forward into the dirt, with barely enough energy to turn her face out of it. She wanted to cry, but couldn't get any tears out. She must be *really* dehydrated. Jesus. If she was wishing for death, maybe she was getting her wish.

Sit up. Go out fighting. Come on, sit up.

" 'You've got to have heart,' " she sang to herself, and laughed. Getting a little *punchy*, kid? A *little*?

With more effort than it was probably worth, she managed to sit up. Now what? She puzzled over that for a minute, then decided to finish the song. It couldn't *hurt*. Other than her throat. Which already hurt, so what the hell.

Singing the song cheered her up, so she went into "Whistle a Happy Tune" from *The King and I*. "Tomorrow," from *Annie*, was probably a little obvious — but, hey. She sang it with enthusiasm. With gusto, even.

Andrea McArdle's reputation was safe.

Before going on, she suddenly imagined some poor hiker going by, hearing a squeaky little croaking of

"Tomorrow" and being terrified by the sound. She thought of Bill Murray in *Ghostbusters* saying, "What a *lovely* singing voice you must have," and laughed weakly.

Not that she had *ever* been able to sing. She was always threatening to sing for people, but she never did. Except to her cat, Vanessa, who would yawn.

Actually, now that she thought about it, when she was in junior high, she had been walking home from school one time, through what she *thought* was a vacant lot, singing "I Have Confidence" at the top of her lungs, when she came upon a group of the very coolest kids in her grade, all of whom were standing around smoking cigarettes. They looked at her; she looked at them. She considered her options — die from humiliation, run away and *then* die from humiliation, shrug self-deprecatingly and continue on her way and with her song. To maintain her last vestige of cool, she chose the latter option, escaping with the tatters of her dignity. "If you'd been singing 'The Seven Deadly Virtues,' you might have pulled it off," Beth had said later, after laughing for about twenty minutes. "Mmmm," Meg had said, less amused.

But, she would sing it now. What the hell. In fact, since *The Sound of Music* was her favorite movie in life, she sang several songs from it. Did her imitation of the Mother Superior singing "Climb Every Mountain," even. The trick, was the quaver.

Gosh, time flew when you were having fun. She looked at the boards, seeing very little light left. Another day over. Christ, was this *ever* going to end?

"Yes, sports fans," she said through her teeth, speaking to an imaginary audience, "it's . . . Your Musical Journey to Hell. And coming up next, we have" —

what? — "that old, that unforgettable favorite, 'Tea for Two.' " She sang it very sweetly, remembering being on vacation when she was about eleven — *her* family, on *vacation*? *U*nbelieveable — and seeing *No, No, Nanette* in summer stock up in New Hampshire somewhere. Her father had sung "Call of the Sea" for about the next *year*. When Meg suggested to her mother that this was very embarrassing, her mother reminded her of the year he'd spent singing "Bewitched, Bothered and Bewildered." "Next year, we'll find a production of *My Fair Lady* somewhere," she said, "I promise. We could live with *that*, right?"

The next year, naturally, had been an election year. Translation: no vacations.

Okay, okay, don't be angry. None of this is her fault. It's just — bad luck. If she'd had any idea that this could happen, she never would have — why did she think Meg and her brothers had Secret Service agents, for Christ's sakes? Decoration? If she really cared about them, she — *stop it*. Being mad at her wasn't going to help. Be interesting to know if the country thought she was a selfish, bad parent, or if they thought it was such a terrible thing that they felt sorry for her. Tough call.

Angrier every second, she picked up the rock she'd been using, taking advantage of the energy to hammer at the chain. And hammer and hammer and hammer. It was almost completely dark now and she missed practically every time, hammering until her hands and arms were so numb and tired that she had to stop, loosening her fingers from around the rock with some difficulty.

Her face felt wet and she touched her forehead. Perspiration. Terrific. How much time was that liquid going to cut off her life? Minutes? Hours? She felt new angry energy and yanked at the chain, using all of her weight, bracing her good leg against the wall. If her stupid hand were smaller, she could pull it through the cuff and be — but it wasn't. She pulled until her muscles wouldn't work anymore, making no progress, then slumped into the dirt to try and catch her breath, her ribs damn near on fire from the effort.

All she had accomplished was more perspiration. Swell.

She lay in the dark for a long time, too exhausted to think about being angry, or scared — or anything.

Except that death was sounding better and better.

Chapter Twelve

She felt cold — or hot — it was hard to tell. Cold, mostly. She huddled down in the dirt, arms wrapped around her body, hugging the thin sweatshirt closer.

Water. What she wouldn't give for a glass of ice-cold water. She licked her lips, her tongue feeling almost as dry. Coke, lemonade, iced tea, milk, orange juice — *liquid*. A slush. Oh, Lord, her *kingdom* for a slush. The water leftover from a can of green beans, prune juice, *anything*.

It was dark, and scary, and she tightened her arms around herself, the chain heavy across her body. Christ, if she could just *sleep*, not have to lie here and — footsteps. Hundreds of footsteps. She sat up in instant terror — pain suspended — pressed flat against the rock wall. An army of them coming to get her. To hurt her. It took almost a minute for her to realize that the sound was only rain.

Rain. She was dying of thirst and water was only fifteen feet away. Jesus Christ. She stared at the boarded-up entrance, hearing blessed, noisy rain. Only, how was she going to get to it?

Think, goddamn you, *think*. She crawled as far as the chain would allow, dragging her bad leg, but still a good ten or twelve feet short. Damn it, damn it, damn. She tried to think, tears of frustration starting. Ten feet would save her life. Damn it to hell.

The hole. Maybe water would soak into the ground, end up in the hole she'd dug, and — she felt for it in the darkness, scraping her hands on small jagged rocks. She found it, finally, as cold and dry as before. She dug some more, using both hands until she was too tired to keep on, the hole as dry as it had been when she started.

Think. She leaned against the wall, still crying, listening to the rain. Would water condense on the rock maybe? Moisture she could lick off? Eagerly, she felt the wall. Cold, dirty rock. *Dry* rock. But, it would take a while, right? Okay, so she'd wait.

Like she really had any options.

She sat there, using her arm as a headrest, trying to think. Ten feet. Ten goddamn feet. If she had a rope, she could tie some cloth to the end, throw it out there, let it get soaked, and — could she *make* a rope? Maybe, if she — and throw it through those damned boards? She'd spent enough time staring at them to know that there were only a few chinks where light came in. And she was going to throw her wad of cloth through one of them? Yeah, right.

Not that *trying* would kill her. She felt for a rock and threw it at the boards, hearing it bounce back towards her. Only, what if she used a bigger rock?

Maybe she could knock a couple of the boards off.

She threw rock after rock, trying to tell by the sound of each what had happened. Nothing, apparently. And the bigger ones she found didn't even seem to go as far as the boards. Terrifying to be so weak that you couldn't even throw a rock ten feet.

She gave up after a while, slumping down to think. She could try to make a rope, maybe. Then, once it was light, she would be able to see the best place to throw it and — what if it stopped raining? What if — making a rope would give her something to *do*, at least.

There was the drawstring in her sweatpants; that was the logical place to start. Except that they were *already* too big. Not that she was going anywhere.

Apples. When you peeled apples, you were supposed to start at the top and try to get all of it in one long piece — her sleeves. If she could rip her sleeves off, then tear each one so it ended up being one long piece — "Oh, good plan," she said aloud, rather pleased by her ingenuity. Less pleased by the sad little rasp of a voice.

She felt for a sharp rock, trying to use it as an awl or something, to separate her left sleeve from the sweatshirt at her shoulder. The whole operation would have been a lot easier if she took the sweatshirt off, but — what if someone came and — what if *he* showed up, and saw her, and — besides, it was cold. And the chain would keep her from taking it all the way off *anyway*. And — Jesus, her life must have really gotten out of control if she could be chained up inside some godforsaken mine shaft off in the middle of nowhere and *still* not feel alone. *Safely* alone, that is.

It was a pretty cheap sweatshirt, and she ripped the rest of the sleeve off without too much trouble. Start-

112

ing at the ragged end, she tore it once around, careful to keep the strip about an inch wide. She kept tearing, slowly, patiently. After all, she had all night. In fact, if one chose to look at it that way, she had the rest of her *life*. She chose not to.

The rain seemed to be stopping, but doggedly, she kept ripping. Nothing *better* to do. She ended up with a piece of cloth about five feet long, the cuff dangling intact. Hanging onto the other end, she threw the cuff towards the boards, hearing it land about halfway over. Not bad. If she weren't nailed in, the damned idea would actually have worked. Although the rain sounded more like a sporadic drizzle at this point. Damn.

"Damn," she said aloud.

With much less energy this time, she started ripping at her right sleeve.

It was light again. Big fucking deal. A nice, bright sunny day. At least, as far as she could tell through the little cracks between some of the boards. No fucking *way* could she have thrown her rope through one of those little cracks. So now, not only did she have a dumb cloth rope she didn't need, but without sleeves, she was that much colder.

What a stupid waste of time that had been. Taking her time — why not? — she wrapped the cloth rope around her neck. *Now* she had a very long and ugly scarf. Swell.

She stared at the biggest crack, at the beauty of the sunlight, then down at the chain on her wrist. Christ. She gave it a halfhearted yank, a couple of tears rolling out.

God, she was tired. Unbelievably fucking tired.

113

Every bone in her body hurt from being on the hard ground for so long and she shifted, trying to find a comfortable position. Or, at least, a less agonizing one.

She hadn't felt hungry for what seemed like years — sometimes her stomach hurt; sometimes it was upset — but maybe she was losing weight and that's why her bones seemed to hurt so much. The ones that weren't already *broken*, that is. She touched her hips, surprised by how sharp they felt. And her ribs. And her collarbones, and — well, if she got out of this, she'd be able to *eat* any damned thing she wanted. As much as she wanted. When*ever* she wanted.

If she got out of this.

She took slow deep breaths, trying to stay very calm. Panic would come from nowhere — jarring, paralyzing panic — where she'd hear her heart against her eardrums, feel her nails cutting into her palms. Rational. She had to stay rational and logical and — what if her throat closed? Everything felt so dry and swollen that she couldn't really swallow anymore, and — what if it just sealed up? Then she wouldn't be able to breathe, or — oh, Christ, what a horrible way to — calm down, calm down. Tracheotomy. She could do a goddamned tracheotomy with — with what? The end of her shoelace. Which there was a word for, not that she could remember the stupid thing. It was plastic-encased, pretty solid. Yeah. She relaxed.

One worry down.

"With millions rising up to take its place," she said, her throat barely working.

What time was it? What *day* was it? *Was* it day? She squinted at the boards. Yeah, there was some light out there. Christ, even her *eyes* hurt when she tried

114

to move them, her eyelids scratchy and dry.

Good thing she didn't wear contacts.

Oh, yes, indeedy, things could be worse.

Think. Think about something good. Something nice.

Awards shows. God, she loved awards shows. From the Teddy Awards on *Mary Tyler Moore*, right on up to the *Academy Awards. The Emmies* were her second favorite.

"And," she said aloud, "for Best Actress in a Television Drama — " She fumbled with the flap on her pretend envelope. "They really *are* hard to open," she remarked to the audience — who chuckled warmly. She opened it, pulling the card free. "And the winner is — Meghan Powers."

Tremendous applause.

She allowed herself to smile shyly, modestly, on her way up to the stage. "Joan, Linda, Heather," she said politely to the presenters, then lifted her Emmy. "They really *are* heavy," she remarked to the audience. Terribly warm chuckles. She let the statue rest on the lectern, smiling modestly once more. "I didn't prepare a speech, I — " Pause for demure reflection. If she was gracious, maybe they'd give her one *every* year. "I'd like to thank the Academy, of course." Oh, to be able to say that and *not* be addressing the faculty at Exeter or someplace. *There*, she'd be saying something like, "I'd like to thank the Academy in general and Mr. Jarvis, in particular, for his splendid array of jam tarts." Kindly smiles, friendly chuckles.

She had been — family legend had it — the kind of child you could put in an empty room, and it would sit there for hours, laughing wildly at nothing. "Meg is very imaginative," her mother would say tactfully.

115

Meg was a bloody simpleton, more likely. Give that child a shoebox, or a piece of string, and she'll be amused for hours. Kind of like Dudley Moore in *Arthur* shrieking with laughter, then saying, "Sometimes I just *think* funny things."

"Like I said," — how colloquial — "I didn't prepare a speech, but — " She pulled out an imaginary sheaf of papers, greatly amusing the audience, "there are one or two people I'd like to thank." Pause to examine sheaf. "My agent. My broker. My parole officer." Audience goes off into gales of laughter. "Working with Mel was — well, unforgettable. And let me assure you that the rumors were — just that." Sympathetic, respectful nods from the audience. "I'd also like to thank my family, and — " Family.

Family. Suddenly, this game didn't seem so funny.

She had to get out of here. She had to get *out* of here. She had to — she was going to die. Any second now, she was going to — she had to get out of here.

She yanked at the chain, crazily, with both hands, yanking so hard that it felt like the muscles were ripping right off the bones in her arms. It wouldn't move. Oh, Jesus *God*, she had to get out of here. Why wouldn't the goddamned thing — she *hated* him! How could he have left her here, and — how could you *do* that to someone? Let her sit here for hours, and days, slowly, slowly feeling herself dying. A new symptom every hour — less movement in her hands, her tongue so swollen that it seemed to fill her whole mouth, dizziness — that goddamned son of a bitch.

She fell over into the dirt, trying to cry, her throat too swollen to whimper even; finally breathing hard and making self-pity noises somewhere inside. Then,

116

she just lay there, drained, not sure if she were going to be able to sit up again. *Ever* again.

This was it. This was abso-fucking-lutely it. And now, she just wished it would hurry up and happen already. It wasn't scary anymore, or something to fight against, or — she was ready. It was too soon — in life — but there wasn't anything she could do to change that, so she was ready. It was going to be *over*.

"I'm sorry," she said, not sure who she was talking to. Her parents, probably. Josh. If her tear glands were still working, she would have cried. "I'm *really* sorry." She hadn't *done* anything, she hadn't *helped* anyone, she had wasted her whole life. Seventeen years of — coasting. Ambling along like she had all the time in the world. No direction, no conviction — *waste*.

And she didn't even give a damn. Just so it would be over. The sun would come up, her family would go on, her class would graduate — and her being there or not wouldn't make much of a difference. People would be *sad* for a while, but they'd get over it. Everyone would. Every*thing* would.

It was going to be peaceful. At least, it damned well better be. She would just let her eyes close and — there'd probably be light, and music, and — she opened her eyes. Music. With *her* luck, she'd get English madrigals or something. Gregorian chants. The Best of Bread. Seventeen years of listening to good rowdy rock and roll and — if she had to listen to stuff like "Bridge Over Troubled Water," death definitely wasn't going to be her kind of place.

Motown'd be cool. Or the Doors, or the Stones, or — "I Love Rock and Roll" was probably asking for too much. But maybe she could get — hey, wait a minute, wasn't she supposed to be *dying* right about

117

now? Christ, instead of chess, she and the Grim Reaper were going to be fighting over the jukebox.

"Put it this way, pal," she said. "You play me any folk or country, and you will *never* work on the East Coast again. On *either* coast."

That'd be telling him. Was Death a him? Oh, no doubt. But her Death wouldn't look like Darth Vader — oh, no. She'd get stuck with a little, fat, effete one. A Republican. If her Death was a woman, it would be a Disneyland tour guide. With Tupperware. Popeet.

If she went to hell — always a possibility — there would be a lot of standing around, singing "We Are the World." *Over* and *over*. Indiscriminate hugging. Waiting in an endless Kmart line. Attention, shoppers. . . .

For someone who was about to die, her mind seemed to be clicking again.

"Death Scene, Take Two," she said aloud.

This time, she was going to think of a better ending.

Chapter
Thirteen

There *had* to be a way out of here. The chain wasn't going to break, or fall off, or unlock, or anything. But there had to be some way — like if she could cut her damn arm *off*, or — wait a minute. Maybe — that might be it.

Heart beating faster, she looked at her hand, not sure if she was overjoyed or nauseated. She could *cut her hand off*. That's how poor little animals got out of traps, right? She'd be free, she could run away, and — blood. All that blood. And what was she going to cut it off *with* — that nice straight orthodonture? Or one of those rocks? Yeah, right.

If only there were some metal around. An old can lid, or — Jesus, what a thought. But that was the only possible — the Idea hit with such force that she actually flinched. A way out. She had actually thought of a — she pulled at the cuff, the base of her thumb keeping it from going any further. She'd lost weight — her hand was a little slimmer maybe — all she had to do was *break* it. Break a few of the bones and her hand would be able to slip right through. It would work. It would actually — she pulled the cuff, studying her hand. Studying what to break, so excited she could barely breathe.

It wouldn't be so hard, she decided. Just a question of the right rock. With a solid edge, but not too sharp — she didn't want to slice herself open. And it couldn't be too blunt because she needed to break the bones at the right spots. Oh, what a wonderful, wonderful plan.

Scrabbling through the dirt, trying to find a good rock, she actually found herself grinning. She *loved* this plan.

And she'd found the rock. Fist-sized, with a slightly flattened edge, maybe half an inch wide. Perfect. She rubbed it across her sweatpant leg, wiping the dirt off. The edge came to a sort of rounded point at one end. Absolutely perfect. She cleaned the rock on the only slightly cleaner sweatpants, getting ready.

If her hand was resting on the ground, the dirt would absorb most of the blow — she'd have to flatten it against the rock wall. Hand pressed down, fingers spread, so she could see the bones.

She flexed her hand, testing it once again at the cuff. It was the joint at the base of her thumb — the bottom knuckle — and the bone leading from there into her wrist that were causing the problem. The knuckles at the bases of her forefinger and pinky might be trouble too. Mainly though, it was her thumb. If there was some way to cut *that* off, she'd be in business.

120

However. With luck, breaking all of those bones would work almost as well.

Hard enough. She had to be damned sure to do it hard enough. If she just bruised, or cracked, the bones, her hand would swell horribly — and she'd also probably never have the courage to smash herself again. Hard. Very goddamned hard. And fast. Any time she'd broken a bone in her life — including recently — it had swollen up instantly, almost before she felt the pain. Big tight swelling, not flexible stuff she could yank through the cuff. So she had to move very, very quickly.

Okay, okay. She had to get ready. Had to do this before the light faded. Slowly, she flexed her right thumb, wondering — with a sudden twist of nausea — if this were going to be the last time she'd move her hand like that in her life. Maybe she'd maim herself permanently, have a crippled — for Christ's sakes, better crippled than dead.

Calmer, she leaned back, moving her thumb, watching the bones' and muscles' responses. Okay, okay. A couple of deep breaths. This was the *only possible* way out. A way he obviously hadn't anticipated. The *only* thing he hadn't anticipated. Bastard.

Now she was ready.

She pressed her hand against the cold rock, trying to decide where her other hand would have the most striking power. Eye level. Just below eye level. Then, she hefted the rock, adjusting its position in her hand until it felt just right.

Okay, okay. One shot. Well, actually, two — to break both places. Okay. One quick break, then another. Don't think. Don't — slam! She heard some kind of yelp come out of herself as the rock crunched into her hand, but was already swinging harder, smashing the rock into the other place. She pulled against the cuff as hard as she could, feeling a scream tear out. But her *hand* didn't come out. Oh, God, it didn't come out. Oh, God, oh, God, oh, God. She smashed the rock down again, panicking, and again and again, wrenching at the cuff with all her weight, suddenly finding herself lying on her back, a convulsion of pain jerking through her hand, then her entire upper body.

She was out. Dear God, she was out. Her hand was twitching and jerking, the pain so hot and horrible that she was whimpering, but she was out. Out!

Hurry! Get *out* of this place! He might come back, to see if she was dead yet. What if he came back? What if he was on his way right now, and — she had to hurry. And half of her body was useless, and — *go*, damn it!

Pulling with her left hand, pushing with her right leg, she dragged herself to the boards, panic giving her energy. Heart thumping with excitement, she peered out through them. There might be a house right out there, or — woods. Forest and mountains, darkening fast.

Okay, okay, just get *out*. She twisted around, her hand resting limply on her stomach, and gave the boards a kick with her good leg. They were rotten. Thank God for *that*. She kicked a couple of them free, then crawled out. *Outside.*

Get away. Don't waste time. Put the boards back so he won't know you got out. Then, *get out of sight.* Don't stop!

Except she was in the middle of the damned woods. Where was she supposed to — *just go!* Get away! She

122

dragged herself towards the thickest part of the woods, feeling too panicked and exposed to think about anything except a place to hide. Someplace safe.

Push with the right leg, pull with the left arm. Push, pull, a foot or two at a time. She made it about fifty feet — well into the woods — before collapsing completely. Don't stop! Keep — except even breathing seemed like too much of an effort. Okay, okay, then rest. *Think.*

It was dark now, and very quiet. A few birds, trees in the wind, rushing. None of which she could really hear over her heartbeat and breathing. Her hand and knee were throbbing, agonizingly, but she was too exhausted to focus on that. The ground felt prickly, even through her clothes, and she realized that she was lying on pine needles. Cool, scratchy needles. So what. She stayed there for a long time, somewhere between sleep and fainting, still unable to catch her breath.

Rushing. The rushing sound was loud, and fast, and — water! She opened her eyes. Where was it? Somewhere nearby, somewhere — all around her, rushing louder, almost deafening. She lifted her head, turning it to try and find the right direction. It was coming from her left, or — behind her. It sounded like it was coming from behind her. She dragged herself in that direction, new adrenaline pumping in.

Every few feet, the ground seemed spongier. Moss, damp ground, rocks. Louder and louder rushing. Closer and — there it was. A fast-rushing stream, barely visible in the early moonlight. She stared at the water, so happy that she would have cried if there had been anything left in her tear ducts. She was going to let herself fall in, but had enough control to remember that water wasn't always safe to drink, that — for Christ's sakes, she was damn near dead *anyway*. It wasn't like she could take the time to crawl around and find *different* water. And this stream had a pretty decent current, which — she was almost sure — was a good sign.

Carefully, she touched the water with her left hand. It was cold. Wonderfully cold. She splashed some across her face, and that felt so good that she splashed more. Across her face, her neck, her chest. She touched a palmful to her lips — cold — fresh — then sipped some, waiting to see what happened.

Nothing happened. And it *tasted* okay. She drank more, then put her whole face in the stream, her skin seeming to soak it up, expand. Okay, okay, take it easy. Don't go crazy with this. Going from no water at all to too *much* water probably wouldn't be too intelligent.

She lifted her face out of the water and just lay in the mud by the edge, trailing her left hand in the water and washing her face again and again. The water was numbingly cold and she lifted her right arm at the wrist, slowly lowering it in. There was one hard jolt of pain, then numb relief. She let her hand float until the current made it hurt too much, then lifted it out.

Safe. Safer, anyway. Lost God only knew where in the wilderness — maybe not even in *America* — but safe. And alive. And a hell of a lot better off than she'd been an hour ago. It was dark, and shiveringly cold, and she hurt — badly; but it didn't matter. Right now, it didn't matter at all.

She must have either fallen asleep or passed out because suddenly, it was light out. The brightness hurt her eyes and for a minute, she couldn't figure out where she was except that she was cold, and wet — and in pain. A *lot* of — she started remembering — and remembering and remembering and *remembering*.

"Jesus," she said aloud, her voice cracking from disuse. Which reminded her that she was probably supposed to be overjoyed. Eternally grateful and all. Sing a song, maybe.

She let her left hand fall into the water, then wiped it across her face, the coldness waking her up even more. Then, she drank a couple of palmfuls, almost able to *feel* her mind clearing. And definitely feeling the pains sharpening. *All* of the pains, her hand now the dominant one. She looked down at it, the shape so swollen and deformed that she came close to throwing up. If she could find anything inside *to* throw up. Her stomach — empty for, Jesus, *days* now — felt shriveled. It hurt. And her knee hurt, and her jaw, and her nose, and *Christ*, her ribs — okay, get a grip, get a grip. She couldn't just lie here, after all. If he came back to the mine shaft and found her gone — she had to get out of here. Move as far and as fast as possible.

What a tiring thought.

Using a nearby rock, she dragged herself to a sitting position — not bothering to fight the requisite groans — and leaned against it, looking around.

Yep, she was in the woods, all right. And, judging from the pitch of the land, mountain woods. *American* woods? Pine trees, other trees, bushes, and stuff. Who the hell knew? She'd never exactly been one to sit around watching PBS nature specials. The only thing she could be pretty damn *sure* of was that this wasn't the Amazon. Probably not the Nile, either.

Okay, think. Be logical. Even though all she wanted to do was sleep some more. Block out all of the pain. He really might show up here any second now and — all that work breaking her hand, just to have him — yeah, she had to get away from here.

She closed her eyes, trying to think. To make her mind work. There had to be a road nearby because they wouldn't have carried her for like, miles. For one thing, she'd be heavy; for another, the odds of their being seen went up that way. So, all she had to do was drag herself back to the mine shaft, find their footprints, and — oh, yeah, *right*. Find the road and have them find *her*. No, she couldn't take the chance. Unless this was the stupid *Yukon* or something, she had to be relatively near civilization. And the nights hadn't been cold enough to indicate that she was way far north like that.

The only slightly logical thing was to go downhill. And stay near the water. It had to go somewhere, right? So, she would just pull herself along — what if she went *in* the water? If she could swim — or float — she could maybe move a little faster, *and* not leave any tracks for them to follow.

"Good plan, good plan," she said aloud. Nothing like a little pep talk. She looked at the stream. It couldn't be all that deep, and she would just stay near the edge anyway. Only, what if there were fish and gross things in there? Of course, if there were *fish*, she could catch them, and — she had to laugh. Even if she could catch one, was she really going to sit down and eat some *raw* like that? Something alive? Even fish sticks made her sick.

In the meantime, he could be on his way here. She took a deep breath and eased herself into the water, yelping from the shock of the cold. She supported her bad hand on her chest, trying to protect it, gritting her teeth against the pain in her knee. *Damn*, it was cold.

In another way, it was a tremendous relief, making her feel more awake than she had in days. And she might actually get *clean*.

"*That'd* be something new," she said. Not that anyone was around to appreciate her sense of irony.

Not that, in all honesty, *anyone* had ever particularly appreciated her sense of irony.

She ducked her head under the water, rubbing her hair with her good hand. Some soap would be swell right around now. Of course, if she were Nature Girl, she would probably be able to *make* herself some soap out of special leaves or something. She had read all of the *Little House on the Prairie* books — you'd think she'd remember some fun facts. At the moment, all she could remember was Jack, the brindle bulldog. And Almanzo eating those incredibly delicious meals. Cracklin' bread, and fried apples and onions, and — thinking about food would not be a good idea. Although she would damn near kill for a bag of Doritos. Cool Ranch style. Hell, she'd kill for a little plate of *okra*.

Pretty much used to the water temperature, she let her body float along the edge, controlling her progress with her good arm, touching algae-slick rocks. Luckily, the current wasn't very fast, but she still banged into more rocks than she avoided, her progress infinitely slower than she'd hoped.

She floated along for what seemed like hours, getting more and more tired. It was so *quiet* out here. Peaceful. Had she ever really been in the woods before? Once, in New Hampshire, she and her family had gone on like, an Audubon trail, but they'd had a tape recorder to tell them what they were seeing and — it wasn't like this. So — quiet. So *big*. The water didn't even seem cold anymore, just sort of numbing, and soft, and — she didn't realize she was falling asleep until her head was already underwater. She fought her way back up to the surface, broken bones forgotten, choking on a lungful of water. Oh, Christ, oh, Christ, she was sinking, she couldn't get — she flailed around in panic, trying to keep her head above water, gasping for air.

The bank. Get over to the bank. She managed to pull herself onto the rocky mud, half in and half out of the water. She couldn't get air, she couldn't get any — she coughed up what had to be half of the goddamn river, and when the bout was finally over, let her face slump into the mud.

Jesus. She lay there for a long time, too tired to drag herself the rest of the way out. Christ, that'd be really stupid — to drown out of exhaustion after everything else she'd managed to do. It might be faster to use the water, but if she could fall asleep in the iciest damn stuff she'd ever been in, then she couldn't take chances. *Christ*, she was tired.

When she woke up, it was dark again. Scary. There was a tree a few feet away and she made her way over to it, hunching against the trunk. There might be animals. Bears, and wolves, and — *snakes*. What if there were snakes? There might even be *poisonous* snakes. Her skin felt crawly, and — bugs! What if she were covered with — she slapped at her back and shoulders with her good hand, in complete revulsion, not feeling anything moving, but — *Jesus*. What if something crawled on her? She would die. She would just flat-out, on the spot, die.

There were rustling noises all around her — animals? Wind? — and she felt around the ground until she found a stick. A heavy stick. She pressed back against the tree so no one could get her from behind and clenched the stick tightly in her hand, ready to defend herself.

It was so dark — darker than anything she'd ever imagined — and there seemed to be eyes everywhere. Looking at her, watching her. *Haunting* her. Maybe there weren't just animals out here. Maybe there were spirits and, and supernatural things, and — they were all going to get her, and — somewhere up above, there was a bird noise and she almost screamed. A bird. Just some stupid bird. No reason to panic. But maybe sometimes, birds attacked people, and — Hitchcock! Swarms of birds flying down to — not *even* birds, swarms of *everything*, all coming to — oh, *Christ*, why couldn't that son of a bitch have just killed her?

She was too afraid to sleep. Too afraid to lie down even. She couldn't look around because she kept seeing eyes and movement, and — but if she *closed* her eyes, she wouldn't be able to see them coming. And she knew they were coming. Even now, he was probably following her and laughing. Hiding somewhere, waiting for her to think she'd gotten away, then jumping out and — she had to get out of here. But, animals and things were nocturnal, and if she moved, she might see some. More to the point, snakes and things would see *her*. Kill her.

There was rustling all around, and she couldn't tell if they were getting closer. Whatever they were. And it was *cold*. Ripping off her damn sleeves had certainly been a stupid idea. Instead of using the cloth as a scarf, should she wrap it around her arms? No, too much work. Could it get so cold that she would die? It was, after all, May — or maybe June? So, unless she was way far north — could she be in like, *Canada*? No, she wouldn't have survived *last* night if she were in someplace like Canada.

There was a crackling noise somewhere off to her right and she stiffened, turning to face it, her stick ready. It *was* an animal, because she heard the noise again, going away from her. Away. Thank God. If she was lucky, maybe little animals and things would be as afraid of her as she was of them. Rabies! What if something bit her, and she — by the time rabies symptoms showed up, she'd be long gone anyway. It'd be more sensible to worry about freezing, and starving, and the ribs that hurt so much that they — if they were broken — might puncture holes in her lungs, and — what would be sensible, would be to sleep.

But it was so dark that she couldn't. Even at home, she had been known to leave the bathroom light on and the door open a crack, "just in case she had to get up in the night and might trip on something." Right. Just in case scary things came to get her, more likely. Which, since there were supposed to be all kinds of ghosts in the White House, was a reasonable fear. One time, when Beth came to visit, she had insisted upon sleeping in the Lincoln Bedroom, and then been full of tales of the many spectres she'd seen. Beth, however, was prone to putting people on.

What did Beth think about all of this? Did she know about it, or was there really a blackout? But, the blackout would have started *after* her mother's speech, and — what about Josh? One of the times, the man had to have been lying, and maybe Josh really was — she didn't want to think about that. She hadn't actually seen him, just seen the door opening — but who else could it have been? Actually, it could have been someone else she knew, or a teacher, or — *don't* think about it. Don't think about Josh, don't think about what had probably happened to Chet — who was one of the swellest agents she had ever had, *don't think.* Just, for Christ's sakes, don't think at all.

Don't think. Don't move. Just wait for morning.

Chapter
Fourteen

She looked up, seeing the stars above the trees. More, and brighter, stars than she had ever seen. The same stars that she had seen in Chestnut Hill, Massachusetts. The same stars she had looked at from Pennsylvania Avenue. Not that she was one of those people who gazed longingly at the dark night sky and wanted to travel to other worlds. She had liked *E.T.* and all, but in general, space could not have held *less* fascination for her. People were supposed to feel small and insignificant and all that when they looked at the stars, but — well, she just thought they were pretty.

She remembered now, lying out on the White House lawn one summer night with her brothers, all of them staring up at the sky. If they looked behind them, they could see the White House; if they looked ahead, they saw the Washington Monument lit up against the bluish-black sky. If they looked *around*, they saw a lot of uneasy Secret Service agents. Mostly, they looked up at the stars and tried to figure out which one was the North Star. Her father was the only one in the family who ever spent time admiring Nature's Beauty, so the Big Dipper was the only thing they could locate with any certainty, but it was nice lying there in the perfectly groomed grass, looking up at the pretty perfect sky. They stayed outside for a long time, not even arguing for once, just admiring the nice sky and thinking summer thoughts. The agents were relieved when Neal finally decided he was hungry and the three of them went scuffling inside.

In Chestnut Hill, it was always lawn chairs. Lying on lawn chairs in the backyard, smelling of mosquito repellent, eating whatever brownies Trudy had most recently baked for them. If her mother was home — and August, with Congress in recess, was the safest bet — her parents would be sitting on the back patio, and lying in the yard, Meg would hear ice against their glasses, low voices, and the ever-present New England sound of the Red Sox on the radio. " 'Hi again, everybody, and welcome to Fenway Park in Boston. It's a *beautiful* night for a ball game, and. . . .' " If she and her brothers took their dog Kirby for a walk around the neighborhood, they would hear the Red Sox game coming through the open windows of almost every house.

She missed that house. Missed their lives. Missed no one knowing, or caring, who the hell she was and what she did with herself. What she *wore* when she did it. Even then, her mother was a hot-shot, "rising star in the Party," but she *was* only a Senator, and there were ninety-nine others. Many of them men and women — almost all men — who had been there longer than she had, and made more headlines. Congress was even better — there were over *four hundred* of them. Of course, they all wanted to be President, but very few of them *made* it. Most of them never even tried.

Meg clenched her teeth — where she still *had* teeth. Life would have been a hell of a lot nicer if her mother hadn't had to try.

Morning again. She had fallen asleep, all crunched up against the tree, and waking up, she was stiffer and colder than she thought it was possible to be. And the birds were very damn loud. She looked around, the woods seeming almost as scary and forbidding as they had all night. But somehow, she would stay awake today. Another night of not being able to fall asleep and staring at utter darkness — being awake was worse than the nightmares she had when she *wasn't.*

Also, tonight, she would have to try and find some kind of shelter. A fallen-over tree, maybe. Boughs she could burrow into for warmth. And here she was, with these worthless cloth strings, and — a splint. Maybe she could use them to make a splint. If she could walk — at *all* — she might actually get out of this. If she could tie a couple of sticks in place, and use another stick as a cane — it just might work.

Energized by this unexpected — and in retrospect, obvious — idea, she looked around for some straight, sturdy sticks. One of the few good things about being in the woods was that there were sticks all *over* the place.

She dragged herself around the clearing until she found two nice straight ones, which she broke to approximately the right size by propping them against a rotting log and kicking down hard with her right foot.

That accomplished, she moved her bad leg out as straight as it would go, feeling reaction shudders from the pain go all over her body. There were two tree roots growing closely together and, on an impulse, she stuck her ankle between them, then used her body to pull her leg out straight. Then, she tried to push her kneecap back into place, not afraid — since she *was* alone — she hoped — to make every pain-moan and groan she knew how to make. Should she try a rock, maybe? Hammer it into — no, *enough* with the rocks already.

How about using her *foot*? She thought about that, then grabbed onto a tree with the crook of her arm, using her right foot to push on the kneecap. The pain got worse and worse, until she was damn near shouting with pain, the swollen muscles fighting the pressure every millimeter of the way. Just when she thought she couldn't stand it for another second, it felt better. Not a lot better, but better. Noticeably so.

She sat up, not moving her right foot away in case the kneecap would slip right back out again. Frowning, she pulled her sweatpant leg tight, seeing what looked like an almost normal knee. Still deformed, but not unrecognizable.

Hunh.

"Good work," she said aloud. She reached for the two sticks, set them on either side of her leg, then unwound the sleeve ropes from around her neck. First, stomach muscles straining, she leaned forward far enough to slip one of the sweatshirt cuffs around her ankle and up around the two sticks to keep them in place. It was hard as hell to tie the thing together with only one hand, but she propped her leg up on a rock and wrapped the cloth tightly around it again and again, then tying several knots.

Finished, she sat back, testing to see if the splint was secure. It appeared to be, without cutting off her circulation, and she couldn't help being a little pleased with herself. Not that it was like, some miracle cure — but it was an improvement, no question about it.

The only problem was that *now* she was too tired to move. If she were *really* clever, she would have made herself a sling and — to hell with it. She'd used up all the rope anyway.

She lay on the ground for a while, resting. When she felt a little stronger, she dragged herself over to the stream to drink. Then, she sat up, looking around for a stick to use as a cane. Once she'd found one, she took a deep breath, aware of how much her knee still hurt. But if it was going to hurt *anyway*, she might as well walk on it. Faster than trying to drag herself; safer than trying to swim. After all, the worst that could happen was that she would fall down. Like, big deal.

Using a tree, she pulled herself up onto her right foot, groaning from the various knifing pains, so dizzy that she had to lean there for a while. When was the last time she'd stood up, anyway? It seemed like years. And the combination of starvation and exhaustion wasn't exactly a strengthening one.

When the worst of the dizziness and spots in front of her eyes faded, she let her left foot touch the ground. It hurt, but not as badly as it might have. She pulled in a deep breath, leaned out with her stick, and hopped over to it on her right foot. One step. Jouncing her hand hurt like crazy, the dizziness was back — and worse, her good leg was trembling almost too much to hold her up. Still, it was a step.

136

"A step in the right direction," she said, to amuse herself. If, in fact, it *was* the right direction.

Lean, hop. Lean, hop. She made it five steps, then had to rest, slumping against a tree. She made it three steps, then rested. Two more, her breath ragged, her ribs hurting so much that they felt as though they might actually burn right through her skin.

Lean, hop. Lean, hop. She fell a few times, her splint jarring loose each time. She would fix it, rub away as many tears as she could, and drag herself back up again.

Tonight, at least, sleeping wasn't going to be a problem.

It was dark, it was light. Dark, light. Lean, hop. Lean, hop. Stagger, fall, crawl. Cry, sleep. What a fucking nightmare.

Her right leg really wasn't strong enough to do all the work anymore and she drank some water, then pulled herself into a pine-needle clearing, checking first for snakes. She had actually seen a couple in the last day or so — mottled brown or black, slithering in the reddish dirt — and she had had to quiver in revulsion, holding her stick as a weapon. Luckily, they didn't seem to want to have much to do with *her* either. None of the animals did — she kept *hearing* things, but she never saw them.

Every sound was terrifying — it might be him, coming after her — but they were usually small sounds. Scuttling. Probably squirrels and rabbits and stuff. She would use her stick to poke the underbrush ahead, hoping to scare out whatever might be in there. So far, as a strategy, it seemed to be working pretty well.

She knew she was supposed to be hungry, and sometimes, she sort of was, but mostly she was dizzy, the ground seeming to move up and down in front of her eyes, trees dipping away from her.

People had gone through worse. She had to keep remembering that. People had gone through things that were much, much worse. People *survived* worse things than this.

It seemed like she had been in these stupid woods for years. Not that the seasons had changed or anything. She leaned forward, lifting her dirt-crusted sweatpant leg — the dirt *was* kind of reddish; was she in the South, maybe? Did it matter? — just enough to look at her real leg. Hair. Actual *hair* on her legs. How gross.

She always shaved her legs. Almost every day. Skiing and tennis were the main reasons. You never knew — it would just *figure* — that the one day you forgot, you would break your leg, and have to go to the hospital, and everyone would look at it in disgust. *She* was pretty goddamned disgusted.

There could be people looking at her right now. Or animals, or — when it was dark, she saw eyes. Eyes, everywhere. Looking at her, laughing — no! Stop it! She couldn't take another night. Last night, pressed into a rock hollow, trembling with fear and cold, too afraid to close her eyes, but even more afraid to look out at the woods, spending the night staring at her good hand, clenched weakly around a rock.

People had gone through worse. Somehow, she had to keep — it would be dark soon. Christ. If she had to spend another — it was so much easier when she passed out. If only she could count on it.

* * *

138

Nothing made sense anymore. She was in the woods, and it was morning, or afternoon, or — her hand hurt. Her hand hurt a lot. And her knee. And her face — she stumbled against a tree, more pain jarring through her.

"God damn it," she said weakly. "God damn *you.*" She took one more step and fell, landing hard on the ground. She stayed there, groaning, the sound like a creaky door. An *old* creaky door.

Finally — ten minutes? ten hours? — she rolled onto her back. It was getting dark. How many nights had she been out here? Four? Five? More? It was too hard to keep track.

She let her head fall to the right and looked around. Dirt. Rocks. Pine needles. Trees. Scary-looking leaf growths, like philodendrons gone wild or something. Creepy-looking. Anything she tried to eat would probably poison her. Not that she was hungry. Exactly. But she was so damned tired. Ten steps was a good hour's work. Pretty soon, she was going to be too weak to move at all.

She rolled her neck enough to look at the sky. Stupid, darkening sky. Stupid stars. Stupid everything.

"Find me!" she yelled, hurting her throat. "Jerks!" she added, more vehemently.

Who find her? The guy? The goddamned incompetent FBI? *Anyone.* Just so she could see a person, hear a voice. It didn't matter what the person did to her — good or bad — just as long as it was a person.

It was dark now, the animal noises starting. Once, she felt something crawl over her and shuddered, knocking it off. A beetle or something. What if there were more? She dragged herself up to move to a safer place, not seeing anything except trees, and rocks, and — lights. She saw lights. Oh, God, she was saved. Thank God.

She limped towards them, barely using her stick, unaware of pain. Lights. She was actually safe. Actually, finally safe. She limped as fast as she could, branches slapping her across the face, stumbling over uneven ground. Then, the lights disappeared. She stopped, horrified, trying to find them. She turned in all directions, squinting at black empty woods, not seeing anything.

"Come back, damn you!" she shouted. "Come back!" But it was dark all around her and she fell down, bursting into weak tears.

She was still crying when she heard the footsteps. Crashing, running footsteps. People coming to save her, or hurt her, or — she sat up, trying to see who it was.

"Hey, over here!" she called raspily. "I'm over here!"

But now, the footsteps seemed to be fading.

"Don't leave me! I'm over here!"

The woods were silent.

"Oh, God." She slumped down, holding her ribcage with her good hand. Yelling hurt.

She was losing it. She was very definitely losing it. She hated to look up anymore because she knew she was going to see things. People, or houses, or — lots of times lately, it was particular people. Him. Her family. Josh. Once, it was a bunch of police officers, and she would have believed it, but they were *Hill Street Blues* people. *Hill Street Blues* people wouldn't be in the *woods*; they were city cops. Besides, she was *pretty* sure that they were actors, that they weren't even real.

Nothing seemed real.

In the morning, she was too weak to stand up, so she just crawled. Reach out with the left hand, pull, push with the right leg. Rest. Cry. Then, reach, pull, push. Sometimes she made it a couple of feet; more often, just inches. Christ, how long was she going to be able to go on?

Reach, pull, push. Each time, it was harder — knowing how much it was going to hurt, how tired it was going to make her. Exhaustion and pain. She couldn't even remember the mine shaft anymore. Just these damn woods. Being covered with dirt and sticky perspiration, crying whether she wanted to or not. She felt so — confused. Like her mind was completely gone. Reach, pull, push, the trees above her swirling around. Swirling, and spinning, and — she came upon the backyard so suddenly that it was almost an anticlimax.

There was a man, with his back to her, chopping wood. With an ax. Terrific. What if, after all this, she had crawled back to the kidnappers' house and — maybe she should — he must have sensed something because he turned, and she saw that it was a boy, not a man, probably about fifteen. Seeing her, his eyes widened, and he took a step back, hanging onto the ax, looking as scared as *she* felt.

Automatically, she lifted her hand to straighten her hair. Or, rather, the thick tangled clumps that had once *been* her hair. She did her best to smile at him, not sure if she remembered how.

141

"I — " Her throat felt as if it were full of crushed glass. "Is that your house?" she asked, managing a weak point from her position on the ground.

He nodded, eyes huge.

"Are your parents home?"

He shook his head.

Naturally. "I, uh — " God, she was tired. So tired she couldn't think. "Do you have a telephone?"

"Well — yeah," he said, looking at her uneasily.

"Good." She rubbed her forehead, her brain feeling as heavy and exhausted as the rest of her.

"W-were y'lost or something?" the boy asked, still keeping his distance. He had an accent. A Southern accent.

Or something. She nodded. "Can you do me a favor and call the police? Tell them" — Tell them what? — "I don't know. Tell them someone got shot and to send every car they can."

"Someone *shot* you?" the boy said.

More like fourteen. "That's to make them come fast," she said, hearing the same patient tone she used when her brothers were being particularly dense. "Ask them to send an ambulance too."

He nodded, not moving.

"Go on now," she said, "okay?"

He hesitated. "Shouldn't I help you — "

"I'll catch up," she said.

He turned to go to the house, eyes still huge.

"Don't run with an ax in your hand," she said automatically.

He nodded, put the ax down, and ran to the house.

Forty or fifty feet. She could make it forty or fifty more feet. Stick or no stick, she could damn well hop it. Under the circumstances. Using a log, she pushed

142

herself up onto her right foot, arms and legs trembling. Safe. She was actually — she wasn't safe *yet*. Now, when she thought about it, was the kind of moment when he would step out of the woods, give her that scary half-grin and — adrenaline pumping, she limped over to the house, scrambling up the back steps, afraid to look behind her in case he and the others were there. Close to absolute panic, she banged on the screen door with her fist, tumbling inside as the boy opened it.

"Please lock it," she said, out of breath. "Lock it!"

He did so, looking scared.

"Are the police coming?" she asked, her heart jumping, closer to hysteria than she had been during this entire nightmare.

He nodded, still clutching the telephone receiver. "I-is someone after you?"

Thirteen. "I think so, yeah." She shivered, crouching down so no one would be able to see her from the outside. "I mean — I don't know. I don't — I mean, I think — " If they were that close, they would have gotten her already, not waited for her to go inside a house. Maybe she was safe. She might actually be — her parents. She had to call her parents. And Josh. And — "Is it okay if I use your phone?"

The boy handed her the receiver. The phone itself was on the wall and she used a counter to pull herself up. A counter. In a *kitchen*. She was actually in a *kitchen*. With a stove, and a refrigerator with children's drawings stuck on it, and nice clean linoleum — a normal, everyday kitchen.

There was a newspaper on the counter and automatically, she glanced down at it. *The Atlanta Constitution*. "Are we in Georgia?"

The boy nodded, apparently too unnerved by all of this to speak.

Georgia. Well, that explained why she hadn't frozen to death. And the reddish dirt. She checked the date at the top of the page. It was Tuesday. It was *June*. Jesus. And no, she wasn't on the front page. Which meant that her mother had really — she had to call home. "I'm going to dial direct, okay? They'll pay you back."

The boy shrugged, still speechless.

"Thanks." She had to think for a minute, both to remember her number and to remember how to dial. To dial *one* first. The dial itself seemed very heavy, the eleven numbers an enormous effort. But when the phone rang and the switchboard answered, "White House," she knew that everything really was going to be all right.

Chapter
Fifteen

Soldiers. Sheriffs, police officers, National Guard. Cars everywhere. The boy, standing awkwardly in the kitchen, giving her a glass of water, shifting his weight from one foot to the other. The boy's *mother* — and a little sister — rushing into the house from the grocery store, alarmed by all of the cars, maybe even more startled by the reason that they were there. And Meg, feeling a strange combination of exhaustion and self-consciousness, too shy to answer questions with more than small "Yes"s or "No"s, waiting for the ambulance, hanging onto the open line to the White House, listening as Preston — with God knew how many people listening in — said calming, comforting things to her — among other things, that her brothers were safe, that Josh was safe. Her parents had left immediately, on their way to meet her somewhere, Meg too tired to pursue the logistics.

The ambulance came and she was bundled onto a gurney and taken outside, surrounded by the tightest cordon of security she had ever seen. At least the press hadn't shown up yet. There seemed to be both doctors and men with guns inside the ambulance, and being surrounded by this group of strange men in a speeding van was so much like actually being kidnapped that she couldn't help being afraid. They all seemed to be talking at once and she knew one of them had told her where they were going, but she couldn't remember what he had said. She kept a little smile on so she wouldn't have to talk to anyone.

Someone put something into her arm — a needle? — which hurt, but she was too tired to protest, too tired to answer all the voices and questions, too tired to watch the IV being set up, or the lights flashing in her eyes. They were doing something to her leg, an air splint ballooning around it, and she woke herself up to watch.

"Did they wreck it up for skiing?" she asked, her voice sounding pathetic even to her. Small, weak. Dulled. "My knee, I mean."

"You're going to be fine," one of the men said, his voice a little bit too soothing.

She nodded, too shy to ask where they were going again, letting her eyes close. They did something to her hand which hurt so much that she had to cry, trying to turn her face away so they wouldn't see. Voices apologized and she felt a hand on her forehead, brushing her hair back. She managed a little smile, acutely embarrassed by all of this.

She happened to meet eyes with a soldier to her right — a *young* man, not much older than she was — and he smiled the same sort of scared little smile at

146

her. She smiled back, relieved to see that someone else was feeling as shaky and nervous as she was.

"I, I look so terrible," she said.

"You look *great*," he said, everyone else seeming to agree with him.

Nice to be humored. She had a pretty good idea of how disgusting she looked. How filthy. "So, what do you think?" she said to the same man. "Am I going to get out of finals?"

He nodded, very seriously, but she heard a couple of the other men laugh. Making a joke, however minor, was tiring, and she blinked a few times, trying to stay awake. It would be too vulnerable to fall asleep in front of all of them. All these men. But it would be nice to — she felt her sweatshirt being lifted, a hand touching her stomach, and had to fight off a scream, doing her best to sit up.

The hand had already left her stomach. "I'm sorry," one of the doctors said. "I was just — "

"Well, you can't!" She shoved the sweatshirt down, clamping her left forearm across it.

"I'm sorry," he said. "I just wanted to take a look at your ribs. I'm worried about the way you're breathing."

She looked at him suspiciously, tightening her arm. "I'm fine."

He nodded, lifting his hands as though showing her that he wasn't going to do anything, and she relaxed a little, but still kept her eyes on him.

"Do you think you can answer some questions?" he asked.

She nodded — slightly — watching him.

"Where are you having the most pain?"

"I don't know, I — " Her tongue felt thick and she

147

looked at the IV again, afraid. "Are you giving me drugs?"

"That's glucose," he said. "And we've given you a mild tranquilizer."

She frowned, not sure if she should believe him or not. "I don't want to fall asleep."

"It's just to help you with the pain."

She frowned, looking around at the other men, checking to see where they were. What they were doing. These are the good guys, a part of her mind was saying, they're not going to hurt you. The *other* part was saying, how do *you* know they're the good guys? She looked back at the doctor, trying to make herself relax.

"I don't mean to be rude to you," she said. "I just — I don't know you."

He nodded. "I'm Dr. Amesley. I live up here in Gilmer County."

Which meant absolutely nothing to her. She studied his face. He *looked* nice enough. Normal enough. Not that *that* meant anything. "I don't remember where you're taking me," she whispered, so the others wouldn't hear.

"To a helicopter," he said, without hesitating. "Which will take you to an Army base, where you'll meet your parents."

She tried, her mind sluggish, to think of military bases in this part of the country. "Bragg?"

He nodded.

Since there wasn't much she could do *but* trust him, she forced herself to relax. Somewhat.

"Is your hand the worst?" he asked.

Tough call, but — she nodded.

148

"What about your head?"

Her *head*? "You mean, my nose?"

"Is that all that hurts?"

"Well — where they got the teeth too." She shifted slightly, not sure why he looked so worried. "Do you think it's broken? My nose?"

The men all seemed to exchange glances, which made her nervous.

"Yes," Dr. Amesley said. "I think it's broken." He lifted his hands, then hesitated. "I'm just going to feel your skull for other injuries, okay?"

She nodded. His hands went right to the side of her forehead where — Christ, it seemed like *centuries* ago — the man in the van had hit her with the gun. His hands, very gentle, moved around to the back of her head.

"Phrenology," she said, and blinked. Where the hell had *that* come from?

The doctor blinked too. "I guess your memory isn't impaired," he said, sounding less worried.

"I guess not." She frowned. There had been some word she'd been trying to think of recently. In the cave? Her shoelace. The stupid thing on the end of her shoelace. It was — zygote. Or — no, *argot*. Except — that wasn't it either. What the hell was it? "Aglet," she said aloud, remembering suddenly.

They were all looking at her.

"On your shoelace," she said, too tired to elaborate.

The doctor kept examining her, asking permission before he did anything, Meg only scared when he felt her ribs, his hands up under her sweatshirt.

"Do you think they're broken?" she asked, struggling not to panic again.

149

"It's hard to say." He took his hands out. "From the way you're breathing, I'd guess that a couple are at least cracked."

All of her bones felt cracked. She nodded a little, feeling a great wave of sleepiness, fighting it off.

"When did you eat last?" he was asking.

"Breakfast," she said, more and more tired, rubbing her face with her shoulder.

"You had *breakfast* today?" he said.

She shook her head, the motion of the ambulance making her even sleepier. "Before school."

"The day you were kidnapped?"

She nodded, hearing more than one gasp, someone saying, "Jesus *Christ*" in a low voice. The doctor was asking another question, but she couldn't keep her eyes open anymore, falling into a confused sort of doze.

It seemed as if they drove for hours, and as if they drove for seconds because then, she was being carried out of the ambulance, into what had to be the helicopter. People were talking at her, but she was too tired to open her eyes, feeling the helicopter lift off the ground. She hated helicopters.

Finally, the motion stopped and hearing many more voices, she forced her eyes open. It was bright outside and there were soldiers everywhere. She heard the word "President" and tried to sit up, so eager that both pain and fatigue were forgotten.

Then, her parents were there and she was hugging them with her good arm, struggling not to cry. But they were, so maybe it was okay.

"I'm sorry," she said weakly. "I'm really sorry."

They were both talking, which was too confusing to follow, and she felt her eyes closing, letting herself

150

slump against them. They wouldn't mind if she — just for a minute — if she — she was aware of being moved — into another helicopter? Air Force One? Aware of new voices, and questions, and her parents holding onto her, but mostly, she just slept, feeling safe, and protected, and *extremely* happy.

She woke up to feel the gurney rolling and opened her eyes, seeing fluorescent lights overhead. A hospital. Maybe they were at the hospital. Her parents were right next to her, holding onto her good hand, and she tried to smile at them. They were saying nice, soft things to her, their faces pale and worried, her mother still crying slightly.

"Are Neal and Steven okay?" she asked, and saw them nodding. "Are we at the hospital?"

They seemed to be saying yes, and she nodded too, about to close her eyes again. Josh. Preston had said — "Is Josh going to be here?"

"I'll have someone get him," her mother said, motioning behind them.

It was both scary and strange to see her crying, and Meg was going to say something about it, but instead, let her head fall back on the pillow, seeing a blur of people against the walls as they passed. Blue uniforms, mostly. Grey suits too. Then, they were in a very bright room, and the people were wearing white.

"I'm pretty drugged out, hunh?" she said, her voice feeling like the slow speed on a record player. She closed her eyes, too tired to wait for a response.

The doctors were doing things to her, poking and probing, flashing more little lights at her eyes.

" — going to hurt a little," a voice was saying.

She opened her eyes. If they were *warning* her, it was going to be something bad.

"I'm just going to numb your arm so it won't hurt when we take the X rays," a man said.

She nodded dully, then recognized him. Dr. Brooks, the White House physician. "Hi."

"Hi." He smiled at her. "I'm very glad that you're here."

She smiled back, sleepily, and let her eyes close again. The needle *did* hurt going into her wrist and she gripped her mother's hand, her father's hand squeezing her shoulder.

"Okay?" Dr. Brooks asked.

She nodded, although it hurt *a lot*. Much worse than novocaine.

"Okay, all finished," he said, the burning pain going away. "In a few minutes, it'll be numb."

She nodded.

"Then we're going to take you down for some X rays."

She laughed weakly. "What are you going to do — a full body shot?"

He laughed too, his hand brushing across the split in her eyebrow. "What happened here?"

"I don't know." She tried to remember, and shook her head. It was hard to remember *anything*.

There was a small sound, like a gasp, and she saw Josh standing by the bed, tears running down his cheeks. Seeing him there, looking the way he always did, wearing a brown shetland sweater she'd given him for his birthday, she had to cry too, so happy to see him safe that she was close to losing the little bit of control she had.

"He told me they killed you," she said weakly. "He told me — I thought — "

He was bending over the bed, kissing her cheek, and she got her arm around his neck, hugging him as hard as she could.

"I," she hugged more tightly, "I'm sorry I look so ugly, I — "

"You look *beautiful*, Meg," he said, and she could hear his voice shaking. "I-I can't believe you're here."

She hung onto him, her eyes closed, a last bit of major worry leaving now that she had actually *seen* him.

There was a low voice — Dr. Brooks? — and Josh bent closer. "They want me to leave now."

She nodded, not wanting to let go of him. "I'll, uh — " She swallowed, not wanting to cry again. "See you in school tomorrow?"

"S-school?"

She laughed, which hurt her ribs. "Got you."

His face relaxed. "Yeah." He leaned closer. "I'll be here if you need me. At the hospital, I mean."

She nodded, the fatigue seeping back, smiling as he kissed her good-bye, feeling her parents take her hand again as he moved away. The doctors were doing something excruciating to her knee — getting *it* ready for X rays? — then Dr. Brooks bent down very close to her face.

"Meg," he sounded both awkward and gentle, "is there anything you need to tell me? Anything they might have — done to you?"

Rape. She felt her parents tense, and shook her head.

"You're *sure*," he said.

She nodded.

"Okay." He straightened up. "We're going to take you down for X rays now."

She nodded, her eyes already half-closed. "Is it okay if I sleep?"

"It's *fine* if you sleep," he said.

Chapter
Sixteen

Something — some*one?* — loomed over her and she slid hard to the right, trying to protect herself, only her left arm responding. Hands fastened around her wrist and elbow, yet another hand touching her face, and she struggled away from them, realizing that she was surrounded. That three, or maybe even more of them, had come in to — to — her mother — one of them was her mother. She made herself relax, waiting to see what was going to happen.

Her mother — it *was* her mother — was saying something, and Meg frowned, trying to focus.

" — safe," her mother said, then something about a hospital.

Hospital. She began to remember the night before — and the night before that, and — Jesus.

"Wh — " She swallowed, her mouth so dry that

her voice didn't want to work. She licked her lips, trying again. "Wh — "

A straw came into her mouth and she choked, spilling water down her front. Water. They must have thought — which was funny, and she laughed, moving away from the straw. "No, I — " She choked again, spilling more water, laughing weakly. "What *time* is it, not — " She laughed some more.

Her mother was holding her hand now. "It's three o'clock in the afternoon," she said, gently sponging the water away.

Afternoon? Meg frowned. "Today? Or — " She shook her head, confused. "I'm sorry, I don't — "

"Shhh," her mother was saying, and she saw that her father was there too.

"I *am* sorry," she said. "I didn't mean to — I mean — I'm really sorry."

They were saying things that blurred somewhere inside her head and she realized, embarrassed, that there were a number of other people in the room.

"I can't remember where we are," she whispered.

"Bethesda Naval Hospital," her father said.

"Oh." She swallowed, feeling tears for some reason. "I thought we'd be right near home."

Her parents said more soothing things to her and she tried to smile at them. She looked down, seeing that she was wearing a hospital gown and froze, not wanting to think of another group of people taking her clothes off, and looking at her. The way all of those men must have — "What happened to my — ?" She swallowed. "I'm not — "

"Your mother and a nurse did it," her father said. "To make things easier."

"Oh." She made herself relax a little, starting to

156

wake up enough to feel pain. *Lots* of pain. Her hand was still the worst, encased in plaster and metal, pushed up at an agonizing angle. There were bandages on her face, and her leg was trussed up in some weird kind of pulley. She took an experimental breath, to see how her ribs were, and felt tight, mediciney-smelling tape. "Am I going to be all right?"

They both nodded, some of the tears in her mother's eyes spilling over.

"It — " She stopped before saying that it hurt, not wanting to sound whiny. But they must have figured it out because a nurse was already by the bed, injecting something into her IV. She was going to ask what it was, but decided that it was easier to close her eyes, let sleep take over again.

She would wake up for a few seconds at a time, see — blurrily — one or both parents, feel pain, and fall back asleep. At first, it was dead black sleep, but then, nightmares began. Being punched, the school and all of the shooting, the mine shaft. She would wake up, muscles rigid, crying, and warm hands — her parents? — would calm her back to sleep.

One of the nightmares was worse than the others — she was chained, unable to move, and rats were crawling over her. Crawling and biting, and — this time, she woke up screaming, fighting to get away. A lot of hands were holding her down and she lay on her back, trembling, tears rolling down her cheeks and soaking the pillow.

"It's all right," her mother said. "You're safe. We're here with you."

"They were — " It wasn't just her parents; there were other people. "I mean — " She closed her eyes, embarrassed.

157

She heard her father's voice, then people with-drawing.

"It's all right," her mother said. "We're the only ones here."

Meg saw that they were, and let the tears fall — slow, tired tears. "I thought rats were on me," she said weakly, and shuddered. Which hurt, and she had to cry some more, ashamed and embarrassed.

Her parents were telling her not to be afraid, that she was safe, that everything was all right, and she did her best to stop crying, working to find a smile.

"I — " She swallowed, her throat hurting. "What time is it?"

Her father checked his watch. "Just past midnight."

That meant that she'd been safe for at least a day. A whole day.

"Here." Her mother was holding a plastic glass with a bent straw. "Sip some of this."

Obediently, Meg sipped, but then started crying again, hating herself for obeying that meekly. Even her parents. Oh, Christ, if only she'd been tougher. She shouldn't have —

"It's all right," her mother said, touching her cheek. "It's really all right."

"I'm sorry," Meg said, still crying. "I really tried. I didn't mean to — I'm sorry."

"Listen to me." Her father bent much closer. "You did *everything right*. *More* than everything. I have *never* been more proud of you."

She looked up at him, wanting to believe it. Also wanting to fall apart; cry the loud, scared tears — the *emotion* tears — she'd been holding back, but she was afraid to start, afraid that she'd never be able to get control again. She pulled in a deep breath, almost yelping at the jab of pain in her side, aware of pain now. *Very* aware. She wanted to ask questions — like, would her hand ever work again, was her knee ruined — but was afraid of the answers. Tomorrow, maybe, she'd ask questions.

The thing to do now, was sleep. It was the only way to get through this.

The next time she woke up, it was still dark. The room went in and out of focus, then she saw her father, slouched in a chair next to the bed.

"How do you feel?" he asked, taking her hand.

"I don't know," she said. "Tired." She swallowed. "What time is it?"

"Five-thirty."

"Wow." She looked around the dark, quiet room, seeing a nurse sitting in the far corner, discreetly ignoring them. "Where's Mom?"

"She went down to check on the boys."

Her brothers. "They're here?"

He nodded.

"Can I see them?"

He nodded again. "In the morning."

She grinned a little. "*Later* in the morning."

He looked at his watch. "Yeah."

It was nice to be quiet, and she looked at him, seeing for the first time how exhausted he was; unshaven, his face greyish and thin. And his hand, although it felt strong holding hers, was shaking a little.

"How long have you been up, Dad?" she asked.

"Two weeks," he said, with the same edge of hysteria she could hear in her own voice. In damn near *everyone's* voice.

"How bad was it?"

159

He laughed shakily. "Pretty bad." He wiped his other hand across his eyes. "Pretty goddamned bad."

Looking at him, she realized that she couldn't imagine it, any more than they could *really* imagine what it had been like for her. Feeling tired again, she pulled his hand closer, leaning her head against it.

"How's the pain?" he asked.

Pretty goddamned bad. She smiled weakly.

"I'll get Brooks in here," her father said, starting to stand up. "He can — "

Meg shook her head. "I'd rather be quiet for a while. Just, you know, sit here."

Her father looked worried, but glanced at the nurse, and sat back down.

"Was there really a news blackout?" she asked.

He nodded. "Pretty much across the board."

Hard to imagine. *Admirable.* "I guess they're all over the place here?"

"Don't worry," her father said. "They won't be able to get near you."

Remembering, suddenly, the time her mother had had a post-shooting, and general, check-up and had had to spend the night in the hospital, and the way the media had actually trained *searchlights* up on her window, Meg looked uneasily at the window in the far corner. The shade was down and it *seemed* dark. "Are they like, filming my *room*?" she asked.

Her father shook his head. "They're not sure where you are."

This room *did* look different from the one her mother had been in. More — ordinary. Sterile. "So, like, we're not in the Presidential Suite?"

He shook his head again. "We decided to put you a few floors higher."

"Are Steven and Neal down there?"

He nodded.

With luck, the lights weren't shining on *them*. "Is there still a blackout?"

"They're not getting anything from *us*, if that's what you mean."

Meg nodded, full of questions, but ready to go back to sleep. "Did she run the country, or transfer to Mr. Kruger?" Mr. Kruger was the Vice-President.

Her father sighed, not answering right away. "She didn't really have a choice, Meg."

Which didn't quite answer her question. "It would be like, a concession? Taking the Twenty-fifth?" Which was the Amendment governing the transfer — temporary or otherwise — of Presidential power.

Her father nodded.

She wanted to ask more questions — sort of — but, staying awake was hard work. "I might sleep again — do you mind?"

"I just want you to get better," her father said. "I just — that's all I want."

When she woke up again, Dr. Brooks was there, checking her pulse.

He smiled at her. "Good morning."

"Hi." She blinked to focus. "Where are my parents?"

He indicated the door. "Just outside." He lowered her wrist. "How do you feel?"

How *did* she feel? "Tired."

"Well, your system's had a pretty rough couple of weeks," he said.

"Yeah." She managed a very small smile.

"How else do you feel?"

161

"I don't know. Confused, mostly."

He nodded.

"And — everything hurts. I mean — " She stopped. "I don't want to be whiny."

"I think you've earned the right," he said.

She glanced at the door to make sure her parents hadn't come back in. "How hurt *am* I? I mean, am I going to be all right?"

"You're going to be *fine*," he said, and looking into his nice white-haired, grandfatherly face, she decided she would believe him. "Do you have any appetite yet?"

Did she? "I don't know," she said. "Not really."

"Well, what we'll do is bring you some broth and crackers, see how you do." He smiled, but his eyes were very sad. "You have a lot of weight to gain back."

There were worse problems to have in life. She waited for him to go on.

"You did a pretty fair job of *re*hydrating out there, but," he glanced at her, "you must have been in pretty bad shape at some point."

She nodded. *That* was for damn sure.

"We've run tests in case you'll need certain medications for anything you might have picked up from the water."

She shuddered. What a thought.

"There's no sign of that so far," he assured her. "The main thing," he indicated the IVs, "is that we want to get you built back up. Repair the electrolyte imbalance, that sort of thing."

She nodded, *basically* understanding what he was talking about.

"We took a few stiches inside your mouth to help the healing process. There was a slight infection, but the antibiotics will take care of that. A couple of your other teeth were loosened, but you're not going to lose them." He studied her face, looking sadder than he'd probably intended. "We had to, essentially, rebreak your nose to set it."

Meg winced, automatically lifting her left hand in the direction of her face, but not touching it. There was a big splint there anyway. "How bad does it look?"

"Not bad at all," he said quickly. "But if you're not happy with it, cosmetic surgery is always an option later on." He gestured towards the rest of her face. "There weren't any other fractures, but we had to take some stitches up near your eyebrow. There's evidence of a mild concussion, but you obviously came through it all right. Actually," he looked uncomfortable, "considering the extent of the beating you sustained, your face is healing very nicely."

"What about here?" She pointed at the tape constricting her ribs. Tape that smelled like a veterinarian's office.

"You broke one and cracked one on the left side, and cracked another on the right side."

She looked down. "It feels a lot worse."

He nodded. "Ribs are bad. You have a lot of bruising in the rib area, as well as the stomach, but there doesn't seem to have been any internal bleeding to worry about."

Save the worst for last. "What about my hand?"

He looked uncomfortable again. "Well, that and your knee are the most serious injuries. The knee was dislocated?"

She swallowed. "I tried to fix it."

He nodded. "That was our impression. You have ligament damage, and the medial meniscus was — "

163

"Will I be able to ski?"

He hesitated. "With surgery, and intensive physical therapy — " He hesitated again. "You're going to need — what I'm going to do, is have the orthopedic people come in here to discuss it with you."

Not exactly encouraging. "What about tennis?" she asked, mentally feeling a good portion of her life come crashing down.

"I don't know," he said. "Lateral movement is going to be — I'm not — we'll have to talk to the orthopedic people about that."

She nodded, unhappily. "Now, my hand."

"With microsurgery, they were able to set the bones pretty well, but — " He didn't quite look at her. "I'd say, count on getting fifty percent mobility back, and depending on surgery and therapy, we'll hope for more."

Fifty percent. Jesus. But at least it wasn't *completely* crippled. And it was better than being *dead.* "Um," she put on what she hoped was a cheerful smile, "sounds like I'm going to be spending a lot of time in hospitals, hunh?"

"Most of it will be out-patient."

She nodded, the prospect of this endless recuperation exhausting.

"It — " He coughed. "It was a very unusual break pattern."

"I used a rock."

He looked startled. "*You* used a rock?"

Strange to realize that she hadn't actually told anyone much of what had happened. But then again, she hadn't been *awake* much either. Odds were, the FBI had been pacing up and down for hours now, waiting to pounce on her. Another tiring thought. "He, uh, he left me in this — I don't know — cave or something, and the chain wouldn't break, so — " She shrugged.

"Oh, Meg," Dr. Brooks said.

He looked so upset that she knew she had to make a joke. "Well, it seemed like a good idea at the time."

"You were extremely courageous," he said.

She shook her head, shyly. "Not really." Then, she changed the subject. "How soon can I go home?"

"Well — it may be a few weeks," he said.

"Weeks?"

"We'll play it by ear," he said. "The important thing is for you to get your strength back."

Then, she would sure as hell cooperate. "Okay," she said. "How about some broth?"

Chapter
Seventeen

Beef broth. Saltines. A glass of milk. Mmmm-hmmm. Her bed had been propped up and a sliding table pulled over to hold the tray. The spoon was heavier than she would have imagined, but she was too embarrassed to have anyone — even her mother — feed her, so she lifted it, her whole arm seeming to tremble with the effort.

Her mother was instantly right next to her. "Meg, I can — "

Meg shook her head. "I can do it." She spilled more than actually stayed in the spoon, but managed to get four spoonfuls down before she had to rest.

"How about some of the milk?" her mother asked.

Too much work. Meg shook her head.

Her mother started to say something, then just nodded, stepping back with her arms nervously across her

166

chest. Seeing her in the light — like seeing her father the night before — had been a shock: Her mother was just as pale and shaky, her eyes so deeply shadowed that it looked like *she* was the one who had been getting punched. She was also — jumpy. Skittish, really. *Different.*

"I guess — " Meg sighed. "The FBI must want to talk to me."

"Well, they can just *wait*," her mother said.

"Yeah, but" — it *would* be nice to wait — "I want them to catch him. I mean — catch all of them." Catch him, in particular.

"Well," her mother sounded very reluctant, "if you're feeling stronger later, maybe — "

"If I put it off, I have to worry about it."

Her mother nodded. "All right, I'll take care of it."

"Thanks." Meg closed her eyes, amazed by how tired she was. How tired she *still* was. She heard people coming into the room, and forced her eyes back open.

Her brothers, her father behind them.

"Hi, guys," she said, trying to make her voice sound normal. Like it always did. Had.

Neal hung back against their father. "Hi, Meggie," he said, almost whispering.

Steven was scowling, which — if she hadn't known that he did that when he was trying not to cry, especially in hospitals — would have hurt her feelings. "Hi," he said, briefly, hands stuffed into his pockets.

Meg glanced at her mother for help.

"Neal," her mother said, "come give your sister a big kiss."

"Oh, please," Meg winced. "I *already* feel sick."

That won her a little giggle from Neal, and something like a smile from Steven.

167

"How are you feeling this morning?" her father asked.

"Well," Meg indicated her tray, "I get to have this delicious soup." She had always hated clear soup. In fact, she hated most soups, but at least minestrone was interesting to look at. She looked around the room, seeing the same uncomfortable expressions she remembered from when her mother had come home from the hospital after being shot, no one knowing what to do, or say — and, in retrospect, she realized that it wasn't fair that the one who was actually *hurt* had to do all the work. Set the tone. "So," she said aloud, "how'd those crazy Red Sox do while I was gone?"

They all looked at each other, either not knowing, or not wanting to *admit* that they knew.

"What do you think we did," Steven said, sounding hostile, "sit around and watch games?"

"You didn't pick up a *newspaper* at least?" she asked, irritated by his tone, even if she *did* understand it. Her head hurt, and she rubbed at it with her good hand.

"As far as I know, they're holding their own," her father said smoothly. "Would you like some ice cream maybe? Instead of the soup?"

She wanted to sleep, that's what she wanted. She shook her head. Neal's staring at her was also getting annoying, and she frowned at him. "You're not at the zoo, okay, Neal?"

He looked very hurt, like he might cry even, and she saw her parents exchange quick glances, then her father put his hand on Neal's shoulder, steering him towards the door.

"We're going to let you get some rest, kiddo," he said to Meg. "Come visit you later."

Oh, Christ, now everyone was all offended. "Look,

168

I didn't mean — " The three of them were gone, and she let out an angry breath. Great, now she was in trouble. She looked down at her bowl of broth, fighting an urge to slam it to the floor. "I didn't mean to hurt his feelings."

"He knows that," her mother said, very soothing.

Now she was being humored. "Yeah, well, I didn't mean to." Christ, her hand hurt. Her hand hurt worse than ever. She clenched her good hand, wishing that she could, at least, smash one of the stupid packets of saltines. "Steven could have said he was happy to see me."

Her mother sighed, reaching over to brush some hair out of her face. "You know how he is."

Yeah, she knew how he was. She didn't have to *like* it. Her knee was throbbing horribly, and she rubbed her eyes, not wanting to cry.

"Meg — " her mother started.

"Are they *ever* going to untie my goddamn leg?"

"After the next operation," her mother said, visibly uncomfortable. "They want to — "

"Great, the *next* fucking operation." Terrific. Now she'd gone and said "fuck" in front of her mother. She covered her eyes with her arm, tenting her elbow over her heavily-bandaged nose, feeling very close to exploding. If she could only get, Christ, even ten *seconds* of privacy, maybe — she uncovered her eyes. "Do you think you could get me a Coke?"

Her mother turned to motion to the nurse, looked at Meg, then moved to get it herself.

"Thank you." Meg re-covered her eyes, taking the deepest breaths she could manage without making her ribs worse. She'd slept like that more than once in the woods, her arm over her eyes to make day seem like night. Then, night, with the noises, and *real* darkness, and — feeling scared, she wanted to move her arm, but decided in favor of preserving the illusion of privacy. Pretending she was home, maybe. Wherever the hell *that* was.

When she smelled perfume, she knew her mother was back, and took a last few seconds alone before lowering her arm.

Her mother set a glass of iced Coke on the table. "Is there anything else you want?"

To be *alone*. Meg shook her head.

Her mother studied her for a minute. "Maybe some time by yourself?"

Meg opened her eyes all the way. "Am I allowed?"

"You're allowed," her mother said, and guided her left hand over to a little hanging box with a white button on it. "If you want anything, or need anyone, just press that."

Meg nodded, eager for the privacy to *start*. "It can be for a while? I mean, as long as I want?"

"If *hours* pass," her mother said, "we may begin to worry about you."

A joke. About *time* someone made one. Meg grinned. "How *many* hours?"

"Six," her mother said. "Eight."

Ten. Twelve. "What time is it now?"

Her mother checked her watch. "Just past noon."

"Can you get the FBI to come at like, one-thirty?"

Her mother hesitated. "If you're sure you — "

"I'm sure," Meg said.

When she was finally alone — even the nurse left — she just lay there, looking up at the ceiling. It was very clean. The whole *room* was, which was probably a good idea, seeing as it was a hospital and all.

For the first time, she noticed that there were a lot of flowers around. Very pretty flowers. There were also some stuffed animals, which certainly had to be from political leaders and people like that who didn't know her. Kind of funny. She looked at everything for a while, especially all of the roses, then closed her eyes. Except that it would be a shame to waste her privacy on sleep, so she opened them again and picked up her Coke, sipping some. Pretty nice to know that she could have something to drink whenever she wanted, as much as she wanted.

Before leaving, the nurse had given her some pills, and even the pain in her hand was better. Fuzzier. She sipped more Coke, absolutely loving the taste. Nice, and sweet, with so much crushed ice that it was almost like a slush. She drank the whole thing, taking her time, enjoying every minute of it. Enjoying the *ice*. Enjoying the silence in the room. If her cat were here, on the bed, this moment would be damn near perfect.

It was hard to tell the story in order. It was hard to remember details. It was hard to stay *awake*. Her parents had insisted upon staying in the room, although the agents seemed uncomfortable about the idea, either self-conscious about asking difficult questions in front of them, or afraid that she would hedge away from difficult answers. A psychologist had come along too, which would have worried her if she hadn't known that that was fairly standard in debriefings like this. He hadn't actually introduced himself as such, but she had picked him out right away — agency people, whether they were FBI, Secret Service, or whatever, were always very distinctive. The same haircut or something. Kind of like astronauts.

171

"And then what happened?" one of the agents was asking.

She woke herself up. "I'm sorry, I don't — when?"

"After you came to the conclusion that you had been abandoned in there."

There. The mine shaft? Christ, if that's where they were, she had a long way to go yet. She sighed, picking up the fresh Coke one of the nurses had brought in.

"Do you remember?" the agent prompted her.

What did he think, that she was stupid? Of *course* she bloody remembered. Her hand was shaking, and she had to be very careful setting the Coke down so she wouldn't spill it. "I — " Was she going to be tired like this for the rest of her stupid life? "I mean, I — "

"I think we ought to finish the rest of this later," her father said, frowning at the agents.

The agents glanced over at her mother.

"I think that would be an excellent idea," her mother said, also frowning at them, and the agents withdrew.

One of them, the leader guy, reached out to shake Meg's hand, and she vaguely remembered him having introduced himself as Special Agent Morehouse. Morgan? Something like that. "Thank you, Meg," he said. "You did very well."

She shrugged, not sure if he were humoring her. "You think you're going to catch them?" *Him?*

The special agent nodded. "Maybe not right away, but — it's only a matter of time."

Maybe. She nodded too, to be cooperative, hearing her father mutter something that sounded suspiciously like "Keystone Kops," as they left the room.

Her mother must have heard too, because she

touched his back. "They will *certainly* come up with something," she said, in the "*heads* will roll" voice Meg rarely heard her use.

"Well." Her father picked up his coffee cup. "Would you like something to eat, Meg? Or to rest? Or — ?"

Decision. "I don't know," she said. She was tired, but — she was getting *tired* of being tired. "Who sent all the flowers?"

"Just about everyone you could *think* of," her mother said. "The hospital can't figure out what to *do* with them, you're getting so many."

"Oh." She didn't have the energy to read, or even ask to see the cards. "Those, um, animals are going to look nice in my bedroom."

Both of her parents grinned.

"It was my first thought," her father said.

Which was pretty funny. Vanessa, who was occasionally on the destructive side, would probably like nothing better than the chance to batter those bunnies around. Then, she thought of something. "Do people like Beth know I'm here? That I'm all right, I mean?"

Her parents nodded.

"Would you like to call her?" her mother asked. "Your telephone is — "

Meg shook her head. "I'm too tired. Later, maybe."

"Would you like to sleep some more?" her father asked.

Yes.

Chapter Eighteen

When she woke up, instead of her parents, she saw Preston sitting in the chair by the bed.

He smiled. "Hey, kid."

She smiled back, very happy to see him. "Hi."

He got up, giving her a kiss on the forehead, then sat down again. "How you doing?"

"Okay." She noticed another large bouquet of roses. "Where did those come from?"

"I don't know, kid. Maybe it was the Flower Fairy."

Meg smiled shyly. "They're really pretty."

Neither of them said anything for a minute, then Preston grinned.

"Phrenology?" he said.

She relaxed, grinning back a little sheepishly. "They told you that?"

"They told *everyone*," he said.

Embarrassed by that, she studied his outfit. A slouchy grey suit — the jacket unconstructed, a pale yellow shirt, and a grey-and-yellow paisley tie. His pocket handkerchief was a brighter yellow.

"Armani?" she guessed.

He shook his head. "Cerruti."

She checked his shoes, and felt her grin widening. "Are you wearing little *boots*?"

He stretched his legs out and she caught a glimpse of dark grey socks above the ankle-high boots. "Indeed I am," he said.

For some reason, she found that hilarious, and it took a great effort not to laugh. "You know what would have been one of the worst things about getting killed?"

"I don't know, Meg," he said, sounding much more serious.

"Not seeing any more of your outfits. I mean," she grinned, "your outfits are usually the high point of my day."

He laughed.

"I'm serious," she said.

"Well, maybe we should work on making your days a little more stimulating," he said.

She laughed too, feeling an immediate twinge in her ribs.

"How you feeling?" he asked.

To lie, or not to lie. "I don't know," she said. "Kind of terrible."

He nodded. "At least you look better than you did the last time I saw you."

She frowned, trying to remember. "I saw you?"

He nodded. "In the emergency room. I brought your

brothers to see that you really *were* all right."

She frowned more, not remembering any of this. "My brothers were there too?"

He nodded. "You were pretty much out of it."

"Was I talking to you?"

He shook his head.

"I talked to you on the phone," she said, starting to remember a little.

He nodded.

"Did I make any sense?"

"You weren't really saying anything at *all*, kid," he said. "I was pretty worried."

"I was so tired." She sighed. "I'm *still* so tired."

He started to get up. "You want me to — ?"

She shook her head. "I'd rather talk to you. Or, you know, have you stay here."

He nodded, reaching over to pick up her hand, Meg noticing — again — how strange and nice it was to feel safe.

"Where are my parents?" she asked.

"Thought they looked pretty tired themselves," he said.

"She must have a lot of work to do too."

He shrugged. "Kruger's on top of it."

"Does the country know?"

He shrugged again. "They know she's not sitting in the Oval Office twelve hours a day."

Did she want to know what the country *thought*? No, probably not. "My father thinks the FBI's stupid."

"It's been a pretty frustrating time," Preston said.

Preston was a master at nonanswers. Although he was usually pretty straight with *her*. "I guess if they *don't* come up with something, heads'll roll?"

"Heads have *already* rolled," he said. "Believe me."

176

Since, except for speeches and stuff, she rarely actually *saw* her mother being the President, it was hard to picture. "I can ask you stuff, right? And you'll tell me?"

He nodded.

"I asked those FBI guys, but they wouldn't really — " She swallowed. "What happened at the school?"

Preston hesitated — which was an answer in itself.

"I saw them both go down," she said.

He nodded.

"I wish — " She swallowed, feeling tears very close. "I really liked Chet. I liked him a lot."

His other hand came over so that he was holding her hand between both of his. "The thing you have to remember, Meg, is that *none* of it was your fault. It's terrible, but it wasn't your fault."

She blinked, some of the tears spilling over. "I stopped walking. I *know* I'm not supposed to — "

"You were *told* to stop," Preston said. "Anyone would have."

"They heard that?" The back-up. Whoever "they" were.

He nodded. "Took a second for them to realize that it wasn't just a reflex on his part."

"The guy said they almost made it with the stun grenades."

Preston nodded.

Meg shivered, not liking thinking about this. "Shouldn't Dennis have *figured* they'd kill him? For knowing too much?"

"He talked a little," Preston said, and she was glad he left off the "before he died" part. "I guess he thought they were just going to wound him."

177

"And then later, they would have like, retired him because of the stress of it all?" she asked, a few more pieces of this whole thing falling into place.

Preston shrugged. "I don't know. No point in thinking about it *now* though."

He was right — she *didn't* want to think about it. In fact, there were a lot of details she'd just as soon *never* know. Which didn't make it any less her fault. "I *knew* I didn't like him. I knew there was something — "

Preston shook his head. "If anything, you thought he was *over*protective."

"Yeah, but, if I'd told you, or my father, or — "

"Yeah, your buddy Josh was all worried about that too," he said. "Says he knew you weren't going to tell anyone, so he should have."

Meg frowned. "It's *my* responsibility, not — "

"He probably would have just gotten a warning to back off, kid. Give you some space."

"He *probably* would have gotten taken off the rotation."

Preston shrugged. "Maybe."

Definitely. What she wanted to do was stop asking questions, but there was still so much she didn't know. "Were other people — I mean — "

"Your back-up guys brought down three of them."

She shivered again. "Were they — ?"

"Two of them," Preston said, nodding. "The other one's in a prison hospital, for now."

"Is he like, plea-bargaining?"

Preston sighed. "I don't think he *knows* much, kid. Whoever planned the thing was — " He stopped, looking uncomfortable.

"Pretty goddamned brilliant," Meg said. And then some.

"Well, no one's *that* smart. They'll get him."

She shook her head.

"The Agency's reputation was pretty tarnished by this one," he said. "*All* of the security agencies, actually. I think they'll do everything it takes."

Meg frowned at him. "You sound like a *press* secretary."

"Wonder why," he said, and grinned at her.

"You *know* they're not going to get him."

He shrugged. "They got the damned group that *funded* the thing."

She perked up. "Really? When?"

"I don't know," he said. "I guess it was the third or fourth day."

Third or fourth day. It was the third or fourth day when they had panicked — or what*ever* it was that happened — and — "Did it leak?"

Preston nodded. "One of the networks."

So because of some damned network, she'd ended up in a mine shaft in the middle of nowhere. "That was *stupid*," she said. "They almost got me killed."

Preston nodded. "I don't think your mother's going to forget it anytime soon either."

"Well, it's not like she can do anything. I mean, freedom of the — "

"Would *you* want to be a major news organization the President had a grudge against?" he asked.

No. "All she can really do is restrict access, or — "

"That's a lot, Meg," he said.

"She can't actually come right out and — "

"They'll get the message," he said.

You didn't get to be President without learning how to handle enemies somewhere along the line. "My father's even less forgiving then *she* is," she said.

Preston nodded. "Especially where his family's concerned."

"Who were they? The, the terrorists, I mean."

Preston scowled, and she was surprised to see his right fist tightening. "Some new damned splinter group."

"Middle East?"

Preston nodded. "Everyone's favorite quagmire," he said through his teeth.

"Are they in jail?"

"Some were detained; others were deported," he said. Cryptically.

Foreign policy was always scary, and Meg wasn't sure if she wanted to know any more details. "Was it — state-supported?" Christ, a *war* could be started over this.

He shook his head. "Doesn't look that way."

"Thank God for *that*," she said.

Preston's face relaxed a little. "Yeah, I'd say so."

"Do you think she would have" — saying "blown them off the map" lacked a certain — "I mean — "

"Your mother is a very prudent woman," he said. "I like to think — " He grinned. "Well, you know me, kid, I'm big on economic sanctions."

None of this was funny, but she laughed anyway. "Can you imagine my father's reaction if that's all she did?"

Preston laughed too. "I'd rather *not* imagine it."

Picturing her father signing on with the Delta Force or something was kind of amusing, but everything was

180

starting to hurt again, so she closed her eyes.

"You okay, Meg?" Preston asked, sounding worried.

"I'm just tired." She opened them. "What time is it?"

"Almost six."

She nodded, not that it really made any difference.

"Feel up for some dinner?"

"I guess," she said, without enthusiasm.

"Couldn't hurt," he said.

She shrugged, and looked in the direction of the door. "Does everyone think I'm going to be psycho from this?"

Preston shrugged too. "I think people are probably just going to be afraid of saying the wrong thing."

"I don't even know what the wrong thing *is*."

"My feeling," he said, "is that you should probably just worry about getting better, *then* worry about how you feel about things."

Right now, all she felt was tired. "An Army psychologist guy was here when the FBI was."

"It's pretty standard," he said. "I wouldn't worry about it."

"He sure as hell took a lot of *notes*."

"I really wouldn't worry. I mean," he glanced at her, "later on, you may want to talk to someone, but — "

"*You* think I'm going to be psycho?"

"No," he said. "I'm just saying — don't rule out the idea — it might be something you'd want to do."

"Thomas Eagleton," Meg said grimly.

He laughed. "Don't date yourself *too* much, kid."

She smiled a little. "Yeah, I guess."

He reached over, touching her cheek. "I'm just going to give you one piece of advice. Do whatever the hell *you* feel comfortable doing, okay? Don't put on an act, don't be a sport, don't do *anything* that isn't the way you really feel."

"That's not exactly *realistic* advice, Preston," she said, sort of amused. "I mean — well, Christ."

He nodded. "Yeah, I know. Just thought I'd suggest it."

"Can I be straight around *you*? If no one else is around, I mean?"

He smiled. "Absolutely, kid."

Chapter
Nineteen

Vegetable soup, custard, milk. None of which she really liked, but she was too shy to say so.

"Is there anything else you want, Meg?" her father asked. "Anything you'd like better?"

She was so tired she couldn't think, so she shook her head, lifting the spoon. Her hand trembled, the same way it had at lunch, and she glanced around to see if anyone — her whole family was in the room — had noticed. Since they were all carefully not paying attention, she knew that they had. She took as deep a breath as her ribs would allow, and tried again, getting a small spoonful down.

"I'm in the mood for a milkshake," her mother said, unexpectedly. She looked at Meg. "Anyone else? Boys?"

"Okay," Neal said in a very small voice, and Steven shrugged.

"Okay," Meg said. "I mean, please."

Neal looked guilty. "Please," he said, his voice even smaller.

Her mother glanced at Meg's father, who shook his head. "All right then." She got up, Meg unnerved by how fluttery she was. "I'll be right back."

The room seemed very quiet as she left and Meg looked at her brothers. "So," she said. "Is school out yet?"

They looked at her father uneasily before shaking their heads.

Of course it wasn't, for Christ's sakes. It was only early June. Then, she thought of something. "Do you get to *go* to school, or do you stay home?"

Both boys looked at her father before answering.

"We stay home," Steven said.

Jesus. "Do you have a tutor?"

Steven checked their father's expression, which was unhappy, before answering. "Not yet."

Pretty grim. "Kind of like being child television stars," she said.

Neal actually giggled, and she smiled at him. "You and Keisha what's-her-name," she said.

Neal looked at the television, Meg noticing it herself for the first time. "Can we watch that tonight maybe?" he asked.

"If your sister's feeling well enough," their father said.

Television, actually, sounded like a swell idea. "I'd like to watch it," she said, and picked up her spoon. What she should probably do, tired or not, was call Josh. Say hello, at least. She put her spoon down, having to concentrate to come up with his number, wishing she had a pencil so she could write it down. Boy, was she tired.

"What is it?" her father asked, looking worried.

"I should call Josh," she said, looking around for the telephone, which was — right where it should be — on the bedside table.

"I think he's here, actually," her father said.

Meg frowned. "Did I know that?"

Her father shook his head. "Probably not. Tonight's the first time you've seemed well enough for visitors."

Weird to think of Josh as a *visitor*. "Can I see him? To, you know, say hi?"

Her father nodded, reaching for the phone, asking whoever it was who answered — the nurses' station? The security force? — to send Josh up, Meg feeling nervous in spite of herself. Shy.

Her mother, a nurse with a tray of milkshakes, and Josh all arrived at just about the same time. Josh stopped to let them go first, giving Meg a chance to get a good look at him. An upsetting look. He was as shaky and tired as her family and Preston seemed, his hair parted strangely, with a cowlick she'd never even known he had. His shirt was rumpled underneath his sweater, and he seemed unsteady on his feet, like they had just woken him up. Which, for all she knew, they *had*.

Seeing her, he smiled. Nervously. "Hi."

She smiled back as he came over to the bed. "Hi. I didn't know you were here. I mean, they just told me."

"Well, I just thought — I mean, it seemed like — " He blinked a few times. "I mean, um," he handed her a small package, "here."

185

"Thank you." It was too hard to open it with one hand, but she could tell by the feel that it was a bag of those orange marshmallow circus peanuts. She grinned. "My favorite."

"Yeah," he said. "H-how do you feel?"

Instead of saying anything negative, she shrugged. "Did they wake you up or anything? You look tired."

"Well, I — " He looked embarrassed. "I guess I kind of just dozed off."

"But, my God, son," she indicated the television, where a sitcom was coming on, "the night is young." Surprisingly, she heard Steven laugh, and winked at him before looking back at Josh.

"I don't" — he was shifting his weight from one foot to the other — "should I — ?"

"Pull a chair over," she said.

"Oh." He looked around. "Yeah."

As he carried one over, she watched her mother jittering around with the milkshakes. She handed the one she'd no doubt ordered for herself to Josh, who held it uncertainly. Then, she picked Neal up, sitting in his chair and holding him on her lap.

Meg couldn't think of anything to say, and Josh couldn't seem to either, so she looked up at the television. An old *Facts of Life* rerun. A sitcom. Christ. *Last* week at this time, she'd been dragging herself through mud and pine needles, dizzy and confused and — Jesus. Last week, the thought of being in a room with her family and Josh would have seemed — it *was* unbelievable.

The show didn't make any sense to her — Tootie was up to some kind of trouble — and the dialogue drifted in and out of her ears as she sipped a little of

186

her milkshake. Vanilla, pretty thick. The sitcom drifted into another, prime time, and she realized that it was Thursday. That — she pulled on Josh's arm.

"What?" he said, instantly attentive.

"Is tomorrow graduation?"

He hesitated, then nodded.

"Are you going?"

"Probably not," he said.

"Oh." She glanced in her mother's direction, then lowered her voice. "Who's speaking?"

Josh shrugged. "Jon's father, I guess."

"Oh." Her knee was really hurting and she tried to ease into a more comfortable position, only finding *worse* ones. She must have groaned because, suddenly, they were all looking at her.

"Are you all right?" her father asked, already on his feet.

"I'm fine," she said.

They were still looking at her.

"I'm *fine*," she said, hearing the tension in her voice, seeing her parents exchange glances. "I'm sorry," she said, more calmly. "Can we please just watch the show?"

Slowly, they all refocused on the television. Unnerving to be the center of attention. And to think that there had been times in her life — *many* times — when she'd felt that her parents — well, one parent in particular — didn't pay enough attention to her. Now, she'd give just about anything to be back to those days. Back to the days when everything hadn't hurt so much too. But she had pretty much *just* taken a pain pill, so whining about it wasn't going to accomplish much. Why the hell, now that she was in

187

the *hospital*, did her knee seem to be hurting *more*?

"Meg," Josh started, looking as though he might be about to leave the room.

"I'm *fine*," she said. "Let's just watch the show."

They watched the end of that sitcom, and another; then her mother took Neal down to get ready for bed, Steven — surprisingly — trailing after them.

Meg's father got up too. "I'm going to go find Brooks, see what he can do for you."

Her knee was hurting so much that Meg didn't protest, watching him go.

Hesitantly, Josh stood up. "I should probably — "

"You don't have to leave," Meg said. Her knee wasn't *his* fault — she could try being polite to him. "I mean — please don't."

He sat back down, not quite looking at her. Christ, did she look *that* bad?

"I, uh" — she touched her hair self-consciously — "I look pretty awful."

"You look *hurt*," he said.

"Well — " She couldn't think of a response to that. "Well, you know."

The room seemed very, very quiet.

"I, um, I hope you weren't here too long," she said. "I mean, no one told me."

He shook his head. "Just during visiting hours."

Which was pretty long. She moved slightly, trying to find a better angle for her leg, biting her lip against the instant flash of pain. She glanced over, hoping that he hadn't noticed. But, of course, he had.

"Should I get — ?" he started.

"No," she said. "Thank you."

The room got quiet again.

188

"I still can't believe you're here," he said, his voice sounding shaky. "It's — I'm *really* glad."

"I can't believe *you're* here. He kept telling me that you were — I thought — " She stopped, not wanting to think about it. About any of it.

"I ducked," Josh said, so quietly that she barely heard him. "When you said to."

"Well — " She frowned, not sure why he looked so upset. "That's good, isn't it?"

He shook his head. "I should have *done* something. I should have — "

"Against *machine* guns? They just would have killed you."

He shivered, without answering, and remembering the whole scene, she did too.

"I'm sorry," she said. "I almost got you — it's all my fault."

"It's *my* fault," Josh said. "I *knew* you didn't like him, and I knew you weren't going to — "

"*I* knew I had Secret Service for a reason — I never should have — " She shook her head. "I'm sorry." Like, big deal. Her *mother* was probably sorry too. Although being just as guilty made it hard to be angry at her.

"You're the *last* person whose fault it was," he said. "You're the brave one who had to go *through* all of it."

Oh, yeah, real brave. Like, just for example, when she'd offered to sleep with the guy so he wouldn't —
"I wasn't all that brave," she said stiffly.

"Yeah, you were." He shivered again. "They're shooting, and grabbing you up off the ground, and you're yelling for *me* to get down."

"I was afraid they — " This conversation was upsetting, and her *knee* was hurting so badly that it was

189

hard not to cry. Impossible, in fact. She turned her head, hoping that he wouldn't be able to see. "Did you, um, drive here?"

"Yeah, I — "

"It's kind of a long drive at night," she said, trying to keep her voice steady. "Maybe you should — "

He was already on his feet. "Is it okay if I come to see you tomorrow?"

The thought of seeing anyone — even him — maybe even *especially* him — was too hard. "I think I — " she didn't want to hurt his feelings — "I need time alone, I think."

"Okay," he said, looking unhappy.

"I'll call you," she said. "When I'm ready."

He nodded.

"Can you make sure no one from school calls me or anything? I mean, you know, if they were going to?" If they could get *through*, even.

He nodded.

"Thanks." There seemed to be tears all over her face, and she wiped at them clumsily with her hand. "I *will* call you. I just — maybe not right away."

He nodded. "Whenever you're ready," he said. "I mean, feel better."

"Yeah. I mean, thanks."

He bent down, gave her an awkward kiss on the forehead, and walked quickly towards the door.

"Josh?"

He turned.

"I think you should go to graduation," she said.

He shook his head. "No, I — "

"You really *liked* that school."

"*Liked*," he said.

He had a point *there*. "I still think you should go."

He looked guilty. "It wouldn't feel — "

"I wasn't even there for two years," she said. "It's not the same for me anyway."

He hesitated, but then shook his head.

"Think about it, okay?"

"I'll think about it," he said.

When he was gone, she sank down into the pillows, not worrying about letting the tears fall, crying mostly about her knee, but also just in general. She was going to press the little white button for the nurse, to see if they could bring her some stronger pain medication, but didn't want them to come in and see her crying.

There was another stupid comedy on and she fumbled for the remote control, turning it off. Without the noise of the television, the room seemed very quiet, and she cried harder, feeling both alone and surrounded. Trapped. As a precaution, she covered her eyes with her arm, then let herself *really* cry, feeling the bed shake underneath her. Oh, God, her knee hurt. Her knee hurt nightmarishly badly. Maybe there was really something wrong. Something new. Maybe she should call — but not while she was crying like this. Christ, how could it hurt so much? How could *anything* hurt so much?

" — just *sit* there and watch my child — " she heard her father's low voice going past her door. That meant that, any minute now, they were going to come back in and — she tried to stop crying, dragging in a slow, rib-stabbing breath. Then, another.

By the time there was a quiet little knock on the door, and her parents and Dr. Brooks came in, she was almost under control. Almost, being the operative word, and she lowered her arm only partway.

"Do you think you can sit up enough to take these?"

191

Dr. Brooks asked, holding a small paper cup of water and another cup with some pills in it.

She nodded as he pushed the button to raise the bed slightly, keeping her head turned so that while they might see that she had been crying, they wouldn't be able to tell how *much* she had been crying.

"Wh-what are they?" she asked, looking at the pills. Not that a tearful little *voice* wasn't a dead giveaway.

"Those should help you get some sleep," he pointed, "and that one should take care of the pain you're having."

She nodded, tipping the contents of the little cup into her mouth, then gulping the water, her hand trembling.

"It's your knee, mostly?" Dr. Brooks asked.

She nodded, tensing in case he was going to have to examine it.

"All right." His hand touched her hand very gently. "Dr. Steiner is on his way up, and we're going to see what we can do to make you feel better."

"I don't — " She swallowed. "Do I know him?"

"Your father and I have met him," her mother said. "He's one of the orthopedic specialists."

"Is he going to move it around?" she asked, already scared. Hurt her more?

"He's just going to have a look," Dr. Brooks said, pumping up a blood pressure cuff on her arm. "Ask you a couple of questions, maybe."

Meg nodded, still scared. But the pills took effect quickly, and by the time Dr. Steiner came in — tall, with glasses and bushy brown hair — she could barely keep her eyes open. He *did* poke around a lot, but the pain seemed faraway, and the questions he asked — when the pain had started getting worse, where, and

192

that sort of thing — took all of her concentration to answer.

They all seemed to be talking somewhere above her — to her, maybe? *About* her? — and she tried to pay attention, but it was too hard.

"I'm going to — I mean, is it okay if I — " It was too much work to stay awake anymore, and she let her eyes close.

Chapter
Twenty

Yet another wakening in darkness, not sure where she was at first, then not sure what time it was. Then, blurrily, she saw her mother by the bed, her father asleep in the chair by the window.

"Okay?" her mother whispered, seeing her open her eyes.

Meg nodded, relieved that her mother understood she was too tired to talk.

"I'm sorry," her mother said softly. "I'm so sorry about *everything*."

Meg nodded, sleepily.

"How's the pain?"

Terrible. More awake now, Meg looked down at the bulky contraption holding her knee in the air. "I-is there something bad wrong with it?" she asked, terrified by the idea.

"Well — " Her mother was choosing her words. "I

guess there's some pressure building up in there."

"What does *that* mean?"

"Well," her mother said, and hesitated. "That they've elected to do the surgery tomorrow, and get you out of traction sooner."

The word "surgery" was scary, and Meg swallowed. "Do I have to be unconscious?"

"They would *prefer* to do it locally."

Meg swallowed again. "Will it hurt?"

Her mother shook her head.

"Will you and Dad be in there with me?"

Her mother nodded, although Meg saw her hands tighten nervously. Her mother was almost as bad as Steven about All Things Medical. Except, in Steven's case, sports injuries. He was the only person she had ever known who actually *did* things like rotator cuff exercises.

"Will the blood and all bother you?" Meg asked.

"Of course not," her mother said. Rather heartily.

Unh-hunh. Almost completely awake now, Meg moved her pillows, her mother helping, so she could sit up a little. "What exactly are they going to *do* to me?"

"Well." Her mother's hands tightened again. "R-reconstruct the ligaments, and, um, clean up any floating cartilage, and — one of the surgeons has worked extensively with the U.S. Ski Team."

Meg felt a flash of great hope and excitement. "You mean, I *will* be able to ski again? And play tennis and all?"

"He's supposed to be the best in the country," her mother said. The President, neatly sidestepping a direct answer.

She was beginning to get a pretty bad feeling about

all of this, but decided not to think about it. Was too *afraid* to think about it.

"It was good to see Josh tonight?" her mother asked.

Not really. Meg shook her head.

"Well, maybe we can have Beth — "

Meg shook her head. "I don't *want* to see people." Didn't want to have them see *her*. "Um, where are Steven and Neal?"

"Asleep downstairs," her mother said.

Which you'd think, she'd be able to remember. She looked over at her father, who was still slouched in his chair, asleep, his face haggard. "Thank God it wasn't Neal," she said, keeping her voice low.

Her mother shuddered, but didn't say anything.

"I mean, Steven would have been bad too, but — " Her head was hurting and she pressed her hand against it, her mother's hand covering hers, very warm and soothing. "Besides, with me — he *wanted* everyone to be thinking about rape."

Her mother's hand stiffened. "Everyone was."

"Yeah." Seeing the genuine fear in her mother's eyes, she managed a little smile. "I swear he didn't. I mean" — she felt the smile tightening — "it was *discussed*, but — "

Her mother nodded, letting out her breath, her hand stroking Meg's forehead again.

It seemed cold, and she wished she were strong enough to sit up for a hug. "I really don't think I'm going to make it through this," she said. "I *really* don't."

Her mother's other hand came over to squeeze her shoulder. "You will," she said. "We all will."

Again, just a bit too hearty. "I don't know," Meg said, and pulled her blanket up higher.

196

"Would you like another?" her mother asked, tucking it around her.

Meg shook her head.

"Why don't you try to get some sleep," her mother said, adjusting the pillows for her.

Meg nodded, her eyes already feeling heavy. Her knee was throbbing though, and she knew she wasn't going to have much luck. Strange to think about what tonight *would* have been like. Should have been. Her last night as a high school senior. She'd only been waiting for — well, since about *third* grade. Someone at school would have been having a big party — probably *was* — and — not that she'd ever been totally into school or anything, but — it *would* have been a big deal. A big step. Only now — she let out her breath.

"Your knee?" her mother asked, sounding worried.

Meg shook her head. Not primarily, anyway. This was more — general — misery. She looked up at her mother, whose expression *looked* the way hers felt. "I wish — " She stopped. Wish *what?* Something real helpful, like that none of this had ever happened? That her mother had lost the election, that they were still in Massachusetts, that — *pointless* wishes? "I wish you were still speaking," she said finally. That everything was *normal*.

Her mother looked confused. "I don't — ?"

"Tomorrow night."

Her mother nodded, picking up her hand. "I'm sorry, I know how — "

"It's not like I *loved* school," Meg said. "It's just — I don't know."

Her mother nodded, holding her hand tightly. "I'm sorry. I *really* am."

197

The room was so quiet that she could hear her father breathing.

"What does the country know?" she asked.

"That you're safe," her mother said. "That you escaped."

"They don't really know details, though."

Her mother shook her head.

"So, there's like, *conjecture.*"

Her mother shrugged, but her hand tightened.

She was much too tired to get into all of this, but — "Do you think they think there's a cover-up?"

Her mother shrugged again. "Let them."

Her mother, indifferent to public opinion? Kind of funny. Especially since she and Steven had occasionally mumbled the word "cover-up" — even out of context — *just* to watch her mother's blood pressure go up. The word "Watergate" was a good one too. However. "Have you spoken to the press at *all?*"

"Well, not — " Her mother stopped.

Not since the "cannot, have not, and *will* not negotiate" speech. Meg didn't say anything.

"I've only released statements," her mother said carefully. "I'd anticipated a press conference in a day or so."

"From *here?*"

"Downstairs, somewhere," her mother said. "I'll just have Linda" — who was her press secretary — "set up — "

"If you do it from here," Meg said, "won't it look — I mean, people'll think — " She sighed. "I mean, I wish — "

Her mother sighed too. "I *can't* speak at the graduation, Meg. It would be — well, 'circus' is putting it *mildly.*"

Which was true. Her mother's being there would turn it into a major media event, and ruin it for — Christ, this was making her head hurt. "If you do it from here, won't people think — I mean, it'll look like I'm lying around all traumatized and — you know, that *all* of us are."

Her mother's glance around the room was more than a little ironic. "Which, Lord knows, isn't the case."

Meg had to grin. "Yeah, but, I don't want them *thinking* that."

Her mother nodded. "Would you like me to have it back at the House? Just a standard press conference?"

"Yeah," Meg said. "I think that would be good. And maybe kind of soon?"

Her mother nodded. "Monday night?"

Which wasn't all that soon. "Um, how about to-morrow night?"

"Well" — her mother glanced at Meg's knee — "wouldn't it be better to wait until — ?"

Meg shook her head. Firmly.

"Okay, then," her mother said. "I'll have Linda arrange it."

"And you won't just talk about me? Or release a picture or anything?" Not that her mother, obviously, could *ignore* the situation. "I mean, you'll talk about normal stuff too?" Little things like — foreign policy, say.

Her mother nodded, bending down to kiss her cheek. "I'll do whatever you want, Meg. I promise."

Meg lifted her shoulders off the bed enough so that her mother could hug her. "I just want to be safe," she said. "I want *all* of us to be safe."

•   •   •

199

The operation was at nine o'clock. The doctors, Dr. Steiner among them, introduced themselves, then disappeared behind the green operating cloth hiding her legs from sight. Her parents and Dr. Brooks were on her side of the cloth, her parents each with a hand holding hers. They were wearing green surgical outfits which, under different circumstances, would have been hilarious.

She hung on, terrified that it was going to hurt, even though she couldn't really feel *anything* below her waist. A nurse was injecting something into her IV and she felt almost immediately calmer. Her parents were telling her not to worry, that she was fine, that everything was going to be fine, but she could hear the surgeons' low voices and — sounds. Suction, and — she clutched at her parents with her good hand, trying not to panic.

"I can hear them *cutting*," she whispered.

Her father moved so that he was holding her hand and her mother's hand between both of his. "We're going to talk to you," he said calmly. "You won't hear anything."

She looked up at him, watching as he talked about the day she was born — night, actually, *late* night — and how happy he was, how fat and wrinkled *she* was, and how they brought her home to her mother's old yellow baby crib, and how they — even the dog, Trevor — would just sit and look at her, and he and her mother would talk about how lucky they were, and how beautiful she was, and how smart they knew she was going to be — sometimes Meg would hear a scary soft sound behind the operating cloth, but she concentrated on keeping her eyes on her father's, listening to him.

200

He talked about the little red cloche hat she had, and her mother laughed, Meg laughing too, even though she didn't remember. He talked about her first lacy Easter dress, and the little white-and-yellow bonnet she wore to go with *that*, and how she was always so good and happy, and *loved* to have her picture taken. And how he would sit her up on his lap, and she would eat Uneeda biscuits, and laugh and laugh.

Sometimes, she would fall asleep for a few seconds or minutes, but when she woke up, her father would still be talking. About how she used to put flour in one half of her hair and walk around singing "Cruella DeVil." About the red plaid dress with a Peter Pan collar she wore on her first day of kindergarten. About the big dishes of mashed potatoes and creamed corn she was always eating. And root beer. Always a root beer. About the tie-dyed "Peace" shirt she wore everywhere — outdated, but hey — with her little blue Keds. About how disapproving she was when Steven was born, especially because he had too much hair. About the first time she went to see her mother in Washington, and how the Speaker of the House let her stand up in the front, after the session was over, and bang his gavel, and how funny she thought that was. About how damned stubborn she had been, *literally* trying to put the square block in the round hole, and when he'd suggested that she try the round green one, she'd said — scornfully — "*Babies* can do *that*." About how much trouble she had pronouncing Yastrzemski.

When the table moved, she woke up completely, afraid that the doctors' scalpels would slip, then realized that the operation was over and she was being wheeled back to a recovery room or something.

201

"Am I all right?" she asked. She couldn't quite understand what the doctors said to her, but was pretty sure she heard the word "encouraging" in there. Which would have to be a good sign.

A lot of people were fussing over her — taking her temperature, pumping up a blood pressure cuff, sponging her face — and she watched from what seemed like way inside her head, too tired to do more than nod and shake her head when they asked questions.

When she woke up again, the first thing she felt was pain. Her leg was out straight, in some kind of strap-on cast, and she groaned before she could stop herself. There was a flurry of activity around the bed, people trying to make her more comfortable, and she put on the best smile she could come up with, wanting to be a good sport. A good scout.

Her mother was holding a glass of water with a bent straw and Meg gratefully sipped some.

"What time is it?" she asked, her tongue less than responsive.

More than one person answered, and she gathered that it was after five. The press conference was at eight, and she looked at her mother. "You're still going, right?"

Her mother nodded.

"Good." She was still pretty tired, so she drank some more water, trying to wake up. She recognized one of the surgeons standing at the bottom of the bed and moved her head to get his attention. "Is it going to be okay?" she asked, indicating the cast.

"Well, we're very encouraged," he said. "There's a good chance that you'll be able to walk unaided."

She blinked. "*Walk* unaided?" She shot a look at Dr. Brooks, who didn't quite meet her eyes. He was a nice family doctor; *of course* he wouldn't have wanted to tell her anything that grim. But, still — it was *her* goddamn leg. They bloody well could have — she looked back at the surgeon. This whole thing was such a nightmare that it was almost starting to be funny. "My leg won't have — un*sightly* scars, now will it?"

"Well," he started hesitantly.

"I believe my daughter's kidding," her father said, and Meg laughed. A little. She was going to be a whole goddamned *bundle* of scars. Scars, and crippled things, and *general* unsightliness. They could have goddamn *told* her that — she covered her eyes with her arm, her fist clenched, wishing that everyone would go away and leave her the hell alone. They *did* back off a little, although there was a big production about getting her back to her room to rest still *more* comfortably.

She kept her arm over her eyes, afraid that she might be going to cry — or yell at someone — or both. Once she was back in her room and everyone but her parents had cleared out, she lowered her arm.

"Meg," her father started, looking unhappy.

"I'm really tired," she said. "I need to sleep for a while." She covered her eyes again, her teeth pressed together almost as tightly as her fist.

Walk unaided. Christ.

Chapter
Twenty-one

By the time she heard her mother moving around, getting ready to leave, she felt under enough control to lower her arm.

"I'm sorry," her mother said. "I didn't mean to wake you up."

"I wasn't asleep." She rubbed her hand across her eyes. "Can you, um, say hi to Vanessa for me? I mean, you know, pat her and all?"

Her mother nodded. "Is there anything you'd like from the house?"

Meg shook her head.

"Some books, or — ?"

"No, thank you," Meg said. Like she would ever be awake to *read* them? "I mean — good luck."

Her mother nodded. "I'll be back soon." She bent down to kiss her good-bye, then straightened up, giving her hand a gentle squeeze.

204

"We'll look for you," Meg's father said, gesturing towards the television and sounding so vague that Meg felt herself smile.

"Okay," her mother said, smiling too.

Meg watched her go, then looked at her father. "She looks nervous."

"She's worried about *you*," her father said. "We both — "

Meg interrupted before he could go on. "I might be getting hungry soon. Where are Steven and Neal?"

He studied her for a second, then nodded. "They're down in the guest rooms. I'll go check about getting you some dinner too. Is there something special you'd like?"

"No, thank you," she said, putting her arm over her eyes.

He had only been gone for a minute when there was a light knock on the door, and she glanced up enough to see Preston. Preston. The *one* person who'd promised to be straight with her.

"Okay if I come in?" he asked, pushing a sheet-covered cart in front of him.

She folded her good arm across her chest, not looking at him.

"Okay, no problem." He pushed the cart up against the wall, out of the way. "Unless you need anything, I can give you a hello later."

"You said you'd be *straight* with me," she said as he turned to go.

He stopped, turning back. "I'm not sure what you — "

"*Walk* unaided?"

He sighed.

"You son of a bitch," she said. "You *did* know."

205

He sighed again. "If you could see what your eyes looked like, *you* wouldn't tell you unnecessarily upsetting things either."

"Not tell me that I'm going to be *crippled?*" Saying the word made her so angry that she clenched her fist to try and keep the anger in.

"I don't know, Meg." He sat down in one of the many chairs, running his hand over his hair. "I guess the logic was, if you didn't know, you'd be up and walking around that much faster."

Yeah, *right.* "The logic *was,* 'Let's play God.' " She gritted her teeth — the ones she had *left* — wanting to smash her fist through something. *Anything.*

"Meg — "

"I mean, it's *my* goddamn leg! What's the deal with my *hand* — they going to cut it off or something? Maybe tell me a week later? *Maybe?*"

He sighed, looking very tired.

"I shouldn't ask *you* anyway," she said. "It's not like you're going to tell me the truth." What was going to happen, was that she was going to cry. Cry, and swear, and — she pressed her hand against her eyes, fighting not to.

"Meg — "

"Don't say *anything,*" she said, hearing her voice shake. "I don't trust you."

"Meg." He let out his breath. "I would *never* do anything to hurt you. I mean, you know that, right?"

She moved her hand to look at him. "Omission can be just as much of a lie."

He nodded.

"It's just like being a prisoner — people telling you *what* they want, *when* they want."

He nodded.

"I — " She swallowed, having to look away from him. "I don't want you to remind me of him." The thought made her shiver, and she looked at him again. "I mean, *you* particularly."

He sat back, looking almost — stricken. An expression she had never seen on his face. "I would never want to," he said quietly.

Jesus Christ, this was *Preston*. One of the very few people in the world who she absolutely, one hundred percent trusted, and loved. Being angry at him was too — if he got angry at *her*, it would be —

"Meg, I would *die* before I let anyone hurt you," he said.

She nodded, the thought too scary to imagine. But she could tell that he meant it. "I'm not mad at you," she said — almost whispered. "I'm just — mad."

He nodded. "You have every right to be, Meg."

"About everything, not just — " She looked down at her leg, exhausted now that the energy of being angry was gone. "How bad *is* it?"

"I don't know," he said, sounding tired too. "They won't *really* know until you get into physical therapy with it."

Which she could have guessed. "Is that soon?"

"Four to six weeks, probably."

At least *that* was specific. She nodded. "Will I be *completely* crippled? In a wheelchair and all?"

He shook his head. "A brace, probably. Maybe a cane."

Jesus. "Permanently?" she asked, her stomach hurting.

"I don't know, Meg," he said. "I honestly don't."

Honestly. She smiled a little. *"Honestly?"*

He nodded, very serious.

"What about my hand? The same basic deal?"

He nodded.

Great. The only *good* thing was that she was too tired to think about it right now.

"I can't tell you how sorry I am," he said. "About this whole damn thing."

She nodded.

"I'll do anything I can to help you."

She nodded. Odds were, she was going to *need* it. She looked over at the sheet-covered cart. "What's that?"

"Well, I don't know. It must be a gift." He got up, whipping the sheet off with some theatricality, revealing a VCR and two stacks of tapes. "Thought you might be a little too tired for reading," he said, handing her a remote-control box.

"Hey, wow." The box felt strange and foreign in her hand. "Thanks."

"And," he said, "we have some lovely tapes for you."

"POW dramas?" she guessed.

He grinned. "Well, let's see." He lifted each tape in turn, pretending to study it. *"The Sound of Music. The Music Man. Oklahoma.* And — what's this? — *Mary Poppins!"* He widened his eyes at her, and she smiled back.

"Are they all musicals?" she asked.

He nodded. *"Many* lovely things. And," he held up two unmarked tapes, "know what we have here?"

"It's a Wonderful Life," she guessed.

"No, but that's a good idea — I'll have them bring it." He winked at her. *"Uncolorized."*

She flushed. She liked to make people listen to her speech about the evils of colorization too.

208

"Anyway," he said, "*these* are all the *Entertainment Tonight*'s you missed."

Jesus. "Really?"

He grinned wryly. "Would I lie to you, kid?"

"So, wait," she said, missing that, "in the middle of everything, you were like, taping *Entertainment Tonight* every night?"

"Except for that first night," he said, not smiling anymore.

"But — like, what if I hadn't — " She stopped, not wanting to get into that, but still curious. "What would you have done with the tapes?"

"I don't know," he said quietly. "It was a sort of — good-luck charm, sort of — I don't know."

Which was really — sweet. Feeling tears in her eyes, she blinked so that he wouldn't see them. "S-sort of like my father always sitting in the same chair when he watches the Red Sox," she said. *And* drinking from the same beer glass and, often, wearing his lucky hat.

Preston nodded. "Yeah. Equally helpful." Then, to her amazement, he actually looked embarrassed. "Put a couple of *Lifestyles of the Rich and Famous* on there too."

Meg laughed, feeling out of practice. "Do my parents know about this?"

"Well — " He winked at her again. "Good-luck charms should be private."

Pretty funny. She played with the remote-control box, aiming it all around the room, pretending to be confused when nothing came on or off.

"How about I get this thing hooked up?" he suggested, picking up a screwdriver from the cart.

She nodded, pushing remote control buttons.

He moved the cart underneath the television, then brought a chair over, climbing onto it, his upper body disappearing behind the set.

"Do you think her press conference'll go okay tonight?" she asked.

"Well," he said, connecting wires, "she'll certainly have a receptive audience."

"People don't — blame her? I mean, the country."

"I think people *empathize*." He tightened the screws. "They know how much all of you have gone through." He bent down for a smaller screwdriver, too casual. "Do *you* blame her?" he asked, before straightening up.

"I don't know," she said. "I haven't decided yet."

He nodded.

"I don't know," she said again. "It'd be kind of like blaming her for getting *shot*. Maybe it's just — I don't know. Bad luck."

He nodded, moving up behind the machine again.

"*Real* bad luck," she said.

"I'll buy that one," he said, behind the television.

"Is her speaking tonight going to be a big deal?" she asked, pretty sure she already knew the answer.

"Well," he got off the chair to check the wires leading into the VCR, "the President has been incommunicado for over two weeks — what's *your* guess?"

Her guess, exactly. "Am I going to look — pathetic?"

"Are you kidding?" he asked. "Whether you know it or not, you've hit folk-hero time."

Meg blushed. "It's not like I — "

"Trust me on this one, kid." Satisfied with the con-

210

nections, he plugged the machine in. "People want to grow up and *be* you."

Oh, *right*. "I'd advise *against* that, myself," she said.

"Well, just don't worry about anyone thinking you're *pathetic*." He turned the VCR on. "Want me to put in *The Sound of Music?*"

"How about *Entertainment Tonight?*"

He smiled. "Sure. Sounds great."

They were watching a story about celebrities who had embraced "daredevil hobbies" — i.e., race-car driving — when her father and brothers came in with dinner.

"Oh, figures," Steven said when he saw the television, then looked guilty.

Meg, however, was amused. "Hey, you know me, I like to be on the cutting edge." She watched as her father set up her tray: scrambled eggs, toast, butterscotch pudding, milk. "Um, thank you," she said as he handed her her fork.

Her brothers, sitting on either side of a small table, were eating the exact same meal, obviously self-conscious. She took a small bite of the eggs, feeling pretty self-conscious herself.

"What are we looking at here?" her father asked, indicating the television.

Meg hesitated. "I was sort of thinking of *The Sound of Music.*"

He nodded, checking his watch so subtly that she almost didn't see him do it. Almost.

The press conference. "Dad, I — " She sighed. "I *really* don't want to. I just — I'd rather not."

"Whatever you're comfortable with," he said. "That's what's important."

211

"I'm *comfortable* with the Von Trapps," Meg said.

Her father smiled. A small smile, but unmistakable.

Preston looked at his own watch. "Tell you what," he said. "How about I go check it out and report back."

"You can go too, Dad," Meg said. "I mean, you know," she gestured towards her brothers, "the three of us can just like, hang out."

Her father looked at all three of them, then nodded. "We'll just be down the hall then," he said, and kissed the top of her head. "Call me if you need me."

When they were gone, the room was very, very quiet.

"Do you want anything, Meggie?" Neal asked, extra-polite.

"No, I — " The fork in her hand was shaking again, and she put it down. "Um, no, thanks."

Neal looked worried. "You should eat."

"Yeah." She tried sipping some of her milk.

"Does your leg feel better?" he asked.

She nodded, although it felt pretty much the same. Worse, even.

Neal looked at the door. "We're not supposed to ask you questions." He jumped and she could tell that Steven — who was just eating his dinner and not looking at either of them — had kicked him under the table.

Meg looked at the door too. "I won't tell them you asked any."

"Why don't we just watch the stupid *Sound of Music*," Steven said, eating.

"I don't care if he asks me stuff," Meg said.

Steven ignored her, scowling across the table at Neal. "Just shut up and eat."

Meg scowled at *him*. "He can ask me whatever he wants."

"I don't want to," Neal said quickly.

Meg sighed. "Well, *obviously*, you do, or you wouldn't — " Don't yell at him. If you're going to yell at anyone, yell at Steven. "Look," she said, more calmly. "I really don't mind if you ask me stuff. I would kind of prefer it, if you want to know the truth."

Neal glanced at Steven, then shook his head.

"I would *prefer* it," she said. Less calmly.

He checked the door. "Was it scary?"

If they weren't supposed to *ask* questions, then she probably wasn't supposed to answer them. "I was alone, mostly," she said.

Steven held out his dish of pudding. "You want this, Neal, or what?"

"I'm talking, Steven, *okay?*" Meg said, irritated.

Steven slapped the dish down. "Yeah, well, he's not supposed to bother you."

"You're *supposed* to make me feel like you're glad I'm back."

"I'm glad you're back," he said, "okay?"

This time, Neal kicked *him*.

"Yeah, well, *act* like it," Meg said, "okay?"

"*Okay*," Steven said.

"Good," Meg said, and it was such a typical way for them to argue, that she had to grin. "Look, can't you just pretend like I was in a car accident, and you're waiting for me to get better is all?"

Steven actually grinned too. "Yo, Meg, you talk *excellent*."

They both laughed, Neal joining in a little late.

"Neal, do me a favor," she said. "Go out there and

ask someone to get us some Doritos and Coke and Twinkies and all."

He hesitated. "Are we — "

"We're allowed," she said. "Hurry it up so we can watch the movie."

Neal hesitated at the door. "Fritos too?"

"Yeah, sure, whatever you want," Meg said. Expansively. "Also, if they sell hats there, can you ask them if they can get me like — a little cap or something? I hate my hair being like this."

Neal looked worried, but nodded, leaving the room.

The room was quiet and since they were all in a good mood now, Meg decided not to start trouble. Even though there were probably things Steven knew that he could —

"I wish it had been me," he said, his voice startling her.

"No, you don't." Meg shook her head. "Believe me, you don't."

His expression was somewhat offended, and even more uneasy.

"I don't mean that you wouldn't be — " She sighed. "It was terrible. I mean, *really* terrible."

He glanced at her leg, then quickly away. "Because of stuff they did to you?"

"Oh, hell, I looked *forward* to him coming in," she said, without thinking. "I mean — " She stopped, realizing how that sounded. "I don't mean I wanted them to — at least then, I had someone to talk to."

Steven checked the door. "Did they *look* scary?"

Her parents were right; she *didn't* want to answer questions. "He looked regular. I mean — he could have been anyone."

"Did they speak English?"

214

"Very well." She grinned wryly. The man had been a goddamn *grammarian*. "Exceedingly well."

"Were they — ?"

Neal came back in, smiling happily. "They said they'd get everything!"

"You know I'm going to get my way for about the next hundred years," Meg said to Steven, who made a sound that was close to a laugh.

"That mean we have to watch this damned thing?" he asked, getting up to put the movie in the VCR.

"We'll have to watch it *repeatedly*," Meg said, Neal giggling. "Hey, fatso," she said to him. "You want to sit up here with me?"

Neal hung back. "We're not — "

"I know you're not supposed to. You want to do it, anyway?"

He didn't move.

"Come on, already," she said, impatiently, indicating the left side of the bed.

He still hesitated. "Will I hurt your leg?"

She shook her head and he climbed over the rail — which yeah, hurt — but it was nice to have someone sitting with her. Less like being in the zoo.

"We ready?" Steven asked, by the VCR.

Meg nodded. "Play it, Sam."

"If she can stand it, *I* can," Steven said to Neal, and turned on the tape.

Maria was just running into the Abbey when Dr. Brooks and a nurse arrived with the food. Seeing Dr. Brooks, Meg felt guilty.

"Am I allowed to eat this stuff?" she asked.

"I'm just happy to see you have an appetite," he said, unpacking a brown grocery bag full of junk food as the nurse gave each of the three of them a plate, a

215

napkin, and a glass full of ice, pouring them some soda, as they nodded polite thank-yous. "Oh," Dr. Brooks smiled, taking a cap out of the bag and handing it to her, "your — hat."

A Slush Puppy cap. Meg grinned sheepishly and put it on. "Thank you."

"It was all they could find," he said.

"It's great," Meg said. Having it on — whether it looked stupid or not — was a tremendous relief.

Dr. Brooks folded the bag and stuck it under his arm, then ruffled Neal's hair. "Watching the movie with your sister?"

Neal nodded, starting to get off the bed.

"No, it's all right. Just be careful." Dr. Brooks gestured towards Meg's knee. "Much pain?"

"It's okay," she said. A lie.

He looked at his watch. "Well, I'll come back in about an hour, see how you are."

She nodded. Nothing like having life revolve around the next pain pill.

"What do you want first, Meggie?" Neal asked, as Dr. Brooks left.

"Twinkies," Steven said, already eating one.

Meg grinned. "Doritos," she said. "Definitely Doritos."

Chapter
Twenty-two

They ate a lot. Enough so that by the time the Von Trapps were singing at the Salzburg Festival, Meg was having trouble staying awake. Of course, she'd been up for — gosh — five or six whole hours now. And the Darvon, or whatever the hell it was that they were giving her, wasn't helping matters any.

"You want to watch another?" Steven asked.

Meg jerked awake. "What?" She must have missed the ending. "I mean, yeah. I guess." Neal was asleep too, leaning against her, and she maneuvered her arm enough to put it around him. *"Mary Poppins?"*

Steven groaned, but got up to put it in.

As the movie started — a dark London skyline, with the familiar soundtrack — Meg smiled. Musicals were so — sweet. So *swell*.

She looked around, waking up a little more. "Wasn't Dad in here?"

"Before, yeah," Steven said.

"Where'd he go?" she asked, noticing that it was dark, except for the small light over near where the nurses usually sat.

"To wait for Mom, I think."

"Oh." She looked up at the movie, at Bert singing and dancing in the park. "Did we talk about the press conference?"

Steven shook his head. "You were sleepy."

She was *still* sleepy. She looked back up at the movie. Now that she thought about it, Bert must have been one of her very first crushes. Her grandfather — it would have been a couple of years before he died — had even given her a little striped blazer, a straw hat, and a cane so she could do the Bert dance. Steven was a baby, so he had only gotten a hat. Once, she remembered, she had taken some ashes from the fireplace to do a chimney sweep dance, but her parents' reaction had been less than enthusiastic.

"Can't believe I like, know all these words," Steven said, as Mrs. Banks sang the "Suffragette's Song."

Meg nodded. "Mom used to sing this."

"Yo, no way," he said.

She nodded. "English accent and everything."

"Yo, really?"

She nodded. "She was always singing musicals' stuff."

"I like, totally don't remember."

"Yeah, well, it was a long time ago," Meg said stiffly.

Steven started to say something, then just looked at the television.

By the time her parents came in, Steven had fallen asleep too and Meg was, foggily, watching Julie Andrews sing "Feed the Birds." Her father gently picked

218

Neal up, carrying him out of the room, while her mother bent down to kiss her.

"How do you feel?" she whispered.

Meg shrugged, half-asleep.

"Do you want to keep watching the movie?"

Meg shook her head. "I'm pretty tired."

Her mother went over to turn off the VCR, pausing to kiss Steven too, before returning to the bed.

"How'd it go?" Meg asked.

"A lot of people care about you," her mother said. "Even more than you know."

Whatever *that* meant. "Did they ask tough questions?"

Her mother shook her head. "Softballs, mostly."

Good old political jargon. Meg let her eyes close partway. "What time is it?"

"Past midnight."

Her father came back in, taking Steven out of the room.

"Do you and Dad sleep downstairs too?" Meg asked. Although mostly, now that she thought about it, they seemed to do all their sleeping sitting up in chairs.

Her mother nodded. "There's more than one bedroom down there."

"When can we go home?"

Her mother hesitated. "Soon, I hope."

In other words, no time soon.

"I know," her mother said. "I'm sorry."

She was curious about the press conference, but she also felt like just closing her eyes and going back to sleep. She wasn't exactly tired, but the pills made her feel — fuzzy. Slow.

Her mother seemed to be saying something, and Meg looked up.

219

"I was just wondering if you wanted anything," her mother said.

Philosophically, an ironic question. Meg shook her head, noticing that her mother seemed pretty shaky and tired herself. "You guys don't have to, you know, stay up with me."

Her mother, about to sit in the chair by the bed, paused. "Do you want privacy?"

Did she? "I just meant you should maybe get some *normal* sleep, and not — " She indicated the stiff chair.

"Your father and I feel better being in here," her mother said, sitting down.

Since it was their decision, Meg wasn't about to argue. "What time did you say it was?"

"A little after twelve-thirty."

"Oh." Meg looked at her telephone. That was pretty late.

Her mother looked at it too. "Would you like to call Josh, or — "

"I kind of thought I'd call Beth." Which she hadn't realized she'd been thinking until she heard herself say it. "Only I guess it's too — "

"I think you should," her mother said. "You'll both feel better."

"You mean, you've talked to her?"

Her mother shook her head. "Your father did at one point."

"Oh." Weird. "That was nice of him." She glanced at the telephone. "I can't call this late — you know how her stepfather is."

"We can have someone place the call *for* you."

"No." Meg shook her head. "I mean, I don't want it to be a big deal, I just — "

220

Her mother moved the telephone closer. "Why don't you just go ahead and call."

Meg reached for it, then pulled back. "Will the FBI or someone be listening in?"

"No," her mother said. Firmly. She got up, handing Meg the receiver. "If you want anything, we'll be outside."

"Oh." Meg looked at the window in pretended confusion. "Do I like, open that and yell out?"

"What?" Her mother looked *genuinely* confused, then smiled. "Right," she said, and gave Meg's hand a squeeze before leaving the room.

Once she was alone, Meg hung up the receiver and looked at it some more. It *was* pretty late. Only, if she sat around, it was going to be even *later*. She picked it up again, flinching when she heard a voice say, "How may I help you?" An operator or someone.

"Were you on there before?" Meg asked. "Did I like, hang up on you?"

"Of course not," the man said, as overly kind as everyone was being to her. Not that White House switchboard people — who would be set up at the hospital — were *ever* rude. "Would you like me to ring a number for you?"

"Uh — " Come on, make a decision. "Yeah. I mean — please." Meg gave him the number, the call going through almost instantly. *Extra*-special fiber optics, maybe.

Naturally, Beth's stepfather answered. Sounding cranky.

Meg swallowed. "Um, may I please speak to Beth?"

"Who is this?" he asked. "Do you know what the hell time it is?"

"Um, yes, sir. I'm sorry, I — " She could hear a

221

voice in the background — Beth's mother, probably — and her stepfather came back on.

"Just a minute," he said.

Meg started counting, getting ready to hang up when she got to ten, but she was only on seven when Beth came on. And, once she heard her voice, Meg couldn't think of anything to say.

"Hello," Beth said again, sounding uneasy.

"I'm sorry, I — " Not knowing what to say made her feel panicky, and she gripped the phone tightly. "I mean, did I wake you up?"

"Meg?" Beth sounded almost stunned. "I mean, *hi*. I mean — Jesus, I don't — Jesus Christ."

"I, um — " Meg had to swallow again. "I just — hadn't talked to you yet, so I thought — I know it's late and all — "

"Where are you?" Beth asked. "I mean, no, that's stupid. Are you — I'm *really* glad you called."

Her friend's voice sounded so strange that Meg felt even more uncomfortable. "You're not like, going to cry, are you?" she asked. Beth *never* cried.

"No." Beth laughed shakily. "I mean, yeah — what do you expect?"

Beth *absolutely* never cried. "Well, do I call you back, or — ?"

"Just relax, okay?" Beth took a deep breath, then laughed a normal-sounding laugh. "You know how emotional my people are."

Her people. Meg had to laugh too. "What, and my people aren't?"

"Oh, yeah," Beth said. "Famous for it."

There was another silence, but this one wasn't as strained.

222

"How, um, how are you feeling?" Beth asked finally.

Meg sighed. "I don't know. I guess I'm going to be here for a while."

There was more silence, Beth apparently finding conversation as difficult as Meg was.

"They don't even seem to know if I'm going to walk right," Meg said, when the dead air made her too nervous. "Only I don't know if that means a brace, or crutches, or what."

"Maybe they're just being cautious," Beth said.

"I don't know. No one gives me straight answers." She tightened her fist around the receiver. "Well. I guess it doesn't matter."

"Meg."

"It's not like I don't have plenty of other things to worry about, right?" Meg gritted her — remaining — teeth. This whole thing really, *royally* — "Did you watch the press conference?"

"Yeah." Beth hesitated. "I thought it was great."

"What did she say?"

"Oh. Well, she — " Beth stopped. "She was pretty angry."

"She *should* be."

"Well — yeah," Beth said. "I just meant — she didn't *sound* the way she looked."

"What's she *supposed* to do, sound all defeated? Jesus, Beth!"

"I guess I thought she'd be more — frazzled," Beth said calmly.

"Not hardly," Meg said. "Not in *public*."

To her surprise, Beth laughed. "I was impressed, okay? Take it easy."

"What did the network people say?"

Beth laughed again. "They agreed with me."

Meg was too tired to be amused. "What were *you*, a guest commentator?"

"Yeah, you should have watched."

Knowing the media, they actually *could* have had Beth on. Best friend of First Family victim and all. "You weren't — were you?"

"Yeah," Beth said. "I was on *Nightline* too."

Which had to be a joke. Although, even under the best of circumstances, Meg couldn't always tell when Beth was kidding. It was usually safe to assume that she *was*.

"Sorry I missed it," she said. Grumpily.

"She *was* good, Meg," Beth said. "Tough as anything."

"What, you mean, mad?"

"Oh, you know. Saying things like 'be*neath* contempt' and 'reprehensible' and all." Beth paused. "And even the *reporters* said nice things about *you*."

Not something Meg really wanted to pursue. "They talked about *other* things, right? I mean, other issues?" Christ, was *she* an issue? What a thought.

"Oh, yeah," Beth said. "She read a statement, said she'd take a few questions on it, then she talked about other stuff."

"So it'll seem like everything's back to normal?"

"*I* got that impression," Beth said, "yeah."

Meg sighed. She probably *should* have watched, but — well, it wasn't like there wouldn't be videotapes of it all over the White House if she wanted to watch it sometime. No time *soon* — but sometime. Maybe.

"You still there?" Beth asked, sounding tentative.

"Yeah."

"Are you, um, allowed to have visitors?"

"I don't really want to."

"Oh. Well, I was just — "

"I don't want people seeing me like this," Meg said.

Beth hesitated. "Does that mean me too?"

"Yeah." Nothing like being callous. "I mean, I think. I mean — " Meg let out her breath. "I haven't washed my hair in three weeks."

"So what?"

"I *hate* it," Meg said. "I hate — I'm not ready. I can't."

"Okay. I was only — "

"It's too much pressure," Meg said, suddenly feeling so panicky that she was afraid she would have to hang up.

"It was just an idea," Beth said. "You know, if you wanted me to."

Meg shook her head. "I *can't*. I'm supposed to know what to say, and I don't, and — no one else does either, and — I fucking *hate* it. I hate all of it."

"Okay. Maybe when you get home, I can — "

"Yeah," Meg said quickly. "Maybe then."

There was a long silence.

"I wasn't trying to hurt your feelings," Meg said.

"You didn't, don't worry."

Right. "Well, I didn't mean to." Meg slumped down into her pillows, so tired that she had to let her eyes close. "I'm sorry, I'm really tired. I shouldn't have called."

"I'm glad you did. I'm glad you're — " Beth stopped. "I'm glad," she said, her voice sounding strange again.

"Me too," Meg said quietly.

225

Chapter
Twenty-three

She spent most of the next couple of weeks watching movies with still-heavy eyes. Various members of her family were usually with her, although Trudy had come up from Florida so her brothers could sleep in their own beds at night. Since they didn't have any grand-parents, Meg and her brothers had always thought of Trudy that way. *She* was at the hospital a lot, during the days, crocheting by the window. Preston was usually around too.

Mostly, she was still too tired to talk much, and she was relieved when no one made her. A couple of times — more out of guilt than anything else — she called Beth and Josh, but there never seemed to be much to say, and the conversations wouldn't last long. The FBI came in, more than once, and she tried to answer their questions and work on the composite sketch, unnerved by how often she got confused. Various specialists and physical therapists had begun putting in daily appearances, and she did her best to cooperate with them. Or at least, stay awake.

Sometimes, she got pushed up and down the hall in a wheelchair, although mostly she would lean her head against her good hand and wait for it to be over. Her ribs were getting better though, and it was easier to sit up. Sometimes, they wheeled her into this stupid sunroom, like it was going to be a magical cure or something. Looking outside was about the *last* thing she felt like doing. And riding up and down the hall was scary because there was so much security — guards, check-in stations, bulletproof glass.

Everyone was very nice, and would talk to her, and she was always very polite, but most of the time, she kept the Slush Puppy hat down low on her forehead so they would know to leave her alone. The hat was especially good if she started crying — which would happen unexpectedly — because that way no one could see.

Waking up from yet another nightmare, so scared that she couldn't quite catch her breath, she saw Trudy hurrying over from the chair by the window.

"Are you all right, dear?" she asked, helping her back down onto the pillows.

Meg stared at her — at the familiar blue knit dress, the pearls, and the pair of half-glasses swinging from a chain around her neck — then realized where she was. "I — " She tried to calm down. "I thought he was in here. Dressed like a doctor." She shuddered, picturing it again — her lying alone in the dark room, not afraid when she saw a doctor come over, until he looked up and she saw the crooked grin.

Trudy was moistening and squeezing out a small

washcloth, then sponging Meg's face. "It was just a dream; everything's all right."

Meg was going to tell her the rest, about how he kept grinning at her, then pulled out the gun, grinning all the while, pressing it into her forehead, getting ready to — she shivered. "Do you think there are more blankets somewhere?" she asked.

"Of course." Trudy bent down, opening a little cabinet below the bedside table and taking out a smooth pale green one, spreading it over her.

The blanket smelled of antiseptic, but Meg pulled it closer. "Where is everyone?"

"Your mother's in a meeting downstairs, and your father's at the house, waiting for the boys' tutoring to be over. They'll be here later this afternoon."

Meg nodded.

"Are you hungry?" Trudy asked. "Would you like anything?"

Meg shook her head, still trying to get rid of the dream. She stiffened, seeing a man with short dark hair at the door, then recognized the Army psychologist guy. He had taken to dropping in lately too.

"May I come in?" he asked.

Meg shrugged, trying to look polite, but not very interested by the idea. So uninterested that she had never bothered getting his name straight.

He came in, nodding at Trudy, stopping near the bottom of the bed. "Just thought I'd see how you're feeling today."

She nodded. Politely. "Fine, thank you."

"I hear you may be going home by the weekend."
She nodded.

"You must be looking forward to that," he said.
She nodded.

He studied her for a minute. "I'm from New Hampshire, you know. Durham."

"It's very nice up there," she said. Trudy looked as though she was going to leave the room, and Meg shook her head, as subtly as she could.

"We used to drive down to the city all the time," he said. "Go to Celtics games."

She nodded. She had never liked basketball much. "They have a very good team."

He nodded too, bending to examine one of her many — still-arriving — baskets of flowers. "Have you been sleeping well?"

"Yes, thank you." Except maybe that was a way to get him out of here. She pretended to yawn a very small yawn. "I'm still very tired though."

He took the hint. "Well, I'll let you get some rest then. Maybe I'll look in on you tomorrow."

She nodded.

When he was gone, Trudy spoke first.

"He seems like a nice man," she said.

Meg shrugged. "I don't like his looks." Not that men in their early thirties with dark hair and high cheekbones were *ever* likely to appeal to her again. She unclenched her fist, hoping that Trudy hadn't noticed.

"Would you like a brownie?" Trudy held out the box she'd brought from the White House the day before.

Meg took one, even though she wasn't hungry. "Thank you." If the psychologist guy had come, that meant it was going to turn into Union Station in here soon, with the therapists and the nurses and everyone.

The worst was when they touched her. And almost all of them did. Sponging her off, changing the bed,

229

taking her temperature, moving the two fingers on her right hand that still worked, moving her left foot, hooking her other arm and leg onto little pulleys and weights so she could exercise them. They even gave her these sort of massages, which she hated more than anything else. All of the ones who actually touched her were women, thank God. But they were still strangers.

She glanced up and saw Trudy watching her with a worried expression. "Um, this looks good," she said, and took a bite of the brownie. It *was* good, but her stomach was so tight that she had to force it down.

"If you don't like him, they could send someone else by," Trudy said.

"Yeah, they had a woman psychologist in here the other day too." Meg put what was left of the brownie neatly on her bedside table, her face feeling as tight as her stomach. "Guess they really think I've gone around the bend."

"They just want to help you."

"Yeah, well — " Meg picked up the remote-control box. "You think anything good is on?"

"If not, we can look at one of your tapes," Trudy said.

They had run through just about every musical or Disney movie ever produced, so now she was watching things like Brat Pack movies and *Mary Tyler Moore* reruns. She was getting sick of looking at the television, but at least it made the time pass a little faster. Not that she really had anything to look forward to.

"Meg?" Trudy asked, uncertainly.

"Um, yeah." Meg handed her the little control box. "Let's look at a tape."

* * *

The doctors established that, indeed, Saturday would be a good day for her to go home. Her mother had arranged to have Camp David set up as a recuperation site, but — despite its privacy — the idea of being in or near the woods was so terrifying that Meg had asked her to do *anything* else. Even the hospital would be better than *that*.

So, they were just going to go back to the White House. And Meg had asked that they please put her in her room, not upstairs in the Solarium or something. Sadly enough, her mother's own convalescence was recent enough so that the staff probably wouldn't have much trouble getting everything ready.

The therapists were letting — making? — her do more, and with the motorized wheelchair, she could even deal with the bathroom herself. The, at her request, mirrorless bathroom. Things like brushing her teeth made her so tired that she would have to rest afterwards, but it was a relief to be able to do that sort of thing in private, finally. They wouldn't let her even try to walk, but sometimes they had her stand up and lean on a railing or something. To get her equilibrium back, mostly. Her right hand wasn't going to work anytime soon, if ever, but once she got a lighter cast for her knee, the therapists seemed confident that she would be able to get around on one crutch. Around a *room*, at least. Meg just did whatever they told her to do, even when she felt so tired and shaky that she practically had to bite through her lip to keep from crying.

Everyone was very happy and excited the night before she was supposed to go home and Meg manufac-

231

tured as much enthusiasm as she could, eating take-out Chinese food, and watching *Tootsie*. Then, Trudy went home with Steven and Neal, and Preston gave Meg a grin and a "Catch you in the morning, kid," and the room was quiet again.

Alone with her parents, Meg let herself stop smiling. Stop faking it. Her parents had moved to the chairs right by the bed, and none of them spoke right away.

"I think that cat of yours is going to be pretty happy to see you," her father said.

Meg nodded. "I'm going to be pretty happy to see *her*."

It was quiet again.

"Are we really going to be able to get out of here without — well, you know. Being surrounded?" Meg asked.

Her mother nodded. "We've indicated that you'll be leaving midafternoon."

Meg couldn't help grinning. "You like, outright lied?"

"Well — yes," her mother said, and blinked a couple of times.

"Word'll get out though. By the time we get to the house, I mean."

Her parents nodded reluctantly.

Meaning that there was probably no way of avoiding a crowd. There had been a huge one when she came to the hospital, but she couldn't remember much about it. *This* time — she pulled her blankets closer, not wanting to imagine it.

"We're going to get you right inside," her father said. "You don't have anything to worry about."

The Szechuan shredded beef and Yu Hsiang chicken

232

were suddenly feeling pretty lousy inside her stomach. She swallowed. "Do I have to say anything? Like, a statement?"

"Of course not," her mother said. "We'll have Linda or Preston brief them."

"What if there are signs?" Meg asked, getting more and more scared. "Or if they clap or something?" Which they had done when her *mother* came home from the hospital.

Her mother reached over to take her hand. "We're going to get there, and go right inside to the elevator. The staff is under *very* strict instructions."

Meg swallowed. "And we'll go right to my room, and I won't have to deal with anyone? Won't it look rude?"

"I couldn't bloody care *less* how it looks," her father said, her mother giving him a warning glance.

Okay, okay, maybe she wasn't the only one who was a little tense here. Meg took a deep breath. "*I* care how it looks, Dad. I mean — " She needed another breath. "*I'm* the one they're going to be looking at tomorrow, not you guys." The eyes of the whole damned *world*, probably. The networks might even — what she needed, although it was going to hurt his feelings, was to talk to her mother for a minute. Alone. "Um, Dad?" She didn't quite look at him. "Would you mind getting me a Coke?"

He barely hesitated. "Sure," he said, and got up.

When she was sure he was gone, she looked at her mother. "What's going to happen?"

"Well," her mother said, "we'll probably take a freight elevator, and — "

"Is it going to be safe?"

233

Her mother nodded. "The security is extremely — "

"I don't mean just tomorrow," Meg said.

Her mother nodded, not answering right away, hands tight in her lap.

"Should I take that as a no?" Meg asked stiffly.

Her mother shook her head. "No, I just think we should take it one step at a time."

"Explore our options?" Meg asked, even more stiff.

Her mother gestured towards the door. "Explore *their* limitations." They, meaning the Secret Service. "It's *not* something you should be worrying about tonight. We'll talk about it later. As a family."

"Oh, yeah," Meg said. "Neal's going to enjoy *that* conversation a lot."

Her mother sighed. "Please don't worry about it, Meg. I *promise* we'll be able to arrange something that we're all comfortable with. I promise."

Oh, yeah, that sounded *real* promising. Meg moved her jaw, the room so quiet that she could hear a phone ringing somewhere far down the hall. "You should have told me about the teeth," she said.

Her mother hunched down, looking visibly smaller. "I'm sorry," she said, her voice so low that Meg almost couldn't hear her.

Meg touched the side of her jaw, remembering the terror of unknown metal objects being forced into her mouth. "It was a surprise," she said, stiffly.

Her mother hunched more, not looking at her. "I'm sorry, Meg. I *never* — that is, your father and I — "

"Yeah, no precedent," Meg said, still holding her jaw. Of course, what it *really* came down to was "cannot, have not, and *will* not negotiate" — "You kind of sold me out," she said, her voice even lower than her mother's had been.

Her mother nodded, looking less like the President than Meg had ever seen her. "I know."

Meg nodded too. "Yeah."

This silence was more awkward than any of the others, her mother rubbing her hand across her eyes.

"I wouldn't accuse you of wanting to do it," Meg said. "I mean — I'm here, right?"

Her mother hunched down, arms folded around herself. "I *expect* you to hate me for it," she said.

Which was more than a little annoying. "I'm a little better person than that, don't you think?" Meg said.

For the first time, her mother looked at her. "Yes. Actually, I do."

Meg nodded. "That's not the part I'm mad at you for. It's the only thing you *could* have done, really. I mean, like, it's already too late at that point."

"Last fall," her mother said. "It would have been better if — things — had worked out differently last fall."

Which was *extremely* annoying. Meg scowled at her. "That's like saying you wish the three of us had never been *born*."

Her mother nodded. "I'm sorry." She looked at Meg, her eyes very bright. "I really *am* sorry. If I'd ever *dreamed* that — I never would have — "

"What about what happened to *you*?" Meg asked. "Would you have run if you'd known that that was going to happen?"

Her mother considered that, then shook her head. "I don't know. Probably." She looked up. "But *not* any of you. Not *ever*."

235

Jesus. Scary to see *yourself* as "acceptable risk." Meg thought of something suddenly. Something that had never really occurred to her before. "You didn't think you'd win, did you? I mean, you *really* — you thought you were like, paving the way."

Her mother took a long time answering. "I don't know," she said finally. "I've spent a lot of hours wondering."

Meg nodded. It probably wasn't a question that had an answer. Particularly not in retrospect. "I wish you hadn't run for Senate. *That's* where it started."

Her mother nodded too.

There was a quiet knock on the door.

"Um," Meg glanced at her mother, then raised her voice, "just a minute, please." She didn't want to keep hurting her father's feelings, but she still had to — "How bad do I look? For the cameras?"

"You look beautiful," her mother said without hesitating.

Not very helpful. "I'm serious." Meg touched her hair self-consciously. The nurses had managed to keep it clean lately, but — well, it wasn't exactly *bouncy*. "I don't want to look — beaten."

"You don't," her mother said. "You're just — very pale."

"How bad is my nose?"

"It looks fine."

"Is it *different*? Is it terrible?"

"Let me get you a mirror," her mother said. "You'll feel much — "

Meg shook her head. *That*, was something she was going to do in private. And not any time soon.

"Mainly, you look exhausted," her mother said.

Which she was. Too exhausted to continue this conversation. Her mother was already tucking her blankets in and, increasingly tired, Meg didn't protest.

"I don't want them all to pity me," she said, as her mother turned her pillow, the fresh side nice and cool.

"Hero-worship is going to be more like it," her mother said.

Right.

"You'd be amazed by how many people care about you," her mother said. "How many people *admire* you."

"Not hardly," Meg said. "I mean — " She shook her head, trying to stay awake.

Her mother spread the extra blanket over her. "I think you should get some sleep."

Meg nodded. No argument there. "Can you have Dad come in and say good-night to me?"

"I'll go get him." Her mother bent down to kiss her cheek, not straightening up right away. "I love you, Meg."

Meg swallowed, then couldn't *not* return the hug, her good arm tight around her mother's shoulder and neck. "I love you too," she whispered.

When her mother finally let go, Meg had just enough time to wipe the unexpected tears off her face before her father came in, looking a little tentative.

"Are you comfortable?" he asked, picking up her hand. "Everything okay?"

She nodded, the extra blanket feeling nice and warm.

"This'll be right here if you get thirsty." He put a glass on her bedside table and she remembered, vaguely, having asked him for a Coke. He sat in the chair next to the bed. "You okay for tomorrow?"

She nodded, beginning to feel very sleepy again.

"Is it all right if I stay in here?" he asked. "Keep an eye on you?"

She smiled, seeing that her mother was already in the chair by the window. "Yeah. That'd be nice."

Chapter
Twenty-four

Leaving the hospital was pretty James Bondish. Wearing clothes — her own clothes — felt strange. Not having been able to shave her leg and all, she *really* hadn't wanted to wear a skirt, and she didn't want to ruin any of her jeans by cutting them to make the cast fit, so she ended up in blue sweatpants and a tennis sweater she'd always loved. And one Tretorn. After spending all that time in that one awful pair of thin grey sweatpants, she felt brave for wearing *this* pair. Falling off the horse and getting right back on and all. Wearing a bra *really* felt strange. Comforting *and* uncomfortable. And embarrassing, since she'd had to have her mother help her put it on.

It felt rude not to be able to say thank you to all of the hospital people, but once everything was ready to go, the Secret Service didn't waste any time, whisking them right onto a large freight elevator, the halls crowded with agents and people from the White House advance team.

She sat very straight in the wheelchair, too scared to try and make conversation, her parents and Dr. Brooks hovering around. The elevator was taking them to a sub-basement or something, so that they could secretly meet the motorcade. Preston, lounging against the side, grinned at her and she tried to smile back.

"A-are you riding with us?" she asked.

"Whatever you all want, kid," he said.

Meg looked up at her mother, who nodded.

The door opened, and they were in a parking garage, the motorcade ready and waiting for them. There were men — and a few women — with guns everywhere, and she suddenly thought about bombs. Terrorists, with bombs, throwing one in front of the car, and they would all be — her father and Dr. Brooks had lifted her into the car, her mother and Preston right behind them. The door closed and the car was moving almost before she was in her seat, her leg being propped up on a special cushion.

She could see light ahead — the outside — and held her breath, terrified. Her parents were on either side of her, her father holding her hand, her mother with her arm around her. They might have been talking to her, probably were, but her heart was thumping so loudly that she couldn't hear them. Couldn't hear *anything*.

They were outside now. Targets. Who *else* could be in black limousines speeding away from Bethesda Naval Hospital? Even though the windows were dark, she could see *out* and the sunlight made her dizzy. Made them that much easier to see. Afraid that she was going to cry — or maybe even scream — she dug her teeth into the inside of her cheek, feeling a couple of tears spill out, anyway. She turned her head towards her mother's shoulder, hoping that none of them had seen.

"Hey, kid," Preston said.

She looked up. Barely.

"Forgot to give you your gift." He put a small, brightly-wrapped package in her lap. Green and white checks, with a green bow. "Meant to give it to you inside."

Opening it with one hand was hard, but she shook her head when her father offered to help her, preferring the difficulty. She managed to rip one end open, then slit the paper down the rest of the way. Inside, was a glasses case. Sunglasses. Vuarnets. Black.

"Better try them on," he said, "or I'll think you don't like them."

Obediently, she put them on, blinking to focus.

"Very nice," he said. "Very Hollywood."

She looked at her parents to see if they agreed.

"Very nice," her father said.

"Greta Garbo," her mother said.

She looked at Preston. "Um, thank you. Thank you very much." Vuarnets were expensive, he shouldn't have —

He shrugged. "You don't look right to me without them."

She felt a little safer behind the glasses, safe enough to peer past her father and out the window for a second. Road. Trees. Telephone poles. The speed at which they were passing by was scary, and she looked down at her leg instead.

"Any pain?" Dr. Brooks asked, sitting on the jump-seat opposite Preston's.

Yes and no. "It feels kind of dead." Numb. She

wasn't supposed to without therapists, but she tried moving her foot a little, which *did* hurt. A lot of the other pain was gone though. Her ribs were okay — as long as she didn't cough. Moving her head didn't make her dizzy anymore, and her nose and mouth felt completely healed. Odds were, they didn't *look* so great.

The main thing, still, was fatigue. In fact, it was a long enough ride — oh, gosh, forty whole minutes — so that a nap wasn't altogether out of the question. The dark glasses made her sleepy too.

"Are you tired?" her mother asked. "Do you want to rest?"

Yes. "No, I'm all right." She sat up, adjusting her sling, and looked around some more.

Her parents' faces were tired and nervous — and very pale for late June. Her mother was wearing a yellow linen dress — nice and crisp and perky. Her father had on his standard summer blue blazer and light khakis ensemble, with a blue-striped tie. Dr. Brooks had on the same sort of outfit except that his coat was white, and rumpled. She saved Preston for last — he had on a purple-and-white-striped shirt with a skinny mauve tie, and beautifully creased cream-colored cotton pants. His shoes were Italian leather slip-ons; his belt was leather too.

Preston smiled at her. "Well?"

"No jacket?" she asked.

"I left it at the house."

"Well — all right," she said, making her voice sound disapproving. Her mother's arm felt very tense around her shoulders and Meg felt stupid for not remembering that it was *her* bad one. "Mom," she leaned forward, "why don't you rest your arm a little?"

"Excellent idea, Katharine," Dr. Brooks said and her mother nodded, removing it with almost-disguised relief.

Nothing like a family of the Walking Wounded. Meg was going to make a joke to that effect, but decided that that would just make things even more tense.

"Trudy's mashing you a batch of potatoes," her father said.

Meg grinned, picturing the scene. Trudy was *nothing* if not a tyrant when it came to people underfoot in the kitchen. "Is she creaming me some corn too?" she asked, still amused.

"I expect she is," her mother said.

Meg had always been big on mashed potatoes with creamed corn. Odds were, Trudy had made up a batch of butterscotch pudding too. And maybe some tacos. And she would make *all* of them drink milk. Sometimes even her parents.

When she saw the first landmark she recognized in downtown Washington, she began to tense up again, the two swallows of juice she'd had for breakfast jumping around her stomach. She could feel herself shaking, and struggled not to, not wanting her parents to worry.

"L-looks pretty much the same," she said. Who the hell did she think she was — Ulysses? It hadn't been *that* long. She couldn't repress one especially hard shake and her father's arm came around her.

"It's going to be fine," he said.

She nodded, but still couldn't stop the trembling. "I-I wish I could walk in, not look all — " She gestured to indicate the wheelchair, which was in the car behind them.

"We're going to get you right into the elevator," her mother said. "Preston'll stay downstairs to give a statement."

Meg nodded, the streets more and more familiar. More and more threatening. She could see tourists — and even Washingtonians — stopping to stare as the motorcade sped by. At least they weren't going to be driving anywhere near the school. She had no intention of *ever* going near *there* again.

Then, they were on Pennsylvania Avenue. The White House was looming up ahead of them and Meg felt the limousine slowing as the security gates swung open to let them through. Which meant they were going inside through the North Entrance.

"Front door and everything, hunh?" she said, her left hand pressed into a tight, nervous fist.

"It's a little quicker," her mother said.

Meg nodded, seeing a lot of cameras and reporters set up outside the entrance. There was a large sign, blue and red on white, hanging down from the entrance way that appeared to say, "Welcome Home, Meghan, and God Bless You."

She nudged her father. "Is that on account of us being so religious and all?" she asked, amused in spite of herself.

He actually grinned. "No doubt."

When the car doors opened, her wheelchair was already set up, and she was helped into it, aware of voices and lights. Possibly — probably *not* — some applause; she was too nervous to look up all the way. There were faces everywhere, mostly male, mostly unfamiliar. Her parents were on either side of the chair and she fought the urge to hang onto them.

" — you feeling?" one of the louder voices yelled.

244

"Um, fine." Her voice was weak and she tried to make it stronger. "Fine, thank you."

She was being wheeled into the North Entrance Hall, where there seemed to be even more noise and people.

" — feel about — "

" — home?"

" — courage in — "

" — your leg?"

Not that she had heard the whole question, but she decided to answer that one anyway, turning in her chair to face the direction from which it had come. The lights were blindingly bright, and she was very glad to have the sunglasses on.

"I'm a little worried," she said, startled by the way the hall instantly quieted down. She gestured towards the cast. "This could add thirty, maybe forty seconds to my mile."

More than a few people laughed.

"Mr. Fielding will be happy to answer questions for you," her mother said, indicating Preston, and suddenly they were in the First Family elevator, the noise and lights gone.

Meg took her sunglasses off and let out her breath, hearing her parents do the same thing.

"I-I guess word traveled fast," she said.

Her mother bent to hug her. "You handled them *beautifully*."

Meg closed her eyes. "I can't wait to sleep."

The elevator doors opened and, as Dr. Brooks pushed her chair out, she saw Trudy and her brothers waiting in the West Sitting Hall.

"Hi," she said.

"Hi," Neal said.

"Yeah," Steven said.

"Well, aren't you three silly." Trudy got up to give her a hug. "Come on, boys, come show your sister how happy you are to see her."

Meg heard claws on polished wood and happy panting, turning to see Kirby, his tail wagging wildly as he tried to climb into the wheelchair.

"Down, Kirby." Her father grabbed his collar. *"Down."*

"I want to see him, Dad." She patted him, Kirby whining with excitement. "Where's Vanessa?"

"She ran away," Neal said.

Meg stared at him. "She *what?*"

"He means she ran down the *hall,*" Steven said and punched him — hard — in the arm. "Stupid."

If she hadn't seen how upset Neal looked, Meg probably would have punched him too. "Where'd she go — upstairs?" Vanessa loved the light in the solarium.

"It's 'cause I was hitting her," Steven volunteered. "I was just hitting her and hitting her, and she — "

"Steven," their father said.

"I know he's kidding, Dad," Meg said. No one ever thought she and Steven were as funny as they did themselves. "Can you like, go find her, Steven?"

Dr. Brooks was pushing her wheelchair down towards her room, and she saw the Chief Usher and a few other people from the staff waiting in the Center Sitting Hall, all of them very solemn.

"Welcome home, Miss Powers," he said in his very deep voice. "It's very good to see you."

She was too self-conscious about the way she looked to meet their eyes, but smiled in their general direction. "Um, thank you. I mean, me too."

For a second, as her father opened her bedroom

door, she was afraid. Afraid that it would be different. That it would seem — not that it had *ever* not been stiff and formal. But, except for the vases of flowers everywhere, it looked pretty much the same. Same four-poster bed, same fireplace, same desk, same bureau, same bookcases. Same rug, same rocking chair, same tall window. The scariest thing was how *neat* it was. Sterile. Not a room anyone *lived* in. She gripped the arm of her wheelchair, afraid that she was going to cry.

"Meg," her mother was saying, "would you like — ?"

"I'd like to be alone," she said, knowing that her voice was too loud. "For — ?" As long as possible. "A while, please."

"Would you like some help — " Dr. Brooks started.

"No! I mean, no problem," she said, more calmly. Someone — her father? — touched her shoulder, but she didn't look up until she heard the door close and was sure she was alone.

Alone. In her room. A place she'd never expected she would be again. The last time she'd been in here — getting ready for school that day. In, as she recalled, a hell of a mood.

Christ, she was sick of crying. That, and sleep, were all she did anymore. She was closest to her bureau, and without bothering to wipe her eyes, she aimed the chair over there. She wasn't exactly great at steering the stupid thing.

She opened one of the drawers, the socks and underwear folded so neatly that it looked almost military. Jesus, had they all been going through her drawers or something? She reached her hand in, messing the rows up. She opened the next drawer — razor-creased T-shirts and tennis shirts — and yanked a few out, throwing them in the direction of her bed and desk. That made things a *little* better, at least. It was hard to reach the top of the bureau from her chair, but she shifted the arrangement of perfume bottles — she *was* mighty fond of perfume — and hairbrushes too. She pulled the nearest bottle down — Charlie — and sprayed some on. Maybe now she wouldn't smell so much like a veterinarian's office.

As she was putting the bottle back, she remembered that there was a mirror up there. A mirror. She thought about it, then pulled herself up onto her right foot to look.

It was a mistake. The stitches had only been out for a few days and there was a red shiny scar going right through her eyebrow and up her forehead. Her eyes were even more red — probably from crying all the time — and her nose was — Jesus. Her nose was actually *crooked*. Hooked, almost. It was *more* than obvious that a fist had been there. And her face actually looked *gaunt*. Like she'd been in a prison camp or something. A prison camp without any sunshine. And her *hair* — forget it.

All of this was so upsetting that she sat down. Quickly. She was going to cry some more, but — it could have been worse. It could have been — what she needed, was Vanessa. But it was too soon not to have privacy. There had to be something else she could — her stereo. To her surprise, she felt herself smile. Yeah, her stereo.

She pushed the little control button on her chair and wheeled over to it. Of course, this being the White House, there wasn't a speck of dust on any of the components. Had they even dusted it while she was missing, or just while she was in the hospital? Not that it mattered, really.

The tape that she had been listening to the day that — everything happened — was still in the cassette player, and she frowned at it. It would be kind of too weird to listen that exact tape right away — but then again, "I Love Rock and Roll" *was* her favorite song in life, and she *always* put it at the beginning of tapes she made. Always.

Okay, she wouldn't listen to the *same* tape, but that was no reason not to hear her favorite song. She fumbled for another tape, managing, awkwardly, to open it. She put it into the cassette player and turned up the volume. All the way.

Hearing the song made her grin. An honest-to-God happy grin.

Being home suddenly felt a hell of a lot better.

Chapter
Twenty-five

After listening to about ten of her favorite songs, she was in a pretty good mood. Almost — almost — a *swell* mood. Songs like "Small Town" by John Cougar Mellencamp, "Hello, I Love You," by the Doors, and — of course — "Jumpin' Jack Flash." "I Want a New Drug" was playing when she finally opened her door, seeing her parents and Trudy across the hall, sitting on the Sheraton settee and chair set. They were all drinking coffee and when they saw her, her parents got up.

"I was just — " She grinned as she saw a small grey-and-white head peek out from over Trudy's lap. "Hey, there."

Vanessa's head stretched out further, her ears pricked forward.

"Yeah, it's me." Meg snapped her fingers. "Come on."

Vanessa scampered over, stopped just out of reach, and began to wash. Very delicately.

"*Vanessa,*" Meg said. Her cat had never liked to be hurried.

"Wait." Her father came over to pick her up. "I'll — "

Meg shook her head. "I don't want to force her." She frowned at her cat, who was now rubbing up against an American Federal end table, still just out of reach.

"The minute we get you into bed, she'll show up," her mother said.

Meg nodded, grumpy now. "I just wish she — "

Kirby came barking down the hall and Vanessa skittered into the Yellow Oval Room, out of sight. Kirby ignored her, greeting Meg all over again, his front paws up on her lap, her mother steering him away from her cast.

Meg patted him. "At least *someone's* glad to see me," she said. "Animals, I mean," she added, before everyone got their feelings hurt. Kirby's enthusiasm made her tired and she was kind of glad when her father hauled him away.

As they all went into her room, her mother bent reflexively to pick up one of the T-shirts from the floor, hesitated, and left it there.

"I, uh — " Meg sighed. Vanessa's not being happy to see her was depressing. "I'd like to go in and get cleaned up."

Her mother handed her a perfectly folded Lanz nightgown, then pushed the wheelchair into the bathroom.

"Do you need help?" she asked, turning on the light. *Bright* light.

251

Meg shook her head, carefully *not* looking at the mirror. Once was enough.

"Well." Her mother took a step backwards. "Well, then, I'll — " She moved forward, giving her a hug that was almost fierce. "It's *very* good to have you here."

Meg shook her head, not hugging back. "It doesn't feel right."

"It will. You just have to get used to things again."

"Yeah, I guess."

Her mother hung onto her for what seemed like a long time, then straightened up. "Well," she said, her eyes wet.

Meg coughed. "I'm just going to get cleaned up now."

"Right." Her mother stepped back. "If you need — "

"Right," Meg said.

When her mother was gone, she realized that she *did* need help — but, Christ, she didn't want to spend the rest of her life having people take her clothes on and off.

When she finally came out, her whole family, Trudy, and Dr. Brooks were all standing around the room.

"Uh, hi," she said.

Her father pushed the wheelchair over to the bed, then lifted her into it, her mother pulling up the sheet and blankets.

"Are you hungry, Meg?" Trudy asked.

She smiled shyly. "I heard a little rumor about mashed potatoes."

Trudy smiled back, and bustled out of the room.

"Stupid's here," Steven said, jerking his head towards the window.

252

Meg looked away from Dr. Brooks and the blood pressure cuff he'd already managed to get around her arm to see Vanessa sitting on the low windowsill. Washing. Just as she was about to ask someone to carry her over, Vanessa jumped down and onto the bed, walking right up her leg cast.

Dr. Brooks frowned. "Oh, my."

"Yeah." Meg grinned, pulling her already-purring cat over for a very close cuddle. "She's kind of a jerk." She gave her a kiss on top of the head, then patted her some more, Vanessa trying to climb into her sling, her head and front paws disappearing from view. Meg glanced up at Dr. Brooks, who she knew was not particularly fond of cats. "Pretty cute, hunh?"

"Mmmm," he said, and checked her pulse.

By the time he had finished examining her, Trudy was already coming in with a tray, and she arranged it over Meg's lap, moving Vanessa aside. It was nice to see familiar — if overly ornate — china, and the arrangement on the tray was just about a work of art: a crystal vase with a small yellow rose, matching crystal salt and pepper shakers, a flat bowl mounded with mashed potatoes and creamed corn, a matching bowl of salad — Boston lettuce, tomato roses, and carrot curls — with, no doubt, Trudy's special honey vinaigrette, a dish of butterscotch pudding, and a glass of milk.

"Does she make tomato roses faster than anyone you know, or *what?*" Meg said to no one in particular, indicating the beautifully cut tomatoes.

"She made them before," Neal said, helpfully.

"*Oh,*" Meg said, as though that explained everything, and then picked up her fork.

"Would you like anything else, dear?" Trudy asked.

"No, thank you — it looks great." It was sort of embarrassing to have them all watching her, but everything looked so good that Meg started eating anyway. "You all don't like, have to *stand* there or anything," she said, tasting the salad. Yup, honey vinaigrette. "I mean, I'm home now, right? You might as well pretend like I'm normal."

"*Pretend,*" Steven said quietly.

At least *he* was acting regular. "Is there a game on today?" she asked him.

He looked guiltily at their father before answering. "What do you mean?"

So much for acting normal. Meg drank some milk. "What do you *think* I mean — hockey?"

"Um, yeah," he said. "I think there's one on later."

He *thought*. "You want to watch it with me?"

He looked at their father again, then shrugged. "No big deal if I don't see it."

Oh, for Christ's sakes. "Okay, but *I'm* going to watch it," Meg said. "I just thought you might want to watch it *with* me."

"Me too?" Neal asked.

"Sure." Meg tried the mashed potatoes, which were delicious. "They in first place?"

"Three and a half out," Steven said.

"Oh." Meg frowned. "The Yankees?"

"Toronto," Steven said.

"Oh." She looked at her father. "Are you going to watch with us too?"

"I'd love too," he said.

"Um, you guys can too," she said to her mother and Trudy. "I just — don't feel like you *have* to."

"Wouldn't miss it for the world," her mother said.

· · ·

Along about the seventh inning, with the Red Sox down eight to two, Meg figured that they were maybe all sort of regretting watching the game. The atmosphere in the room probably would have been more than a little cranky, but Preston had shown up during the third, and kept saying jolly things. Even when the Red Sox rallied for five runs, then had the bases loaded in the bottom of the ninth before someone popped up for the third out.

There was a long, and rather deadly, silence in the room.

"Never a dull moment," Preston said, and Meg's father and Steven scowled at him. Anyone *else*, they would have smacked.

"They never give up," her mother said. "They're to be admired for that."

Her father and Steven didn't say anything.

Since he wasn't about to yell at *her*, Meg looked at her father. "Maybe it's because you weren't in your lucky chair," she said.

He shrugged. Pleasantly. "It's only a game."

Next to him, Steven pretended to commit hara-kiri, then fell to the floor. Meg — at least — was amused. Maybe things were different now, but "it's only a game" was something people in her family occasionally *said*, but never meant. Not down deep inside. Particularly, of course, when the Red Sox were involved.

"Maybe," her mother said, "we should — " The phone next to Meg's bed rang, and she answered it, then looked at Meg. "They have Beth on the line for you."

255

Meg thought about that, then nodded. If she got tired and had to hang up, Beth would understand. As she took the phone, she saw everyone in the room tactfully leaving. Who would ever have thought that having people be constantly, completely considerate would be sort of tiresome?

"Hello?" she said into the phone.

"Thirty seconds to your mile?" Beth said.

Meg felt herself blushing. "What was I supposed to say?"

"It was pretty funny," Beth said. "You in your sunglasses and all."

"Preston gave them to me," Meg said defensively.

"The man has taste."

"Yeah." Still embarrassed, Meg shifted her position. Vanessa, who had been *very* comfortably asleep on her lap, flounced away to the bottom of the bed and curled up again. "Was it a special report, or just like, on the news?"

"What an ego," Beth said.

"I'm just asking."

Beth sighed a very deep sigh. "They interrupted regularly scheduled programming."

"Pretty weird," Meg said.

Neither of them spoke for a minute.

"So. How you doing?" Beth asked.

"I don't know. Okay, I guess."

"Is it okay being home?"

"Yeah, I guess," Meg said. "We just watched the baseball game."

"Did they win?"

"No."

"Was Steven mad?"

"Yeah."

256

"Was Vanessa glad to see you?"

Meg looked down at the bottom of the bed, where Vanessa was already deep in sleep. "Not really."

"Well — she's like that," Beth said.

"Yeah."

Another long silence.

"Well," Beth said. "I just, you know, wanted to see how you were doing."

"Yeah."

"People up here said to say hello to you. I mean, the next time I talked to you."

Meg nodded. "My father said I got cards and stuff from a lot of them."

"The Greater Boston area?"

"Yeah, kind of." According to her father, she'd gotten a card or a telegram or something from almost every teacher she'd ever had — even the ones who hadn't liked her much — and from people who had gone to school with her, and from practically every neighbor they'd ever had. As well as something from almost everyone her *parents* had known in Boston. In the *world*.

"Have you seen Josh or anyone?"

Meg sighed. "No."

"Oh," Beth said, sounding a little embarrassed. "Well, maybe it'll be easier now that you're home."

"Maybe," Meg said. "Um, look. I'm getting sort of tired, and — "

"Okay," Beth said. "I just called to see how you were doing."

"Yeah."

"You, uh, you looked good on television, Meg. Really confident."

257

Meg frowned at the phone. "You don't have to humor me."

"Oh, yeah," Beth said. "I *constantly* humor people."

Which was valid — Beth was, as a rule, quite blunt. "Did you see where my nose used to be?"

"I thought it looked pretty much the same."

"You should see it up close."

"It looked okay to me."

More silence.

"Well," Beth said. "I guess you're pretty tired and all?"

"Pretty damn tired," Meg agreed.

After hanging up, the phone seemed too heavy to lift to the bedside table, so Meg let it stay on top of the blankets, adjusting her pillows so she could lie down. It was *definitely* naptime.

They had tacos for dinner. Which were hard to eat one-handed. But everyone was relaxed enough now so that Steven and Neal laughed when two of her tacos in a row broke in half and fell all over her plate. Laughed *at* her. Meg thought it was funny, but her parents frowned at her brothers.

"Would you like to watch television," her father said after dinner, "or — ".

Meg shook her head. "I think I just want to read a book."

"Anything special?" her mother asked.

Meg shrugged. "Just not a mystery." Blood and guts and guns weren't anything she wanted to deal with. Ever again.

Her parents went to gather up a stack of novels — some of which she had been given in the hospital, but been too tired to bother opening — and carried them

in. In the hospital, even *People* had seemed like stren-
uous literature.

"Do you want anything else?" her father asked.

"No, thank you." She looked at Trudy. "Um, dinner
was delicious."

Everyone pretty much cleared out and she examined
the stack of books, selecting *The War Between the
Tates*, by Alison Lurie. She'd read another book of
hers, *Foreign Affairs*, and liked it a lot.

Her parents kept coming in to check on her — or
maybe just *look* at her, it seemed like — and Trudy
kept bringing her things to eat and drink. But mostly,
it was very quiet and peaceful, and she just read her
book. Kind of weird to have reading seem like such a
special treat. A couple of times, she dozed a little, and
that was peaceful too.

It was past ten, and there was a knock on the door.
Trudy with more treats, probably.

Meg lowered her book. "Come in."

The door opened and she saw Neal, wearing his
Return of the Jedi pajamas — which were way too small,
one hand behind him.

"Hi," she said.

He nodded, hanging back.

"What's going on?"

He stayed by the door. "Do you want anything?
Mommy said to ask."

"No, thanks," she said, then sighed. "Come on,
don't stand there on the threshold — you know I hate
that."

Quickly, he stepped inside. "I'm sorry."

"What's going on?" she asked, again.

He shifted from one foot to the other, not looking
at her.

"What is it?"

He looked guilty, his hand still behind his back. "Don't be mad."

"What do you mean?"

"I took something."

Judging from his expression, it must have been half of Fort Knox. "Okay," she said uneasily.

"Something of *yours*."

She shrugged. "Okay, no big deal."

He hesitated, then brought his hand out, dropping a rock on the bed. More than a little confused, Meg picked it up. It was the rock she used as a paperweight on her desk; mostly quartz, with bits of mica or something. She'd never really retained Mo's Table of rock categories, or any of that.

"You took my rock?" she said, not sure why he was so worried.

He nodded. "I'm sorry."

She was about to say "It's just a *rock*," but considering how upset he was, that would have been tactless. "Um, like I said, no big deal." She held the rock up to the light, studying it. She'd found it about five summers before when they'd taken one of their vacations up in New Hampshire, renting a house on a lake. One of those quiet lakes, where motorboats were forbidden and all. "Remember when I found it?"

He nodded, and she thought about it too. The house had had a rickety little dock and — not that they were the world's greatest swimmers or anything — they would dive off it and see if they could find things on the lake bottom. This rock had looked especially pretty, and she and Steven had spent almost a whole afternoon trying to dive down far enough to get it.

260

"Funny how they always looked prettier when they were in the water," she said.

Neal nodded.

"If you like it so much, why didn't you just *ask* me for it?"

"You weren't here," he said, not looking at her.

Oh. "I don't mean *recently*. If you liked it, why didn't you ask me like, *years* ago?"

"It's yours," he said.

"Yeah, but — " Somehow, she could sense that this was going to be a losing conversation. "Can I give it to you?"

He shook his head.

"Take it," she said. "It'll make me happy."

He hesitated, then picked it up, holding it almost reverently. "Remember how me and Steven couldn't hardly dive at all?"

"Well, you were just a little guy." Meg grinned. "And *Steven* was a klutz." One of the days they were there, Steven had even managed to hit his head on the dock, and her parents had had to rush him to the emergency room with a mild concussion.

"I knew *you* could get it," Neal said. "I *knew* you would."

Yeah, it had only taken her about six hours. "You were that sure, hunh?"

He nodded.

Funny to think of him wanting it all those years, and never saying a word.

"Remember how you always used to bring me things?" he asked.

She could *sort of* remember, but not really. "Yeah," she said.

"Like when I was too little to go, and you'd bring me movie candy?"

That, actually, she remembered. He'd always been wild about Junior Mints. She, personally, despised them, but had always had a couple to be polite.

"And the funny pioneer soap? From the field trip?"

She remembered that, too. Sturbridge Village. "What about the three-colored pen? That I got downtown?" In Boston, one of the first times she and Beth had been allowed to take the subway into the city by themselves. "I could never figure out why you liked that pen so much." He seemed awfully quiet and she looked up, startled to see him crying. "Neal? You okay?" She motioned for him to sit on the bed. "Come on, sit up here."

"I'm not supposed to," he said, crying.

"Just come on."

He got up next to her and she put her arm around him.

"I didn't mean to hit you," he said.

What? "When?"

"Ever," he said. "I didn't know how bad it was."

"It's not like you ever *hurt* me. I mean — " She shook her head. "When *we* fight, it's different."

"Steven isn't going to hit people anymore either," he said.

That'd be the day. "Well, that's good," she said, and tightened her arm. "Please don't cry, okay? I mean — I'm home, right?"

He looked up at her. Actually, he was getting tall — his head didn't have to tilt up nearly as much as it used to. "I was crying a lot when you were gone."

She smiled a little. "So was I."

"I saw Steven, but he got mad."

262

Meg refrained from asking if Steven had hit him. "Well, it was a hard time for everyone." Be nice if *that* were past tense.

"I was really scared," he said.

She nodded. "You and me both, cowboy." She let out her breath. "You and me both."

Chapter
Twenty-six

The next day, Josh called and, feeling guilty, she said that yeah, sure, he could come over for a while, no problem. She regretted it almost before the words were out of her mouth, but by then, it was too late.

So, she got dressed, allowing Trudy to cut the left leg off one of her pairs of jeans, and having Steven "borrow" for her an old Radcliffe sweatshirt of her mother's that she'd always coveted.

When Josh arrived, she, her father, and her brothers were up in the Solarium, watching the end of the Red Sox game. In *this* one, they had been ahead five to nothing, gotten behind eight to five, and finally won nine to eight — just as Josh came in, carrying a box of chocolates.

"Yo, *candy*," Steven said cheerfully. "Excellent." As long as the Red Sox won, *how* they did it never seemed to matter to him. No matter how tortuous it was.

"Uh, yeah," Josh said, handing the box to Meg, then putting his hands in his pockets. He coughed. "Did they win?"

"*Of* course," Steven said. "They're too *excellent* not to always win."

Talk about selective memory. "Thank you," Meg said to Josh. "They look delicious."

"You don't know that," Steven said. "You haven't *opened* them yet."

Their father smiled, getting up. "Come on, guys, let's go out and throw the ball around."

"Yeah!" Neal said, jumping up.

Her father touched her shoulder. "Anything you need, kiddo?"

Meg shook her head.

"Well, if you do, I'll be right outside." He put his hand out to shake Josh's. "Good to see you, Josh. Come on, boys."

Steven sat down on the couch, linking his arm through Meg's. "I must stay with my sister," he said solemnly. "My sister *needs* me."

Their father sighed. "Steven."

"I *must*," he said.

Meg looked over at him, amused. "Go away."

"But, Sister dear — "

"*Go away.*"

He laughed, and went after Neal and their father.

"He seems pretty chipper," Josh said.

And *then* some. Meg nodded.

"So, uh — " He coughed. "So."

"Sit down."

"Yeah." He sat in the chair next to the couch.

It had been a pretty long time since they'd seen each other, and it *felt* even longer. Meg resisted the urge to cough too. "So," she said.

"You, you look good," he said.

Time to get that glasses prescription changed, maybe. She reached for the box of candy. "Thank you for these. Should we open them?"

He shrugged. "Sure."

Instead of struggling one-handed, she gave the box to him. "Beth says hi."

He unwrapped the plastic. "When's she coming down here?"

"I don't know. No time soon." She turned off the television, which made the room seem so quiet that she turned it back on.

"You want to watch something?"

"Not really." She turned it off again. "I mean, unless you do."

He shook his head, handing her the open box of chocolates.

She took one. "Thank you." Vanilla cream. "How are Nathan and everyone?"

"Okay," he said, selecting a piece for himself. "I mean, you know, fine."

"Um, tell them I said hi."

He nodded.

"Thanks." Starting to remember how tired she was, she closed her eyes, trying to will the feeling away.

"Would you like to rest?" he asked.

Yes. "It's not that," she said. "It's just — I'm sorry."

"You don't have anything to be sorry about."

As far as she could see, she didn't have too many things *not* to be sorry about. But, it was probably time

266

to change the subject. "So, um, graduation was good," she said. "You went, I mean."

He nodded.

"Well — that's good," she said. "You, um, you working at the golf course?" Which was his regular summer job.

"Some, yeah," he said.

"Getting any good tips?"

"Stay out of coffee futures," he said.

Okay, that was funny. She smiled, and he smiled back.

"You making any *money* over there?" she asked.

"Yeah, some," he said.

For school. It wouldn't be much longer before he would be leaving. Before *everyone* her age would be going away to school. Or doing whatever adult thing they were going to do.

"Well, that's good," she said aloud. "You'll be able to use it."

He looked uncomfortable. "I don't know, yeah."

Unable to think of anything else to say, she reached for the box of chocolates and, left arm across her body, offered it to him. He shook his head and, not hungry herself, she put the box back on the coffee table.

"How's your leg?" he asked.

"I don't know," she said, and looked at the cast. "Pretty much the same."

"This cast looks smaller."

"It is a little, yeah," she agreed. As conversations went, this had to be one of their worst of all time. "You're getting a pretty good tan."

He glanced at his arms, very brown against his white Lacoste shirt. "Yeah, kind of." He looked towards the hall, where there was an exit to the roof. "It's still pretty sunny. You want to go outside for a while?"

No. "I'm kind of tired," she said.

"Just for a minute?" he said. "I could — "

Jesus! "I *don't want to*," she said. "Okay?"

He nodded. "I'm sorry. I didn't mean to — "

"You didn't," she said. "I just — " Christ. This was too much work. "You want to watch something on television?" Television was easy; television was safe.

"Sure," he said, reaching for the remote-control box, not quite looking at her. "Whatever you want."

He didn't stay for dinner. She knew she was supposed to ask him, but all she really wanted to do was be taken back to her room, close the door, and be alone. Trudy, as always, prepared her a wonderful tray, but she felt too numb to do much more than rearrange the food with her fork. After assuring her family that she was fine, that she just needed to rest, and could they please make sure she didn't get any phone calls, they left her alone. It was too scary to sleep in the dark room, so she had her father turn on the bathroom light on his way out.

She slept, waking up on and off — when they checked on her, when Vanessa got restless, when the blankets felt too hot. Even when she was awake, she was too tired to bother turning on the light, too tired to do more than watch the red numbers on her clock change. At one point, when her mother was in to check on her, they managed to scare the hell out of each other — her mother not expecting her to be awake, Meg not expecting to see her standing by the bed.

268

Her mother recovered first. "I'm sorry, I didn't mean to startle you."

"You didn't," Meg said, trying to sit up. She looked at her clock, which read 2:47. "Pretty late."

"Well, I just wanted to be sure you were sleeping all right," her mother said.

"You are going to *really* go back to work tomorrow, right?" Meg said. "Not hang out with me?"

"Well — I don't know," her mother said. "I'm not — "

"It's not like I'm an *invalid*. I mean like, things should get back to normal." If possible.

"Well," her mother said, and looked uneasy.

"You're *only* going to be downstairs."

Her mother nodded.

"Good," Meg said. If they all *did* normal things, maybe she would *feel* normal. Unfortunately, normal for *her* meant resuming physical therapy the next day. The Nautilus room — which only her father used with any regularity — had been set up with some new "injury-specific" equipment. Swell.

"It was hard having Josh here today?" her mother both said and asked.

There was an understatement. Meg nodded.

"Well, what if we had Beth — "

"I really don't want to see people," Meg said. "I'm just — not ready."

Her mother nodded.

"I'm kind of tired." Meg reached back to turn her pillow, her mother moving in to do it for her.

"Do you need anything?" she asked.

Meg shook her head, lying down.

269

"Well — I'll see you in the morning," her mother said. "Sleep well."

Meg nodded. "You too."

The therapy was awful. Exhausting. The therapist was a nice nurse named Edith, whom she remembered from the hospital, but Meg didn't talk any more than she had to to be polite, just concentrating on finishing the exercises and the electro-stimulus stuff, which was supposed to promote healing, and getting back to bed. The bathtub she used had been set up with an arm and a leg rest, but she still needed a little bit of help, which was embarrassing, even though it was only Trudy, with a nurse sitting outside the door just in case.

"Well, dear," Trudy said, tucking her back into bed. "Would you like anything?"

Meg shook her head. "No, thank you."

"Would you like me to keep you company?"

Meg shook her head. "No, thank you. I just want to rest."

Trudy looked worried, but nodded, giving the blankets one last tuck before leaving the room.

So, mostly, she slept. Dr. Brooks came by to check on her, her family was in and out, and in the middle of the afternoon, she woke up long enough to eat half a grilled cheese sandwich and a small bowl of mushroom soup. Other than that, she slept.

She managed another small meal — chicken, a baked potato, some salad — for dinner; then let Steven watch, while she half-watched, the baseball game in her room. Then, back to sleep.

The scary part was how fast the happy novelty of being home was evaporating. Replaced by, for the most

270

part, paralyzing fear. She wasn't even sure what she was afraid *of* — some combination of the past, present, and future — or *lack* of a future — but she knew she was afraid. She didn't want her family to know how bad it was, so she was careful to seem calm and cheerful. On the mend.

She stayed with her pattern of almost-constant sleep because it was the only way she could function. It wasn't even so much that she was *tired*, but sleeping meant that she didn't have to be scared. Didn't have to pretend that everything was fine, no problem, not to worry — and other such platitudes. Obviously, her family wasn't stupid enough to believe that she had been suddenly cured, but no one pressured her either.

She was lying in bed after a physical therapy session, holding a glass of fresh lemonade she was too tired to drink when Preston came in. He had been in and out over the last week or so too.

"Hey, kid," he said cheerfully, putting a new hardcover on her bedside table. "How you doing?"

"Fine, thank you," she said.

"Yeah." He sat down, his look penetrating. "Therapy going okay?"

She nodded.

"Good," he said. "Word has it they're going to get that leg into a more comfortable cast soon."

She shrugged. "I guess."

"That'll be good — you'll be able to get around better."

She shrugged.

"Well." He indicated his outfit. "What do you think?"

"It's nice," she said, not really looking. Pants, a shirt, tie. That sort of thing.

He sat back, studying her. "You know, kid," he said, "could be just me, but it seems like you're maybe beginning to internalize a little."

"I'm just tired," she said.

"How about a change of scene? We'll go sit on the Truman Balcony."

The balcony any psycho with a good pair of binoculars could see onto. She shook her head.

"Think some fresh air'd do you good," he said.

"No, thank you," she said, politely.

"Well, I'd give it some thought maybe."

She nodded, so he'd drop it.

"It's nice and sunny out," he said.

She nodded.

"Hate to see you looking so pale."

She glared at him. "Back off, okay, Preston?"

"Sure," he said. "I just hate to see you going *down-hill*, you know?"

"I'm just tired," she said.

"Okay." He tilted his chair back, looking up at her chandelier. "Given any thought to sitting down with Gary Crowell?"

The Army psychologist guy. *"No,"* she said.

"He knows his stuff, Meg. He's worked with a lot of the embassy people, after — "

"I don't like him," she said.

"What about someone who's been through the same sort of thing? Someone from one of the hijackings, or — "

"I don't even want to talk to people I *know*," she said, "forget people I *don't* know."

"Sometimes it's easier when you don't know the person," he said. "Nothing to hide that way."

"Yeah, well, I'm not interested."

272

"Okay." He sighed. "Just can't stand seeing you turn yourself into a little time bomb."

"I'm just tired," she said.

"Okay."

"I'm *really* tired," she said, hoping that he would take the hint and leave already.

"I know you are." He folded his hands behind his head, still looking up at the ceiling. "You know," he said, "at some point you've got to let yourself start thinking about it."

"Thinking about *what*?" she asked stiffly.

He shrugged. "I don't know. The future, primarily."

What future? She didn't say anything.

"Come on, Meg, talk to me," he said. "Give yourself a break."

She scowled at him. "I don't *have* a future. In case you didn't notice."

He turned his head enough to look at her. "Mention this to your parents yet?"

"No." She managed a weak smile. "I don't want them to worry."

He nodded. "Why spoil their tranquility."

"Oh, yeah, right," she said. "Tell them I'm not even glad to be back?" That sounded terrible. "I mean, I'm *glad*, but — " But what? "It's sort of like I didn't come back *to* anything."

"How do you mean?"

She frowned. "You don't understand?"

"I want to be *sure* I understand."

"I'm not going to have a life," she said. "Even if I were *allowed* to go anywhere, I can't — I mean, even if they *could* protect me, I wouldn't be able to — what are they going to do, come here and tutor me *college*?"

He shrugged. "It's not the best scenario, but — "

"Don't say 'scenario,' " she said, remembering the guy. "*Worst* scenario," he'd said, "I start liking you," and — she shivered, not wanting to think about it.

"Sorry," Preston said. "Can't help falling into press secretary talk sometimes."

She shrugged.

He looked at her thoughtfully. "Funny word to give you bad associations."

She felt herself shiver again.

"Meg — "

"I'm going to sleep," she said, "okay?"

"You'd feel better if — "

"I'm *going* to," she said, covering her eyes with her arm. "*Okay?*"

He sighed, standing up. "Okay."

Chapter
Twenty-seven

She was careful to hide it, but over the next few days, she could feel the pressure building. Even sleep wasn't working as a cure because the nightmares were back, worse than ever. Most of them were about the guy — or even just his grin, like some scary Cheshire cat — but falling, seeing people she knew get killed, and being trapped in places were regular themes too.

Her appetite was pretty much gone and every day, the therapy exercises seemed harder and harder. She tried to keep a constant "don't worry, I'm fine" smile pasted on, but knew she wasn't really fooling anyone. And she still wasn't taking phone calls. From *anyone*.

Preston was around a lot, but she avoided being alone with him since she knew he could, *would*, make her talk. Upset her. Whenever Dr. Brooks came in, he would look very serious and worried, but he didn't push her. Her family was being quiet and careful too. Thank God.

It was very late — she wasn't sure what night it was — when she had the worst nightmare so far. She was chained to that iron bed frame, the room smaller and darker than she remembered, and he was coming at her — more crazed than he'd been with the gun that time — apparently planning to kill her with his bare hands. He was breathing hard, like an animal, and when she saw his eyes, she screamed, because they *weren't* eyes, they were fire. Not *even* fire — more like red light. Burning red light. She screamed again, screamed as he started laughing, his hands around her throat.

"Who did you *think* I was?" he asked.

"Y-you don't exist," she said, some awake, sane part of her brain aware that this wasn't happening, that it couldn't be — "This isn't real."

"I *do* exist," he said, and as she watched his eyes, his face reddened and lengthened, turning into the honest-to-God devil, his laugh more and more high-pitched.

She was too terrified to say anything, too terrified to *move*, and he came at her again, a rope stretched out between his hands, laughing.

"You'll never get away from me," he said, wrapping the rope around her neck. "You'll be with me *forever*."

She tried to scream, but the rope was already too tight, already cutting off her air.

He laughed some more, laughed wildly. "You know who I am? Do you? Do you know who I am? That's who I am!"

She screamed again, was still screaming when she realized that the room was much brighter. That she

276

was in *her* room, and her parents were there, holding her.

"It's all right, Meg," her mother was saying over and over. "Wake up, Meg, it's all right."

Maybe it wasn't her room, maybe it was a trick, maybe —

"*Wake up*, Meg," her mother said gently.

She looked at her parents, at her room, at Steven standing near the door, his eyes huge. Normal eyes. She looked at her parents, who also had normal eyes. Normal eyes. She tried to get her breath, her heart thumping so hard that the force seemed strong enough to knock her off the bed.

"I-I think I'm having a heart attack," she gasped.

"Shhh," her mother was holding her close, "you're all right. It was just a dream."

"He's coming to get me! He can get in *anywhere!*"

"You're safe," her father said. "I promise."

"You don't know him!"

"I *promise*," her father said.

She trusted her father. Her father never lied to her. She looked at him, wondering with a sudden terrified quiver if *his* eyes were going to change, if all of them were going to turn into — "Are you *sure?*" she asked.

"I'm sure," he said.

She let herself relax a little, the dream beginning to fade. "You're *sure?*"

He nodded, and she sank down into the pillows, pulling in slow, deep breaths. They were all looking at her with such concern that she managed a small laugh.

"You're not going to believe this," she said weakly, "but I think I just had a Born-Again dream."

"A what?" her mother asked, as her father said, "I

277

don't understand." Steven didn't say *anything*.

Meg just shook her head, too tired to explain.

"Would you — " her mother started.

"Yeah," Meg said, gesturing weakly towards the VCR. "Could you put in *The Sound of Music?*"

"Of course," her mother said. "Whatever you want."

"Good," Meg said, watching her father search through the stack of tapes on her desk as she tried to stop trembling. "Because I think I need to see some nuns."

Her parents sat up with her for a long time. They watched the movie, not talking much, the memory of the dream slowly disappearing as Meg stared at the screen. By the time Maria was singing "My Favorite Things," Meg was relaxed enough to let her eyes close.

"Feel better?" her father asked.

Meg grinned sheepishly. "Yeah."

"Good," he said, and got up to turn the movie off, the room seeming very quiet.

"How would you feel about going home to Massachusetts for a while?" her mother asked. "You could see your old friends, and — "

Oh, yeah, like they'd be safe *there*. "I'm just tired," Meg said. "I'm going to be *fine*."

Her mother nodded. "I know. We just thought you might feel better if — "

"I *don't* want to go anywhere," Meg said. "I'm not going to ruin everything."

Her father patted her hand, very calm. "Your mother and I just want to make things easier for you. We thought going home for a while might — "

"I'm *trying* to get better," Meg said defensively. "I can't help — "

"We just want to make it easier," her father said. "That's all."

Meg sighed. "I don't want everything messed up because of me. I don't want to go home and — I mean, we live *here* now. I just — I want things to be *normal*. I mean, anything else means they got what they wanted. That they — I don't know, changed the order of things."

Her parents both nodded.

"Besides," Meg said. "If we're not safe *here*, we're not going to be safe anywhere else. I mean, you *know* we're not."

They nodded.

"I want things to be *normal*." She looked at her mother. "You especially. Work, I mean."

Her mother nodded.

"I just — I don't know." Talking was making her tired. Again. Her parents must have been able to tell because her mother started arranging her pillows, while her father turned the light out. "Can you make sure the bathroom light stays on?" she asked. "So I can sleep?"

Her father nodded, moving to turn it on, leaving the door ajar about a foot.

"Thank you," she said, and closed her eyes.

She did her best to feel better. To eat normal meals. To smile. To *function*. She had to go back to the hospital that week — in a helicopter from the South Lawn, not a motorcade — and have a different kind of cast put on her leg. This one was very light —

mostly fiberglass and straps — and she was given a tall crutch too, which her physical therapist would be teaching her how to use. The doctors still seemed pretty divided on her "walking unaided" or not. Not that it affected *them* much.

She was also taken to a dentist, who did the preliminary work for the permanent bridge she was going to need to replace her teeth on the left side. Yeah, she could hardly *wait*. The whole trip was very tiring — and scary — and she resorted to the sunglasses-on/slight-friendly-wave strategy when they got back to the White House and her parents — with what looked like half of the entire Secret Service — took her inside, past the press.

"Long day," her father said, once they had her back in bed, with a small dinner tray that she was too tired to eat.

And *then* some. Meg nodded. Most of the time that they had been outside, transferring to and from the helicopter, she had been so scared that she had had to keep her eyes closed behind the sunglasses, her good hand wrapped tightly around the arm of the wheelchair.

"Anything else you want?" her father asked.

For this day to be *over*. Meg shook her head, slowly picking up her fork.

Although she was exhausted from having Edith teach her how to try and use the crutch, she went up to the solarium the next afternoon for her "change of scene." The Red Sox played at one o'clock, and since Roger Clemens pitched, and pitched *well*, Steven was pretty jolly.

"You want some chow?" he asked, happily watching

the recap of the game — a solid shut-out victory.

Meg shook her head. "No, thanks. I mean, go ahead."

"Should I like" — he looked at her wheelchair — "take you downstairs?"

She shook her head. "I'm tired, I'm just going to hang out for a while." Once the game had seemed safely in hand, her father had taken Kirby, and Neal, out for a walk on the lawn. Her mother was in a meeting or something.

"Well — okay," Steven said. "You can like, call," he motioned towards the phone, "if you, you know, want anything or anything."

"And you think *I* talk excellent?" she said.

He laughed, doing a pretend pitcher's warm-up toss at her, then headed for the door.

When he was gone, it was more quiet than she wanted it to be, and she picked up the remote-control, turning channels until she found another baseball game. This one was National League and therefore, not as interesting, but she left it on anyway.

Slouching down to watch, she felt the usual wave of depression starting, not sure if she had enough energy to fight it off. She was *never* going to feel better. *Days* were passing, and she still — hearing someone at the door, she prepared a game little "don't worry about *me*" smile, then looked up to see Beth. A somewhat tentative Beth, holding a small blue giftbox. No *wonder* her parents had kind of been making themselves scarce this afternoon.

Feeling even more tired, she sighed. "They went behind my back, didn't they?"

Beth grinned and came into the room, wearing jeans, pink Keds, and a very pink bowling shirt. "Is

281

that anything like 'Hello' 'How nice to see you' 'What a pretty outfit'?"

"I *told* you I didn't feel well enough to see people."

Beth shrugged, gave her a shy hug, then sat down in an easy chair. "Hey, the President calls and tells you to do something, you *do* it."

"Beth to the Rescue," Meg said grimly.

"*There's* a hell of a chapter title." Beth leaned over to hand her the present. "Here."

"Thank you." Meg turned the box over in her hand, but didn't open it. "She shouldn't have gone behind my back like that."

"Who knows," Beth said. "Maybe she was trying to help you."

"Maybe," Meg said, her face feeling stiff. She looked at Beth, frowning. "You don't wear a *hat* to come see me even?"

"It's with all of my luggage, of course," Beth said solemnly.

"What, are you moving in?"

"Yes," Beth said. "I'm taking over the Department of Housing and Urban Development."

Meg sighed.

"*Now*, you have to ask me something nice."

Meg sighed again, trying to think. "How was your flight?"

"Just the swellest," Beth said cheerfully. "How are *you*?"

Meg shrugged.

"If you don't mind my saying so, you don't look so good."

Meg frowned at her. "I mind your saying so."

"Are you eating?"

"Oh, yeah," Meg said. "This is just what I need."

"Do you *ever* see sunshine?"

"I got to go to the hospital the other day." Meg put the present down, unopened. "Look, just so I'll know. What did my mother say to you?"

"That you maybe needed some cheering up." Beth grinned. "*Ob*viously, she was mistaken."

"Yeah." She didn't — really — want to be rude, so she tried to smile back. "You, uh, you want anything to eat, or drink, or anything? I can call downstairs."

"No, thanks." Beth looked at her. "If you don't want me here, just say so."

"It's not that." It *was* that, actually. "I just — " Time to change the subject. "How's your family?"

"Fine. How's yours?"

"You should know — you *talk* to them all the time," Meg said, before she could stop herself.

"Just looking for your perspective," Beth said, very cheerful.

"So you *do* talk to them all the time?"

Beth laughed. "Jesus, Meg. Take it easy, why don't you?"

"How often have you talked to them?"

"Twice, Lieutenant."

Meg frowned, not amused. "When?"

"Your father called from the hospital to let me know you were all right, and your mother called me yesterday." Beth paused. "You want transcripts?"

"Do you talk to Josh too? And Preston?"

"Yeah, it's kind of a nightmare having people care about you." Beth indicated the television. "Big fan now?"

"It's something to *do*."

Beth nodded. "Look," she said, "if you really don't want me here, the shuttle leaves every hour."

283

Meg sighed, not sure *what* she wanted. "I'm not much fun to be around."

Beth shrugged. "Were you *ever*?"

To her horror, Meg felt her eyes filling with tears, and had to look away.

"I'm sorry," Beth said quickly. "I was just kidding."

Meg nodded, mortified to feel a couple of the tears spill over.

"Oh, Jesus, I'm sorry." Beth moved over to sit next to her. "Meg, I really — " She touched her shoulder hesitantly. "I thought if I — I didn't mean to upset you."

"I'm *terminally* upset," Meg said.

Beth nodded, leaving her hand on Meg's shoulder.

"So I feel better being left alone."

Beth nodded again. "Can I hang out and be upset *with* you?"

"Oh, yeah, sounds fun," Meg said.

"This," Beth pointed to herself, "is a girl who knows how to have fun."

Meg had to grin. "Right."

"So what do you want to do?"

"I want to watch the game," Meg said.

Beth leaned back, swinging her feet onto the coffee table. "Then let's watch the game."

Chapter
Twenty-eight

Her family and Trudy were in and out during the next couple of hours. Her father and brothers to watch some of the game — National League, or not; Trudy to bring them fudge-marshmallow bars and milk; her mother "just to say hello." When her mother came in, Meg didn't look at her, answering questions in monosyllables, and her mother left the room relatively quickly.

"For Christ's sakes," Beth said, frowning over at her. "She was trying to make you happy."

"She just likes to call all the shots," Meg said, and gritted her teeth. "She always has."

"Oh, come on, Meg."

"You wouldn't be mad at *your* mother?"

Beth smiled sheepishly. "I'm *generally* mad at my mother."

Which was true — Beth and her mother had started clashing around the time Beth was ten, and never really slacked off since. "At least *your* mother has never almost gotten you killed."

"Meg, come on. It isn't like she — "

"I don't want to talk about it," Meg said. "Okay?"

"Yeah, but — "

"Please just stay out of it."

"At the moment, I seem to be in the *middle* of it," Beth said.

"*I* didn't put you there." The silence was deadly enough so that Meg felt guilty. "I *told* you I shouldn't be around people."

Beth nodded. "You weren't kidding."

They both stared at the television.

"Seems like you keep feeling worse instead of better," Beth said.

Meg sighed. "Yeah. Looks that way."

"Well, is there anything — ?"

Meg shook her head. "I don't think there's anything anyone can do."

"You can't just quit."

"I don't have any *better* ideas."

Beth considered that, then looked down at her watch. "When's dinner?"

"Is that supposed to be a better idea?"

"It's not a worse one," Beth said. "Come on, let's head downstairs, see if it's ready yet."

Meg shook her head. "I have trays."

"Always?"

Meg nodded, picking up the remote-control box. "You want to watch some videos?"

"You *always* have trays?"

286

Meg let the little box fall. "In case you haven't noticed, I'm having a tough time."

"So let's try eating at the table," Beth said. "You might feel better."

Meg shook her head. "I'm too tired."

"Do you *eat* your trays?"

Meg sighed, feeling more and more tired. "They're made of metal, usually."

"My God." Beth clapped her hands to her chest. "She made a joke."

"Look, if you're hungry," Meg reached for the phone, "I'll just — "

Beth stood up. "Let's go downstairs. I haven't seen your family in a long time."

Meg sighed again. "Are you going to pressure me the whole time you're here?"

"Is this pressure?"

"Yes."

"Then, yeah," Beth said. "I probably am." She handed Meg her crutch. "Come on."

"You don't understand how tired I am."

"You're right, I probably don't." Beth put her hand out to help her up. "Come on."

Since she knew Beth wouldn't stop pushing her until she gave in, Meg put her left hand out, letting Beth pull her up to her feet. For a few seconds, she was dizzy, and had to hang onto her friend's arm for support. Then, she shifted her weight to the crutch, the thought of making her way to the door too awesome to face right away.

"You all right?" Beth asked.

"I'm not faking," Meg said defensively.

"I know you're not, buddy." Beth rested her hand

on her back. "Think you can get to the elevator?"

Meg scowled at her. "You're not going to make me do the *stairs?*"

"That would be sadistic," Beth said.

Meg nodded, taking it one slow step at a time, resting every so often. Her wheelchair was right by the door and she paused to look at it.

"Don't want to get *used* to the damned thing," Beth said.

"I *need* the damned thing," Meg said.

"No, you don't."

The little hall leaving the solarium sloped down to the Third Floor Sitting Hall — *very* convenient for wheelchairs — and rather hard going with one crutch. "You're an M.D. now?" Meg said, out of breath.

"Yes," Beth said. "My stepfather was very pleased."

Meg didn't have enough energy to respond to that, leaning against the wall, the elevator seeming very far away.

"You want to rest?" Beth asked.

Meg shook her head, pulling in a deep breath and grimly crutching her way across the hall to the alcove where the First Family private elevator and staircase were.

Beth pushed the elevator button. "You're tougher than you look."

Meg looked up, breathing hard from what had seemed like monumental exertion. "If I had a free hand, I'd slug you."

"Then I'm lucky you don't have a free hand." The elevator doors opened and Beth stepped aside. "After you."

Meg crutched inside, then sank against the wall.

Beth pushed the button for the second floor. "Home-stretch now."

Meg didn't answer her, resting.

When they got off the elevator, Beth gestured towards a closed door to their right: the White House Cosmetology Room.

"Want to stop off and get a manicure?" she asked.

Meg shook her head.

"Come on, that was funny."

"Hilarious," Meg said, slowly crutching towards the West Sitting Hall.

Her father, on the couch reading, glanced up, looking startled to see her.

"Anything wrong?" he asked.

Meg shook her head, sitting heavily at the round mahogany table they used for breakfast sometimes. Especially on weekends. "Beth was wondering when dinner is."

"Oh." He was maybe going to say more, but didn't. "Any time now, I think. Let me go get your mother and the boys."

As he left, Meg leaned her head on her arm, very tempted to fall asleep. Her mother came down the hall from the Treaty Room, holding her reading glasses in one hand, a thick folder in the other, a group of various aides and advisors clustered in the Stair Hall, just outside the Treaty Room.

"I *thought* I heard your voice," she said, looking surprised.

"Excuse me." Beth got up from the table, heading towards Meg's room. "I'm going to wash up for dinner."

Meg's mother hesitated, then sat down in the chair Beth had vacated. "I'm sorry," she said. "I know you don't really feel ready for visitors."

289

Meg looked down towards the group of advisors, mostly men, in grey suits. "Hey, *you're* the President," she said, shrugging. "It's your show."

Her mother ignored that. "I thought you needed to see her."

"Thank you," Meg said. "I'm not able to make these decisions for myself."

"Meg, I'm just — "

"Trying to help," Meg said. "Yeah."

"Yeah." Her mother stood up. "Have your father let me know when dinner's ready."

Beth was her usual self at dinner — fairly hyper, quite glib, and rather entertaining. Which was good, because everyone else was pretty quiet.

"So there we are," Beth said, nodding thank-you as a butler served her some salad, "in Tunisia, right? And Meg, of course, has *no* money. So, we go to this bar. A men's bar, really. And — " She paused, looking at Meg. "Would you like to tell the rest?"

"I wasn't listening," Meg said, eating a piece of ham. With her hand and all, her father or someone always had to cut the meat *for* her.

"Oh," Beth said, and grinned. "Then maybe we should speak of other things." She looked across the table at Steven. "Think they're going to win the pennant?"

"No," he said.

Beth nodded. "Now *that* is what I called dogged optimism. It's — it's inspirational."

He helped himself to some more baked beans. When Trudy cooked on a Saturday night, they *always* had baked beans. "Still don't think they're going to."

"Well, that's that Puritan heritage of yours," Beth

290

said sadly. "You really can't help yourself."

Meg shook her head, starting to be amused by this. "What a jerk."

Beth looked at her sternly. "Being a Puritan doesn't make him a jerk. Be more tolerant."

"Yeah," Meg said. "America is a melting pot."

"It certainly is," Beth agreed. "What a clever observation."

Meg laughed. "Jesus." Her parents were, reluctantly, used to them swearing, but she looked guiltily at Trudy. "Excuse me."

Meg's father smiled. "What kind of summer have they been having up there?" he asked Beth.

"Well." She gave that some thought. "It's been endless fun and happiness. I'd have to say."

"Kind of like here," Meg said.

"Well, not *quite* as fun," Beth said. "But then, I don't have your sunny disposition."

Meg grinned, motioning for Neal to pass her the potato salad.

"Graduation was pretty fun too," Beth said. "I came in first," she paused, "*and* second in the class, so I was pretty busy, but — " She shrugged, indicating helplessness in the face of her own success.

"Your family must have been very proud," Meg's mother said, her expression amused.

"Well, they were a little disappointed," Beth said. "They were hoping I'd come in *third* too."

"Ba-dum," Steven said and pointed at Neal who made a cymbals sound, a little late.

Meg couldn't not grin, passing her plate to her father for some more ham. Beth was, undeniably, a girl who knew how to have fun.

"So," Beth said, sitting back and plucking significantly at her sleeve, where the name "Louie" was embroidered. "What are we going to do after dinner?"

Meg, having just picked up her fork, put it down. "You're not going to make me *bowl*, are you?"

Beth looked down at her shirt, the pocket of which read: Clover Lane Bowling Championships, 1972. Duckpins, apparently. "You didn't notice my shirt?"

A shirt so pink that it almost certainly glowed in the dark. "Are you kidding?" Meg said. "Every ship within fifty miles changed course."

"Oh, now, don't exaggerate," Beth said. "Four miles. *Maybe* five."

There was, in fact, a bowling alley in the basement, and whenever Beth visited, she *always* insisted upon playing a few frames. Every once in a while, Meg and her brothers played for the hell of it, and once, Meg had had the rare privilege, and unforgettable pleasure, of seeing her parents play with the very patrician House Majority Leader — who was a close friend of her mother's — and his wife. One of those evenings when she would have damn near sold her soul to have a camera nearby.

"I feel we *must* play," Beth said. "Right after dinner."

"Us too?" Neal asked.

"Of course," Beth said, and looked down at Meg's crutch. "If you *want*, you can sit in your damn chair." She looked at Trudy. "Excuse me."

"Oh, yeah, sounds great," Meg said, handing her plate to Steven for another helping of baked beans, nodding when Trudy put a piece of brown bread on there too. As she took her plate back, she saw her parents exchange happy glances, and she flushed. Her mother, as a rule, had too much dignity to say "I told

292

you so" — but maybe it *hadn't* been such a terrible idea for Beth to come down and visit.

By the time dinner was over, Meg was so tired that it was an effort to sit up in her chair.

"Would you like some more cake?" Trudy asked. "Some ice cream?"

She shook her head. "No, thank you." Shaking her head made her even *more* tired, and she held back a yawn, resting her chin on her propped-up hand.

"You want to maybe skip bowling tonight?" Beth asked. "Watch some television?"

"I, uh — " She didn't want to be rude. "I'm sorry, I'm *really* tired." So tired that sitting here at the dinner table was beginning to make her feel panicky. "I kind of — I think I need — "

Her mother glanced at one of the butlers who instantly brought over her wheelchair, Meg nodding gratefully. The idea of moving was exhausting, but her father was already up and helping her into the chair.

Feeling guilty, she looked at Beth. "I'm sorry, I — I just can't — I'm really sorry," she said.

Beth shrugged, but was obviously uneasy. "No problem. I'll see you later."

Meg nodded, wishing desperately that she was already in bed, relieved when her parents took her down the hall, her mother helping her into her nightgown, then under the covers. As her father turned out her lamp — the bathroom light on — she was so glad to be in the safety of her bed that she almost started crying. Then, when her mother bent to kiss her good-night, she *did* start crying.

"This is why I can't have visitors," she said weakly. "It's too hard."

"It's all right," her mother said. "Beth understands."

No one understood. Meg pulled a Kleenex from the box by her pillow — a concept depressing in and of itself — wiping at her eyes. "I don't want her to be mad at me," she said. "I just — *I can't.*"

"Beth will be fine," her father said. "Don't worry about a thing."

Don't *worry*? Jesus, was he from another *planet*? She closed her eyes, tears squeezing out. "All right," she said, trying to keep her voice steady. "I just have to sleep."

"Okay." Her father bent to kiss her too. "We'll see you in the morning."

"*Please* don't let anyone come in here," Meg said, fighting back what felt like an *explosion* of tears inside. "I just want to sleep."

Her parents nodded, then quietly left the room.

Chapter
Twenty-nine

When she was sure she was alone, she let the tears come, turning her head away from the door, praying that no one would hear. She cried until she was so exhausted that she couldn't do anything *but* sleep, her arm over her eyes in case someone came in.

If nothing else, she slept *soundly*, not waking up — or maybe even moving — until Trudy knocked on her door the next morning and came in with her breakfast tray.

"Good morning, dear," Trudy said, putting the tray down on Meg's desk, then moving the curtains to let in some light. "How do you feel?"

Awful. Meg sat up with some difficulty, hoping that her eyes weren't as red as they *felt*. "I-I'm all right. I mean, good morning."

After helping her into the wheelchair so she could go get washed up, Trudy set up the tray for her —

orange juice, broccoli and mushroom quiche, toast triangles, a dish of strawberries and cream.

"I, uh — " Meg picked up her juice glass, still feeling as shaky and tired as she had the night before. "Is Beth still here?"

Trudy nodded. "Would you like her to come in?"

"Well, I — " The room seemed very bright and she wished Trudy would pull the shade back down. "I don't really — I guess so." She looked at her clock. Ten-fifteen. That meant that she would have to do the goddamned physical therapy in — Jesus, there was *no* way she could face that today. "I, uh, I don't feel very good. Can you tell them I'm going to stay in bed today? That I can't — I *really* don't feel good."

Trudy looked at her clock too. "Maybe after you — "

"Can you *please* tell them? I *need* to stay in bed today."

Trudy nodded, her eyes so sad that Meg couldn't look at her, focusing down on her breakfast.

"Thank you," Meg said. "For breakfast too."

After Trudy had been gone for a few minutes, there was a quiet knock on her door.

Her parents, to *make* her do her therapy, probably. "Who is it?"

"Me," Beth said.

Christ. "Okay," Meg said, feeling both embarrassed and defensive about being in bed with a tray.

Beth came in, wearing jeans and her old — but, Meg knew, beloved — Denver Carrington T-shirt. "Hi," she said, her hands awkward in her pockets. "How do you feel?"

Meg shrugged, not really looking at her, ashamed of how red her eyes — she knew, from her trip to the bathroom — were. "You, uh, you get breakfast and everything?"

Beth nodded. "Trudy went all-out."

Meg nodded too, although she hadn't really touched her *own* breakfast. "Uh, sorry about last night."

Beth shrugged. "Your brothers and I did some bowling."

"Oh. I mean, that's good," Meg said. "I guess they're not having much fun lately."

"Yeah," Beth agreed.

It was quiet for a minute.

"You should at least eat the strawberries," Beth said. "They were really good."

Meg nodded, and moved the dish closer, but didn't pick up her spoon.

"Look, I — " Beth stopped. "I don't know what I should do."

Go home. Meg shrugged, looking at her breakfast.

"Meg — " Beth let out her breath. "I don't know. You're a lot worse than I thought you'd be."

Meg looked up, furious. "It's not my fault!"

"I meant *feeling* worse, not *being* worse."

Oh. Meg scowled, but looked back down, her good hand clenched around the side of her tray.

"Look, just tell me what to do," Beth said. "I'll do whatever you want."

"I kind of — " She *really* didn't want to hurt Beth's feelings — "I want you to — " Oh, hell.

"I *know* you're not ready to see people yet," Beth said, her voice very quiet. "And Christ, the last thing I want to do is — " She stopped, her voice getting even quieter. "Did it ever occur to you that maybe *I* sort of needed to see *you?*"

Beth, whose goal in *life* was to be ever cool and

297

invulnerable? Beth, who — at the moment — looked rather small, and upset. "I don't know," Meg said.

"Well, think about it," Beth said.

Meg thought about it. Thought about how *she* would feel if something terrible happened to *Beth*. Thought about how much she would want to see *her*, be sure she was all right. "I'm sorry," she said, looking down. "It's just so hard."

"Dragging yourself through the fucking *woods* was hard," Beth said. "Hanging out with *me* is easy."

Meg smiled a little. "Oh, yeah?"

"I promise not to pressure you," Beth said. "You just tell me what you can't do, and we'll go from there."

"What I *can't* do?" That question was so all-encompassing that Meg smiled a little more. "How much time do you have?"

Beth grinned, sitting down in the rocking chair. "This girl has nothing *but* time."

They didn't do much. In fact, about the most Meg could manage was to watch some reruns. *Family Affair*. *Bewitched*. *Mister Ed*.

Beth looked at the *TV Guide*, then at her watch. "Hey, we're in luck — the *700 Club* is on!"

"Fun," Meg said.

Beth grinned, and flipped the channel to *The Addams Family*.

They were watching *Lassie* when her father and Trudy came in with lunch — chicken soup, BLTs, and — of all things — Trudy winking at her — Cokes.

Meg's father looked at the television. "Maybe we should have just brought you two some Jell-O."

"There's *always* room for Jell-O," Beth remarked, to no one in particular.

Meg's father smiled, then looked at Meg. "Bob" — Dr. Brooks — "is going to come in in a while? Say hello to you?"

Meg nodded, drinking her Coke.

They watched television for a long time. Dr. Brooks came in, checked her over, said jovially that a nice day of rest might be "just the ticket," and left; Steven came in with Neal, looked at the television, said, "Yo, you aren't going to watch the *Cubs* game?" and they left. Her mother called from the West Wing, "just to say hi."

"We're getting stupid, Meg," Beth said, as they watched *I Dream of Jeannie*. "I can *feel* it happening."

Meg nodded. She was, indeed, feeling pretty stupid. Anesthetized. "You want to call it quits?"

"Are you kidding?" Beth said. "With *The Brady Bunch* coming on next?"

Oh, yay. "I hope it's the one where Peter's voice changes," Meg said.

Beth shook her head. "I hope it's the one where Alice's cousin comes and makes them exercise."

It was the one where Jan is allergic to Tiger's new flea powder.

By the time the episode was over, Meg was so tired that she could barely see straight, but it was *good* tired.

"What's on now?" she asked, yawning. "Anything good?"

Beth also yawned, and looked in the *TV Guide*. "*Three's Company*."

"Perfect," Meg said.

* * *

299

When it was dinnertime, Beth looked over at her. "Well. What do you think?"

Meg sighed. "Okay, but that's *it* for tonight."

"Fair enough," Beth said.

So, Meg put on sweatpants and *her* — not quite *beloved*, but certainly well-*liked* — Denver Carrington T-shirt, and they went down to the Presidential Dining Room. They compromised, Meg riding the wheelchair down there, but crutching into the room.

She was too tired to participate in the dinner conversation, but luckily, Steven and Neal had spent the afternoon playing basketball with Preston and off-duty Secret Service agents, and were all charged up, agreeably yapping away throughout the meal. Beth was pretty quiet too, suffering — almost certainly — from a severe situation comedy overdose.

"Steven and me played *excellent*," Neal said, his mouth full of scalloped potatoes. "We — "

"Try some chewing and swallowing," their father suggested from the end of table, sounding much less annoyed than he ordinarily would have. *Before*, anyway.

Neal chewed and swallowed. "They couldn't stop us at *all* practically."

Steven laughed. "Yeah, you should have seen Baby Skyhook here. He's a wild man."

Meg grinned, picturing it. Steven had been coordinated before *birth*, but Neal was kind of a late-bloomer.

"So, hey." Steven pointed his fork at her. "We watching the game tonight?"

Meg shook her head. "I kind of think I'm sleeping tonight."

"Yo, you *traitor*," he said, and pointed his fork at Beth. "You watching?"

Beth shook her head too. "Sorry."

"Traitors," he said grimly. "I'm *totally* surrounded by traitors."

Meg grinned, finishing up her last piece of asparagus. Steven was pretty funny when he wanted to be.

"I bet those girls are going to watch the *Yankees*," he was saying to Neal. "I bet they're going to watch the Yankees and *clap*."

Beth laughed. "You know it," she said. "And the Mets are on the coast tonight, so we can watch *both* games."

Steven collapsed in his chair, pretending to faint. "Smelling salts," he said weakly to Trudy, who was sitting to his left. "Where are my smelling salts?"

"You just sit up and eat your dinner," she said. "Don't be so silly."

Meg found *that* amusing too. Trudy had always been one to crack the whip of authority, especially during meals. Her mother offered her more salad, and she shook her head, her eating energy depleted. But she sat through the rest of the meal, smiling at the right times, nodding or shaking her head if anyone asked her a question.

"You look like you've just about had it," her mother said, as Trudy — shooing away the butlers — served dessert.

Meg nodded.

"Are you sure you don't want some, dear?" Trudy asked her.

Butterscotch pie, no doubt delicious. Meg shook her head. "No, thank you. I'm full." She reached for her crutch, not looking at Beth. "In fact, I kind of think — "

"You're right," Beth said, getting up. "The Yankees game starts in about five minutes."

Shaking her head when her father moved to help her, Meg pushed herself to her feet, Beth going out to the hall to get the wheelchair.

"We'll be down to say good-night?" her father said.

Meg nodded, crutching her way to the hall.

The next morning, bright and early — if eleven o'clock was bright and early — Edith, the physical therapist, arrived. She was very nice, in her thirties, with blonde hair and glasses, but Meg sure as hell hated the therapy. Hated every minute of it. Each time, she had to fight the urge to throw a Presidential-progeny tantrum and intimidate Edith into not coming back. However, the odds of Dr. Brooks letting her skip two days in a row were slim.

Beth came down to the Nautilus room to watch, and Meg let herself be strapped into the weight machine, which was called an Orthotron, or something like that. Cybex. It was used a lot in sports medicine. Oh, yeah, like *she* was going to be playing sports again.

"Okay," Edith said, once she had set the resistance on the machine. "Can you do three sets of ten?"

No. Meg set her jaw, and forced the weight up with her right leg. Ten times. Ten more. Slowly, she started the final set, already perspiring, her leg shaking in protest. The weight was incredibly heavy, and even though she had seven repetitions to go, she had to stop.

"Come on," Edith said, very kind and encouraging. "You can do it."

302

Meg shook her head, breathing with some difficulty. "It's too hard."

Beth was sitting on the recumbent bicycle, her ankles propped up on the wheel, reading *Dispatches* by Michael Herr. As a concession to Meg's having to exercise, she had put on a pair of sweatpants too. Bright red. "Come on, keep going," she said, not even looking up. "You want to ski or not?"

Meg forced the weight up again, scowling over at her. "Can't you at least pedal that damn thing?"

Beth turned a page. "*I* don't want to ski."

Meg scowled and pushed the weight up again. Five more to go.

"That's it," Beth said as she managed another, and then another. "Keep it up."

"Easy," Meg forced the weight up, out of breath, "for *you* to say."

"Two months, Meg. Two months, and it'll be snowing out West."

Meg scowled at her, and finished the set of ten.

"Very good," Edith said, smiling at her. "Good job." She had a little bit of a *Romper Room* quality, but she *was* nice.

Beth turned a page. "Do ten more."

"*You* do ten more," Meg said, accepting the white towel Edith gave her, and wiping her face.

"Thanksgiving," Beth said. "Mountains all over the East will be open by Thanksgiving."

Meg gritted her teeth and started another set, keeping a hard, constant rhythm.

"Ski," Beth said conversationally to Edith, who looked a little nonplussed. " 'Ski' is the magic word. Say 'ski' and she'll do just about anything."

Seven, eight — Meg glared at her — nine, *ten*. She

let her leg fall, too out of breath to say anything.

"What does she do now?" Beth asked. "Pull the weights *down?*"

"Well" — Edith blinked a few times — "yes."

"Good." Beth nodded her approval, then focused on her book. "Sounds good."

Meg watched Edith set the machine for the opposite workout, her glasses slipping down. "The damn shuttle leaves every hour."

Beth nodded. "So you hear."

The machine was ready, and Edith checked to make sure the Velcro strap was fastened tightly around Meg's ankle, then stepped back.

"Three sets of ten?" Meg said.

Edith nodded.

Meg set her jaw, and began.

When the session was finally over and Edith had strapped ice packs to the arm and leg Meg had exercised — the regular routine — Edith left the room with a fluttery "I'll just see if Dr. Brooks — I'll be right back." Meg looked over at Beth, who was still reading.

"What happened to not pressuring me?" she asked.

"That wasn't pressure," Beth said. "That was *inspiration.*"

Right. "You make her nervous," Meg said, gesturing towards the door with her arm cast.

Beth shrugged. "She'll get used to me."

"You're staying that long?"

Beth laughed.

"Having fun?" Meg asked, tired enough from the exercises to feel good and grumpy.

Beth took a bookmark out of her red terry-cloth headband, and closed the book. "It looked pretty hard."

"I'm not even exercising the things I *hurt* yet."

Beth shrugged. "So, when it's time for that, you'll be in good shape."

"They don't even think I'm going to *walk* right, forget ski."

"You're already walking," Beth said.

Meg gestured towards the crutch. "You call that walking?"

"It's a start."

Meg slouched down, pressing the towel against her face, feeling heavy with fatigue. "You *really* don't understand how hard it is."

"It's going to be a long time before you do *anything* that isn't hard."

Meg lowered the towel. "That's cheering."

"Yeah." Beth looked at the door. "What happens now?"

"They come in and shoot electricity into me."

"Where?" Beth asked uneasily.

Meg sighed, very tired. "I put one hand in water, and the other in the socket."

Beth laughed. "Sounds healthy."

Meg sighed again. "They shoot it into my knee mostly," she said, gesturing towards a little machine with wires and suction cups, "and my hand a little too. It's supposed to stimulate healing."

"Oh." Beth looked at the machine dubiously. "Does it hurt?"

"Stings, sort of."

"Oh." Now, she looked at Meg. "This really isn't much fun, is it?"

"Not much fun at all," Meg said.

Chapter
Thirty

That night, pursuing the list of things Meg could and could not do, they went up to the solarium and watched *Murphy's Romance* — which Meg was sucker enough to have always loved — and ate popcorn, upon which Steven put altogether too much Parmesan cheese. Neal went a little heavy with the seasoned salt too.

After the movie, Meg crutched her way to the third floor elevator, then switched to the wheelchair for the ride downstairs, her crutch across her lap.

"So," Beth said, once they were on the second floor, pushing her in the wheelchair. "You tired?"

"I don't know." She'd had a *very* long nap that afternoon. "A little."

"You want to go downstairs? Look at the East Room and all?"

Meg shook her head, tensed in her chair. "If I go down there, I have to have agents."

"Oh." Beth thought about that. "You want to go outside for a while?"

"I *told* you," Meg said, "if I — "

"I meant the balcony," Beth said, indicating the Yellow Oval Room.

Meg shook her head, tensing more.

Beth sat down on one of the settees in the Center Sitting Hall — obviously a girl with nothing *but* time. "It's okay if you can't," she said. "I'm just wondering why."

Christ, was she stupid? "They can *see* me," Meg said.

"What, from the street?"

Meg nodded, the thought so terrifying that, even in the windowless Center Hall, she felt exposed. Afraid.

"We always sit out there when I come," Beth said. "And we *never* see anyone."

Meg hunched a little in the wheelchair. "We see people walking."

"We see little tiny shapes way far away," Beth said. "Besides, I thought that's why your parents have the lights kept low out there."

"That's to save energy."

"And here *I* was, thinking it was for privacy," Beth said.

Which was, of course, exactly what it was for. Meg sighed.

"If you don't like it, we can come right back in," Beth promised.

Meg sighed.

"Is that a yes?"

Meg sighed again, but nodded.

"Good." Beth pushed her wheelchair into the Yellow Oval Room, then moved the Chinese porcelain urn — complete with potted plant — that blocked the combination window and door to the Truman Balcony. As she opened the door, fresh summer air blew into the room, smelling warm and clean. "Hey, it *is* nice out," she said.

Meg nodded, hoisting herself up onto her crutch, concentrating on not being afraid. Or, at least, not letting Beth *see* that she was afraid.

"Need help?" Beth asked.

Meg shook her head, tremblingly making her way outside. *Outside.* She lowered herself onto the white wrought-iron couch — her parents had the balcony set up as a sort of porch, keeping her eyes down.

"Here." Beth took a cushion from one of the little white chairs and put it on the low coffee table. *Cocktail* table, more often.

Meg lifted her leg onto it. "Thanks."

"No problem," Beth said. "You want me to go get some soda or something?"

And leave her *alone* out here? "No," Meg said quickly.

"I'd only be gone a minute."

"*Please* don't," Meg said, ready to panic.

"Okay." Beth sat down. "No problem."

Meg took a few deep breaths, trying to relax. To get the courage to look *up*.

"Maybe it *is* a little chilly out here," Beth said, very casual. "You want to go inside?"

"I'm *fine*," Meg said, gripping the iron arm of the couch.

308

"If you're — "

"I'm *very* sure," Meg said. This was the White House; they were safe. No one could see them. They couldn't be too much *safer* than where they were, even if — she opened her eyes. "I-I am kind of thirsty — would you mind getting us something?"

Beth hesitated, then nodded. "Sure thing," she said, and got up. "Be right back."

Alone on the balcony — safe or not — Meg could feel herself shaking. Feel her heart beating. *Nothing* was going to happen. She was safe. *Here*, anyway. She forced herself to look up and out at the view: at the bright fountains on the South Lawn, at the Washington Monument, at the distant very dark blue of the Tidal Basin, the Potomac beyond. The Jefferson Memorial was ahead; the Capitol down the Mall to the left; the Lincoln and Vietnam Memorials to the right. She couldn't see *all* of them — but it seemed that way. Felt that way.

She took some more deep breaths. *No one* could see her. Maybe no one was even *looking*. And even if they were —

"Hi," Beth said, her voice muffled by the tortilla chips bag between her teeth. She put two tall glasses of lemonade and some napkins down on the table. "Look good?"

Meg nodded, letting out her breath.

Beth sat down. "Nice out here."

Realizing that her hand was cramping around the arm of the couch, Meg released it. "Yeah." She picked up her glass, and they sat there for a minute.

"You can talk or not," Beth said. "Whatever the hell you want."

"Not," Meg said.

Beth shrugged, opening the bag of chips. "Whatever you want."

They sat there for a long time, long enough to finish the lemonade and half of the chips.

"I can't talk to *anyone*," Meg said.

Beth nodded.

"I mean, I told the FBI stuff, but — " But, nothing *personal*. "I mean, I didn't *lie* to them, but — I don't know."

" 'Just the facts, ma'am,' " Beth said.

Meg nodded.

"What about your parents?"

Meg shook her head. "They're so upset that I don't — I mean, my mother especially."

"She must feel pretty guilty," Beth said.

Meg nodded.

Beth started to say something, then stopped.

"No," Meg said, anticipating the unspoken question. "I'm not all that mad at her. Just sometimes."

Beth nodded.

"I can't seem to talk to Josh either," Meg said. "I mean, about *anything*."

Beth shrugged. "You guys were having trouble talking before this even happened."

True. Meg nodded.

"It's probably better that you'd already broken up," Beth said. "This would have *really* messed things up."

Meg nodded. "I still want to be friends with him. I mean, you know."

"So we'll have him come over while I'm here," Beth said. "Maybe that'll make things easier."

Maybe. Meg nodded, looking out at the dark night,

310

and the bright monuments. Then, she looked back at Beth, who shrugged. Receptively.

"How much do you know?" she asked. "About what happened?"

"I don't know," Beth said. "Pretty much, I guess."

"Details?"

"I *think* so," Beth said, uncertainly. "I mean, you know, everything that was in the papers and *Newsweek* and all."

Meg frowned. "I haven't seen any papers." Although she was pretty sure that the White House had released the simplest version possible. Just enough to be plausible. "Did my mother tell you stuff?"

"Some," Beth said, nodding. "Preston did too."

She didn't like to think of people talking behind her back. "When was *that*?" she asked stiffly.

"He was with the car that picked me up at the airport."

Oh. That made sense — obviously, Beth hadn't taken the *subway* to the White House. Meg frowned some more. "So, basically, you know what happened?"

Beth nodded.

Of course, she hadn't even told her *parents* everything. None of the more — personal — things. She looked over at Beth, who shrugged again.

Oh, hell. "I got drunk with him," she said. Something *no one* knew.

"One of — them?" Beth asked.

"Just this one guy. He was the only one I ever really saw."

Beth nodded.

"It was after he ripped my knee up — I don't know how long." Meg stopped. Getting into this was a mistake. Maybe she should just go inside to bed, and —

"What happened then?" Beth asked.

Meg shook her head, looking out over the South Lawn.

"Come on, Meg," Beth said. "You have to tell *someone*."

Meg took a deep breath, then let it out. "I got drunk with him. He had this bottle of J & B, and he wanted me to have some too."

Beth nodded.

"My *father* drinks that."

Beth nodded.

"I don't know what his motive was. I mean, maybe he thought I'd get sick, and he could laugh, or — I don't know."

"Pretty weird," Beth said.

It was Meg's turn to nod. "I got *literally* drunk. I mean, I never really have before." She looked over uncertainly. "You think there's something wrong with me?"

"For not getting *drunk* before?"

Meg shook her head. "No, for — talking to him."

"Doesn't sound like you had much choice," Beth said.

"No, but — " Meg shivered. Thinking about this was — "I was so sure he was going to rape me."

Beth didn't say anything, but Meg saw her shoulders hunch up.

"Every time he came in, I thought — only then, I — " Meg stopped. "Don't tell anyone this."

"I won't," Beth said.

"Don't tell *anyone*. Not about *any* of this."

"You know I won't, Meg."

Which Meg *did* know. "I kind of" — this was hu-

312

miliating — "I offered to — I asked him if my, you know, would keep him from — well — "

"Sounds *smart* to me," Beth said.

Meg shook her head, ashamed all over again.

"He was going to *kill* you."

Meg nodded.

"What happened then?" Beth asked, after a pause.

"He, uh, said it wouldn't make any difference."

"That was honest of him."

Meg looked up. "He *was* honest." Like about Josh? "I mean — I can't explain it." Beth didn't say anything, and she took a deep breath. "I *would* have done it. I mean, if I thought — " She met Beth's eyes. "Don't *ever* tell anyone."

"I'm not going to," Beth said.

"You can't. They'd think I — "

"I'm not going to," Beth said, "but everyone would understand. I mean, if something's going to save your *life*, you do it."

Meg nodded, automatically looking at her hand.

"Yeah," Beth said, following her gaze. "Like that."

"Yeah." Meg looked away from it. "I think that night saved my life. I mean, talking to him and all."

Beth nodded.

"I think he kind of — I think he *liked* me."

Beth nodded.

Meg looked around, even though she knew they were alone. "Can I tell you something worse?"

"Sure," Beth said.

"I liked *him*." She could feel herself blushing. "I don't mean I *liked* him" — yeah, she did — "but, he — he reminded me of Preston." Horribly enough.

Beth's eyebrows went up. "Of *Preston*?"

"Yeah." It was cold and Meg folded her good arm

around herself. "I mean, not *exactly*, but — " But what? "Like if he had an evil twin."

Beth laughed. "An *evil twin?*"

Meg didn't laugh. "I'm serious."

"Yeah, I know. I just — *Preston?*"

Meg nodded. "He was really smart. And really — calm. And — a little amused all the time, you know?"

Beth nodded too.

"He got my jokes."

"No *wonder* you liked him," Beth said.

"I didn't like him, I — " She sighed. "Yeah, I did. I mean — " She tried to think of a good comparison. It was too upsetting to associate him — in any way — with one of her favorite people in the world. "Like, like if you had a *really* sadistic big brother who you followed around *anyway.*"

"Jesus," Beth said.

"I know I'm not explaining it right." Meg glanced over, trying to read her reaction. "He could have killed me. He *should* have."

"Yeah, but — " Beth shook her head. "He didn't exactly put you on a bus to Washington."

"No," Meg said slowly, "but — "

"Preston *would* have killed you."

Meg stared at her, instantly afraid. "What?"

"I don't mean Preston would hurt you," Beth said. "Ever. I just — he wouldn't *leave* someone like that. Leave them to suffer."

"Yeah, but — " Meg blinked a few times, trying to digest that. "I got away."

"He didn't *plan* it that way," Beth said, her arms tightly folded. "I mean — he chained you up. He *nailed* you in. I mean — *Jesus.*"

314

"You mean he *wanted* me to die like that? *Really* horribly?"

"I don't know," Beth said. "But I wouldn't be grateful to him for something *you* did yourself."

Meg thought about that; remembered lying in the dirt, the heavy chain clamped around her wrist, slowly, slowly feeling her life disappear. Hour by hour, minute by minute even, she'd felt — "I guess it wasn't very — humane," she said.

"I guess *not*," Beth said.

Thinking about it, about the enormity of being able to sit out on the balcony, quiet and safe, her family just a few rooms away, Meg shivered again. Hard. "I'm really not supposed to be here, am I?" she said.

Beth seemed to shiver too. "No."

There didn't seem to be much to say, so Meg leaned back, looking at the few stars she could see beyond all the lights. Funny to think how many, many more there were beyond the ones she could usually see.

"You're looking pretty tired," Beth said.

Meg laughed weakly. So what else was new?

"You want to call it a night?"

Meg nodded, reaching for her crutch.

Chapter
Thirty-one

Beth sat in on the physical therapy for the next several days. Often, she gave slightly skewed sports advice; otherwise, she just read whatever book she was holding. Meg gritted her teeth and lifted and pulled and pushed the various weights. Edith was very pleased. Dr. Brooks and the various orthopedic surgeons were too.

After exercising, and sitting through the electro-stimulus therapy, Meg would take one of the uncomfortable baths, then get into bed with a very small lunch tray. Usually, she would take a nap. Then, Beth would "convince" her to get up and have dinner with everyone and after that, they would watch a movie or a baseball game with Steven and Neal. Generally, her father or Preston would sit up there with them too. And, increasingly, Preston didn't remind her of anyone but himself. Thank God.

Things were getting enough back to normal so that Steven and Neal started having their friends over sometimes. Steven's best friends were Vinnie and Ed, who were both punks. Cute punks, but still punks. In Meg's opinion. Neal's closest friend was Ahmed, a nice little boy with thick glasses, who always wore a turtleneck. Always.

Her parents and Trudy were *around*, but not obtrusively. Her mother was pretty much one hundred percent back to work, which Meg thought was a relief. Even though she was — Meg sensed — spending a hell of a lot of time sequestered with FBI agents and the like. They hadn't made *much* progress, but they had done things like find the mine shaft. Which turned out to be — not that Meg really wanted any details — precisely that: an abandoned mine shaft way the hell in the middle of the woods. Regardless, although the trip to Geneva had been indefinitely postponed — late fall, perhaps — and they weren't exactly having state dinners all over the place, at least there were signals that the White House was back in business. So to speak.

At night, after Steven and Neal went to bed, she and Beth would sit up in the solarium, or out on the Truman Balcony, talking or not. Beth didn't push her, always receptive, but never pressing for details. So, Meg found herself telling her more than she would have otherwise. What had happened, how she felt, how afraid she had been. She never really talked about how afraid she still *was*, but Beth probably figured it out. Especially since she still refused to go down to the First Floor even, forget outside.

On Sunday morning — Dr. Brooks had decided that it could be a day of rest — Meg was the last one to get up. By a long shot. Late enough so that it was prudent to eat lunch instead of breakfast. On, happily enough, a tray. Beth appeared in her room shortly after the tray did.

"What's on for today?" she asked, wearing shorts, a wild blue-and-yellow Hawaiian shirt, and her black high-top Converse All-Stars.

Meg shook her head. "You're too cool for me."

Beth looked down at herself, and grinned. "Well, *everyone* knows that." She sat on the bottom of the bed. "So. What are we going to do?"

Odds were, Beth wasn't going to let her spend the day resting in bed. "I don't know." Meg made herself eat a spoonful of her Mexican omelet. "What do *you* want to do?"

"It's really nice out," Beth said. "Let's sit out on the roof. Get some sun."

Meg sighed. Okay. "Out on the Promenade maybe? Near the solarium?"

"Sure," Beth said. "Why don't we call Josh too? See if he wants to come over."

Meg thought about that, then reached for her telephone. "Okay."

Josh, it turned out, had the day off from his job at the golf course, and so the three of them ended up sitting out on the Promenade on chaise longues, Meg feeling self-consciously pale in her shorts and T-shirt and casts. Especially next to the two of them.

"Fifteen SPF," Beth said, handing her a tube of suntan lotion. "*Minimum.* Maybe even twenty."

"Thank you, Doctor," Meg said, and put some on her face, neck, and exposed leg.

"Can you get your arm okay?" Josh asked.

Probably not. She shook her head and handed the

tube to him, Josh smoothing on the lotion very gently.

"Thank you," she said.

"No problem," he said.

"We all have our shades?" Beth asked, already wearing a pair of white cat-eyes.

Meg, who had decided to drape the pair Preston had given her rakishly from her collar, put them on.

Josh took the folded baseball cap out of the back pocket of his shorts, putting it on. It was the same cap he'd been wearing the day everything happened, and looking at it made Meg feel sad. More sad than scared, since she knew he'd had that cap all through high school and loved it. At one point, the coach had tried to make him take a new, less battered one, but he had — a mistake, in Meg's opinion — refused.

"Am I tan yet?" Beth asked, holding out her arms.

"Bronze," Meg said.

"Good." Beth lowered her arms. "So are you."

"Unh-hunh." She looked at Josh, who was putting on some of the suntan lotion. "I, uh, I'm glad you weren't working today."

He looked very happy. "Me too."

That said, Meg lay back on the chaise longue, the sun feeling nice and warm. "You know," she said, "we're missing the Red Sox game, being out here."

Beth didn't even lift her head. "Neal's going to come out every now and then, keep us up-to-date."

"Do you think of *everything*?" Meg asked.

"Yes," Beth said. "I do."

They had a pleasant afternoon, talking a little, but mainly just lying in the sunshine. Neal, as advertised, appeared every half hour or so.

"Steven say to tell you Burks just *hammered* that baby!" He bellowed over to them on his third trip out.

319

Meg lifted her head. "He took a *hammer* to a *baby?*" she said, pretending to be confused.

"Home run, probably," Josh said, without looking up. "At *least* a double."

Beth shook her head. "Boys are so smart."

"I know," Meg said. "It's amazing." She turned back towards Neal. "What's the score?" she yelled.

"They're winning!" he yelled back, and went away again.

They lay in the sun some more, Meg feeling very comfortable, and a little sleepy.

"We need some food," Beth said. "And something with *ice.*"

Meg opened her eyes. "Just yell in to Steven and Neal. They can have someone — "

"No, I'll go downstairs." Beth got up. "Be right back."

Meg watched her go, feeling sort of nervous about being alone with Josh. Awkward. Which was, no doubt, precisely why Beth had left. She glanced over, seeing that he looked uneasy too.

"You're feeling better?" he asked. "I mean, lately?"

She nodded.

"You *look* better," he said.

"Thanks." She tried to think of something to say. "You do too. I mean, you have a really good tan."

"Caddie tan," he said.

Which meant sock, sleeve, *and* shorts lines. Like the tennis tans she'd always had. Except that she didn't particularly want to think about tennis. "Um, what have you been doing lately?"

He shrugged. "I don't know. Work, mostly."

"You're having *some* fun, right?"

"Nothing too exciting."

320

"You *should* have fun," Meg said. "I mean —
Christ."

He shrugged, not really looking at her.

"Josh — "

"I *miss* you," he said.

She nodded self-consciously.

"It's okay if I say that?"

She had to smile. "Yeah."

It was quiet for a minute.

"Is it, um, mutual?" he asked.

She looked at him, at his nice, kind face, then
nodded. "Yeah," she said. "It is."

Hesitantly, he reached out, touching her arm, his
hand feeling very warm. "I just want to be friends. I
mean, if that's all *you* want."

Here came the pressure. She let out her breath.
"That's all I can *handle*, Josh."

He nodded.

"I *do* miss you," she said. "It's just — everything's
still kind of an effort."

He nodded, giving her arm a squeeze, then letting
go.

"It doesn't mean I don't want to see you," she said.
"I'm just — taking it slowly."

He nodded, and neither of them said anything for
a minute, Meg wondering what the hell was taking
Beth so long to get back.

"So," Josh checked her expression, "it'd be okay if
I maybe gave you a call sometimes? On my day off,
or whatever?"

She tensed. "I can't *go* anywhere. I mean, not even
downstairs. Or — "

"This is nice," he said, indicating their chairs.
"Being in the sun and all."

321

She relaxed a little. "Yeah. This is fine."

"And," he said, "you *know* how much I like watching your family's favorite baseball team."

This, from the guy she had seen wearing an old Washington Senators T-shirt — *very* old; it must have been his father's originally — and, many times, wearing a Baltimore Orioles cap. "Right," she said, relaxing more.

"They're *always* entertaining," he said.

She smiled.

"I remember *one* time when I was watching them," he said, "they had this nine-run lead, and — "

"Josh, you are on *unbelievably* thin ice," she said, cutting him off.

He grinned, and subsided.

"*So* thin that — "

"I think Greenwell's better than Mattingly," he said. "Really."

Now *that* was more like it. "Much better," she said.

"And Bucky Dent's bat *must* have been corked."

Meg laughed. "Okay. You're forgiven."

"Hey, check it out!" Beth called, carrying a full plate and some napkins, Felix — Meg's favorite among the butlers — behind her with a tray of iced tea. "Trudy made petits fours!"

Meg loved petits fours.

"You know," Beth said, once she was settled back on her chaise longue, with her tea. "There really *are* worse places to live."

"Yeah, really," Josh said, eating petits fours.

Meg thought about that, then sighed. "Yeah," she said. "There probably are."

* * *

322

That night, although clouds had rolled in and it was sort of misty and cool, Meg and Beth sat out on the Truman Balcony, Meg drinking Coke, Beth drinking Evian. The Washington Monument and the Jefferson Memorial looked all the more impressive, but somewhat eerie in the light fog.

"You and Josh looked like you were having an okay time today," Beth said.

Meg nodded.

"Did you talk? You know, when I left?"

Meg grinned wryly. "I *knew* you left on purpose."

"Well, hell," Beth said, and also grinned. "So you talked?"

"A little, yeah."

The fog was thickening, a few raindrops beginning to fall.

"You going to be more specific?" Beth asked.

Meg laughed, drinking some Coke.

"I tell *you* the many details of *my* social life," Beth pointed out.

"Like the time you and Preston had your secret tryst in the Cayman Islands?"

"The *Canary* Islands," Beth said.

Meg laughed.

"I have my *bank* account in the Cayman Islands."

Meg laughed again.

It was raining harder, the sound quiet on the cement driveway and grass lawn below them.

"Anyway," Beth said.

Meg shrugged. "He wants to be friends. Maybe come over on his days off."

"That sounds okay."

Meg nodded. "As long as he doesn't push me."

323

Beth nodded too, looking out across the lawn, the trees bobbing slightly in the wind.

"He'll be going away pretty soon," Meg said.

Beth nodded, looking over at her.

"I mean, *everyone* will." Everyone *else*.

"You want to talk about that?" Beth asked, her voice noticeably offhand.

Did she? No. "Not really," Meg said, and sighed. "I'm not even ready to *think* about it."

Beth nodded, and they watched the rain.

"Getting cold out here," Meg said.

Beth nodded, and handed her her crutch.

Chapter
Thirty-two

Beth was going to leave on Thursday, and on Wednesday night, she suggested that they go outside. For real.

"Oh, come on," Meg said. "I like the balcony."

Beth was already putting on a hooded sweatshirt and taking another out of Meg's dresser for her to wear.

Meg sighed, putting it on. "If I leave the private quarters, I have to have agents."

Beth handed her the phone. "Here. Let them know we're coming."

It was strange to have agents with her — except for going to the hospital, it had been a long time. And she wasn't sure if she felt guilty, because of poor Chet, or a little afraid of them. Four of them, one a woman, came outside with them, and Meg was pretty sure that there were a few more lurking ahead of them somewhere.

"We aren't just going to sit in the Rose Garden?" Meg asked, as Beth pushed her wheelchair along the cement oval.

"Too boring," Beth said.

"You'd better not take me over to the tennis court."

"It's nice over there," Beth said. "Trees and all."

Meg slouched down in the wheelchair. "Goddamn it."

When they were at the edge of the oval, Beth stopped the chair and Meg got up, crutching over to the court, which was almost unnaturally quiet. She looked around, feeling miserable, and sat in one of the courtside chairs. Beth sat down in another.

"You've got a lot of nerve making me come out here," she said.

"You've got a lot of nerve *coming* out here," Beth said cheerfully.

Meg stared out at the empty court, then down at her leg, feeling a surge of tremendous hatred for the son of a bitch who had ruined all of this for her. Who had ruined her whole *life*.

"Nice weather we're having," Beth said.

Meg scowled at her.

"Just an observation," Beth said.

They sat there, Meg feeling both furious and devastated, keeping her left fist clenched.

"So?" Beth said.

Meg sighed. "I was going to be a tennis player."

"Oh, you were not," Beth said.

"What do *you* know about it?"

"*You* were going to be a tennis player, like *I'm* going to win an Academy Award," Beth said.

Meg frowned. "You don't even act."

326

"I know," Beth said, and looked sad. "That's why it's going to be even *harder* for *me*."

Meg kept frowning at her. "So what's your point?"

"I just think you were destined for other things, that's all."

"Like what?"

Beth shrugged. "I don't know." Then, she grinned. "I wouldn't be surprised to turn around and see you be the House Majority Leader."

"*Never*," Meg said.

"Who knows."

"Yeah, well, *that* one you can count on," Meg said.

"Maybe." Beth grinned again. "How about Assistant District Attorney somewhere?"

"*Assistant?*"

"She has an ego and *a half*," Beth said to no one in particular.

Meg flushed. "I do not."

"Oh. Okay. You don't."

"I don't," Meg said defensively.

Beth nodded.

"Besides, I'm not going to school *anyway*."

"They'll figure something out," Beth said. "I mean, Steven and Neal are getting to go places again."

"Places like the *movies*."

"It's a start."

"I guess so." Meg sighed. "Hell, even if they *would* let me, I couldn't do it."

"You're still scared?"

There was a stupid question. "Wouldn't *you* be?"

Beth nodded.

"Besides, it's only a month away. I have to have operations, and all kinds of therapy, and they *still* don't — "

"So take a year off," Beth said. "Or, at least, a semester."

Meg stopped, briefly, feeling sorry for herself. "Go in January?"

"Why not?" Beth asked. "That's what people who get wait-listed do."

"Yeah, but — I'd be *behind*."

"Behind what?"

"Well — " Meg frowned. "You're supposed to — "

"What, the world'll stop if you don't graduate in *precisely* four years?"

"No, but — "

"What do you think the odds are that *I'm* going to finish in eight nice, neat semesters?" Beth asked.

Meg grinned. Slim to none. "Well, I'm kind of more — "

"Conventional," Beth said.

"Yeah," Meg said.

"Well, you Puritans are like that."

"Yeah." Although she could always make up the lost semester — or two — during the summers and — then, the obvious, simple solution occurred to her. "Hey, I could go part-time. Here in the city." And George Washington University was *literally* a couple of blocks away from the White House. Surely, her parents and the Secret Service could work something out. She looked over at Beth, feeling — almost — excited. "That might be — okay," she said. "Sort of."

"Well, don't be *too* enthusiastic," Beth said.

Meg grinned, but then thought about the *reality* of the situation. The way people would stare at her, or maybe come after her, or — the way the press would —

"What," Beth said, seeing her expression.

328

Meg looked around uneasily, even though the tennis court was dark, and quiet, and secluded. "I don't think I can go out in public. I mean, even if I *were* safe. Everyone'll — I mean, I couldn't go anywhere *before* without people staring, and hanging around and all."

"I guess it'll be a lot worse now," Beth said.

"I guess," Meg said, wryly. And nothing like having a crippled hand and leg to make herself even *more* conspicuous.

Beth was looking at her leg too. "You'll go *nuts* if you don't get out of here at some point. I mean, even if you are — well — "

"A pariah," Meg said.

"Well — not *that* bad."

Worse, in all likelihood.

"I don't think there's anything *evil* about it," Beth said. "I just think — people are worried about you. They want to know you're okay and all."

Meg nodded. Judging from the stacks of mail that were still swamping the Correspondence Office, that was probably true. She hadn't had the energy to look at more than a few — Preston generally had some with him — but had been startled by how genuinely heartfelt they were. Letters from people all over the country — and other countries, people she had never *met*, from places she had never been, who wrote about how hard they'd prayed, how happy they were she was safe, how they just wanted to let her know how they felt. Very nice, sweet letters.

"All these people wrote that they cried," she said. "You know, when they heard I was safe."

"I'm sure they did," Beth said quietly. "It was really something."

"You *saw* it? I mean, you were watching television?"

Beth shook her head. "My stepfather was. He called us." She grinned. "He *hugged* me, if you can believe it."

"Who announced it — Linda?" Linda was her mother's press secretary, blonde and aloof, and always *all* business.

Beth nodded. "Yeah, you should have seen it. She's got this big grin on, and the press room's clapping, and — everyone was pretty happy. I mean, it was sort of scary because I guess the networks heard something was happening, because they cut to it *before* she came out, and you've got Dan Rather saying that they knew the President was en route *somewhere*, and there would be an announcement any time now, and then Linda comes out with this big — " She stopped, her eyes very bright. "Well," she said, and looked away, whisking her sleeve across her eyes.

"Pretty dramatic," Meg said.

"Pretty *amazing*," Beth said.

They sat there for a minute, Meg thinking about how strange it was that something that was so very personal could also be so very public.

"I have to face them," she said. "The press, I mean."

Beth nodded.

"It'll be scary."

"Do an exclusive with someone," Beth said. "Someone you like."

Meg shook her head. "I owe them for the blackout — I should talk to *all* of them." All of them who had *honored* the blackout.

"I think that's a good idea," Beth said. "Clear the air."

Meg nodded, and they sat there some more, looking out at the tennis court.

"I, uh — " Meg coughed. She was never one to get emotional. If possible. "I'm glad you came. To see me and all. I mean — " She coughed again. "Thank you."

Beth grinned. "Kind of a nightmare for you to say that?"

Meg shrugged, embarrassed.

"What I like," Beth said, "is that you're not uptight. It's refreshing."

Meg managed a sheepish smile, not looking up.

"I'm glad I came too," Beth said. "I mean," now *she* looked uncomfortable, "you know."

Meg nodded, and they both looked in different directions.

"I'm afraid," Meg said, after a while.

Beth nodded. "I am too."

Not expecting that, Meg looked over. "You are?"

"Well, yeah. I mean — " Beth's expression was pretty embarrassed too. "I don't want anything to happen to you."

Meg couldn't think of anything to say, and Beth couldn't seem to either.

Finally, Meg broke the silence. "Well."

"Yeah." Beth stood up. "Let's go watch a movie."

Despite its being her favorite show in life, because of all the violence, Meg hadn't watched a *Hill Street Blues* tape since — everything. "Want to watch some *Hill Street*?"

"Do you?" Beth asked.

"Yeah," Meg said. "Let's give it a try."

When Beth was gone, the house seemed very quiet. Much more so than usual. They had watched two *Hill Street Blues* episodes the night before, and after Beth left that morning, Meg spent the afternoon and eve-

331

ning watching more episodes, sometimes alone, sometimes not.

At about eleven, her mother came in, looking very
tired.

"Working all this time?" Meg asked. She had only
been with them briefly at dinner before hurrying back
to the West Wing.

Her mother studied her before answering. "A lot of
catching up to do."

Meg nodded. Probably a *hell* of a lot.

Her mother looked at the television, where Meg was
almost through with her second six-episode tape.
"Aren't you beginning to overdose on this?"

"Yeah." She knew each of the episodes so well that
so far, even during the occasional hostage scene, the
violence wasn't bothering her. Much.

"Did Beth call and let you know she got home all
right?"

Meg nodded.

"It was good to see her."

Meg nodded.

"Well." Her mother bent to straighten her pillows.
"Is there anything you — ?"

"Thank you for calling her," Meg said. "I guess I
did need to see her."

Despite the fact that she was a politician and spent
most of her life putting on smiles, her mother's *happy*
smile was always a special surprise. "I'm glad you feel
better."

"Yeah," Meg said. "I think I do."

Her mother's smile was more like a *beam*. "I'm glad."

"How's, um, everything going? With the country
and all." She hadn't exactly been keeping up with
current events lately.

Her mother didn't answer right away. "It looks like they're holding their own."

Like the poor old Red Sox, who were *still* three and a half games out. "Well, that's good," Meg said. "I mean — " She patted Vanessa, who was curled up by her leg cast. "I like knowing who's in charge. It makes me feel — safe." She busied herself with the remote-control box, fast-forwarding past some commercials.

"I *do* think we're safest here," her mother said slowly. "That they're working very hard."

Meg nodded. The Secret Service was nothing if not driven in its efforts to keep them protected now. Steven had been allowed to go out to a couple of movies, and Neal had gone to a birthday party.

"Beth and I were talking about, you know, rising above," she said.

Her mother nodded.

"Like, that I've got to do *something*. And not just — I don't know," — Meg tried to think of the right word — "*languish*." Close enough.

Her mother nodded, sitting down in the rocking chair.

"I want to go away to school in January. Give them time to get things set up, and for me to — " She gestured towards her casts.

"Okay," her mother said, her voice less enthusiastic than her expression.

"I *want* to," Meg said. "I want to be normal."

Her mother nodded. "I *want* you to be."

"Are Steven and Neal going to be able to too? Go to school and all?"

Her mother nodded. "Your father and I are working with Gabler." The man in charge of the White House Security Detail.

"Think he can arrange for some security at GW? So I can take a couple of classes this fall maybe?"

"Another decision," her mother said.

"Yeah," Meg said, her voice purposely firm. Confident. "I don't want to get too far behind."

Her mother nodded.

Of course there was the little problem of her not being registered there. "Can you arrange to have me *admitted* there too?"

Her mother grinned. "Maybe I can pull a couple of strings."

Meg grinned too. "Thought that might be in your jurisdiction."

"Consider it done," her mother said.

Good. Meg took a deep breath. "One more thing."

"Okay," her mother said.

"I want" — *did* she? — "I think I want to have a press conference."

Her mother looked surprised. "You *do*?"

Meg nodded.

"Get everything out in the open, so they won't mob you later?"

Meg nodded.

After a minute, her mother nodded too. "The idea has merit."

"Yeah," Meg said. "I mean, I know they'll keep bugging me, but if I answer everything *once*, I don't have to again, if I don't want to." Ever.

"It makes sense," her mother said. "Your father and I can — "

"How about just Preston?" Meg said. "Like, so I can do it by myself."

"Okay." Her mother smiled. "Sure."

"Thanks," Meg said. And, hey, while her mother

was in such a generous mood — "Can I have a car too?" So what if she didn't drive. "And an apartment in New York, and — "

"How about a nightclub?" her mother suggested. "We could give you your own nightclub. And maybe apartments in London, and Paris, and — "

"Thanks." Meg grinned. "I'll let you know if there's anything else."

"You do that," her mother said.

Chapter
Thirty-three

Preston agreed to set the press conference up for Tuesday morning. CNN was going to carry it live; he wasn't sure about the networks. She hadn't thought that the whole thing would get so major, but when she called Beth to get her opinion, Beth said that she should go for it. That she should take a trip to the Cosmetology Room, even.

Josh came over on Monday afternoon — it was raining, so she knew he wouldn't be working — and helped her pick out an outfit. Actually, he didn't help much at all, saying things like, *"That's* pretty," and "Yeah, that's pretty too." Preston made the final decision, choosing a dress that he thought would look especially nice against the background curtains in the White House Press Room. And, he said, a splash of color at her neck and she would "knock 'em silly."

That night, Meg watched part of the Red Sox game up in the solarium with her father and brothers, but started feeling so nervous that she excused herself and went down to her room to rest. Her father came down after her, tucking her in, bringing her a Coke, being generally supportive.

He sat down on the edge of the bed. "Big day tomorrow."

Meg nodded, sipping Coke.

"Sure you don't want your mother and me in there with you?"

She nodded. "I want to do it myself."

"Okay," he said, patting her shoulder. "But don't be afraid to change your mind — even once it starts."

"What," she said, "get up in the middle of it?"

He shook his head. "We could have a code word."

Maybe she'd been watching too many *Hill Street* episodes, but that struck her funny. "What," she grinned, "say '*Gosh*, it's *hot* in here,' and you guys'll come running in?"

He nodded seriously. "Something like that, sure."

The image was so funny — her parents bursting in — live — that it was hard not to laugh. "I think I'll pass, Dad."

"The option is always there though."

Meg nodded, even closer to laughing.

"Been a pretty tough summer so far," he said.

Ah, understatement. "It's been a pretty tough *year*."

He nodded.

"Do you think things are going to be all right?"

"It seems only fair," he said.

Meg nodded. They were *due* for a good spell.

"I really am proud of you," he said. "More than you'll ever know."

"Uh, thank you," Meg said, managing *not* to do her patented cough of embarrassment.

"If you want," he said, "maybe tomorrow night, you and your mother and I can sit down and look over the GW catalog. See what sort of classes you'll want to take."

What a nice idea. She smiled at him. "I'd like that, Dad. I'd like that a lot."

The switchboard woke her up early the next morning. She lay in bed without moving, feeling very tired, and a little sick to her stomach. She had had a couple of nightmares — none, luckily, that woke her up screaming — and this press conference idea was beginning to seem like a big mistake. However.

"What do you think?" she asked Vanessa, who yawned a big yawn, a *squeaky* yawn, and stretched. *There* was a "no comment" if she'd ever heard one.

She sat up, stretching a little herself. Like the saying went, she was already *on* the merry-go-round, so she might as well enjoy the ride.

She took the best bath she could, shaving her leg and so forth. Not that it would really matter — Preston was going to have a cloth-covered table set up so she could sit down and her cast wouldn't show. And no *way* was she going to wear her sling.

The dress was beautiful — a deep, rich red linen. A little Republican, but what the hell. The collar — shirt-dressy — *would* look better with a scarf, but she wasn't sure if she had the nerve to wear one. The élan. Maybe she would go the New England route and settle for some discreet pearls. She *did* like her pearls, which she had gotten for her sixteenth birthday.

338

Finally dressed, and feeling self-conscious, she crutched her way down to the Presidential Dining Room. The crutch, she suspected, spoiled the line of the dress. She paused in the doorway, seeing her family and Trudy already in there. They looked up with the usual concern.

"Good *morning*, peasants," she said cheerfully. *That* got their attention. "Yes, it is I this A.M. The Queen." This A.M. It was official — she had become Sergeant Esterhaus's clone.

"You look beautiful," her father said.

"Well, thank you," she said.

"You change parties or something?" Steven asked, eating some toast.

How nice to share a sense of humor with someone. "Yes," she said. "In fact, I'll be announcing my candidacy today." She crutched her way into the room, sitting down more clumsily than she would have liked. "No, it's okay," she said as Trudy started to get up. "I'm just going to have some cereal."

Neal came over with a box of Captain Crunch.

"Well, thank you, youngster," she said. "Will you pour it for me, please?"

He did, uncertainly.

"Well, thank you." She handed him her napkin ring. "Here's a prize." Her stomach felt too uncertain for her to eat, but she poured some milk over the cereal anyway, Trudy pouring her a glass of orange juice. "Thank you."

"Would you like some toast?" her mother asked. "A muffin?"

"What I *really* want is some clotted cream." She picked up her spoon, decided that she had no appetite, and tried some juice instead.

"Would you like a different kind of cereal?" Trudy asked.

Meg shook her head. "Actually," she swallowed, "the Queen doesn't have much appetite."

"That is so cool," Steven said. "Talking in the third person and all."

Meg grinned. "If you're lucky, maybe I'll teach you how."

"Excellent," he said, and helped himself to a muffin.

After breakfast — half of her juice — she *did* make a little visit to the Cosmetology Room. Let them go crazy with mousse and such. When they were finished — television makeup tricks galore — she only pretended to look in the mirror and admire their work. No point in getting even *more* self-conscious.

It was getting late — the press conference was supposed to start at eleven — and Preston was out in the Center Hall, waiting for her. When he saw her, he pretended to faint.

"Is that good or bad?" she asked.

"It's *very* good." He brought over her wheelchair. "Come on, I'll give you a ride down there."

"I'm going to *walk* in," she said.

He nodded, and she sat down, holding her crutch across her lap.

Her family was in the West Sitting Hall; her parents looking tense, Neal curious, Steven bored.

"Aren't you supposed to be working?" Meg asked her mother.

"Later," her mother said.

Meg put on a very stern frown. "Well — *all right.*"

"Break a leg," her father said, then winced.

Meg, however, was amused. "Wouldn't *that* be a disaster," she said, and saw Preston glance at his watch.

"Right." She looked at her family, feeling sort of like she was going on a very long journey. "Well. See you later."

Steven looked up from patting Kirby. "Yo, we'll watch the Cubs game this afternoon."

"Sounds good," Meg said.

When she and Preston were in the elevator, she let out her breath.

"You think my parents are really going to stay up there?" she asked.

He grinned. "Maybe."

"No one'll know they came downstairs though, right?"

He nodded.

She looked at him for a minute. "You *don't* remind me of him."

He smiled. "I'm glad."

Feeling very nervous, she decided to check out his outfit. A chalk-striped double-breasted dark grey suit, a light pink Perry Ellis shirt with matching pocket handkerchief, and his tie — silk-foulard — was *magenta*.

"I know," he said, seeing her expression. "You think the tie's a little much."

"Well, Jesus, Preston," she said. "You don't want to be a *fop*."

He laughed.

"I hope your *socks* aren't pink."

He lifted his pants leg and she saw that they were dark grey. His shoes were conservative too.

"Well, *good*," she said.

They were downstairs now, a small squad of agents joining them as Preston pushed her chair towards the West Wing and the Press Room.

She looked at the agents, trying to think of something to say. Break the tension. "What do you think," she asked one of them, "is his tie a little over the top?"

The agent laughed, but didn't — she noticed — answer.

"That means yes," she said to Preston.

They were getting close to the Press Room, and Meg was finding it hard to catch her breath. There were people everywhere, mostly press staff, and the best she could do was smile when they spoke to her.

Linda came out of the briefing room, looking anxious. As ever.

"Good," she said, sounding unreasonably relieved. "You're here. Are we all set?" she asked, turning away before Meg had a chance to answer. "Good. Good luck. I'll go open it up, Preston." She disappeared back into the briefing room.

Preston grinned, resting his hands on her shoulders. "You're going to knock them silly, kid."

Meg swallowed, regretting ever getting into this. She had practically never been *in* the Press Room, let alone up in front of everybody. "How many microphones are there?"

"Not as many as it looks like," he said.

Meaning *a lot*. Satellite feeds and all. "An FBI guy'll be there, right, in case there's something I'm not supposed to answer?"

Preston nodded.

She swallowed again. "Are you ever nervous before you go in there?"

"Almost always," he said. "But you *look* beautiful."

The sounds of conversation in the room had abruptly ceased, indicating that Linda was behind the podium, speaking to the press. The outside hall seemed to be brighter, which meant that the television cameras were rolling, the lights on.

Oh, boy.

Preston smiled at her, a nice, encouraging smile. "Ready to go, kid?"

Meg took a deep breath, and lifted herself up onto her crutch. "Yeah," she said. "I'm ready to go."

About the Author

ELLEN EMERSON WHITE spends *way* too much time in Fenway Park, which may account for the somewhat dark subject matter of this book. She is the author of several books for young adults, among them *The President's Daughter*, *White House Autumn*, and *Friends for Life*.

Ellen Emerson White grew up in Naragansett, Rhode Island, and was graduated from Tufts University in 1983. She now works full-time as a writer, dividing her time between Boston and New York.